Large Print ISBN 978-1-80048-761-1

Hardback ISBN 978-1-80280-869-8

Ebook ISBN 978-1-80048-764-2

Kindle ISBN 978-1-80048-763-5

Audio CD ISBN 978-1-80048-756-7

MP3 CD ISBN 978-1-80048-757-4

Digital audio download ISBN 978-1-80048-759-8

Boldwood Books Ltd
23 Bowerdean Street
London SW6 3TN
www.boldwoodbooks.com

WILL THEY, WON'T THEY?

PORTIA MACINTOSH

B
Boldwood

First published in Great Britain in 2021 by Boldwood Books Ltd.

Copyright © Portia MacIntosh, 2021

Cover Design by Debbie Clement Design

Cover Photography: Shutterstock

A CIP catalogue record for this book is available from the British Library.

Paperback ISBN 978-1-80048-762-8

For Kim
A mum in a million

1

'I know,' he says simply – almost menacingly.

'Know what?' I reply.

I sound innocent enough, but my eyes tell a different story.

Lying here, in bed with him, with just a thin sheet barely protecting my modesty, I wriggle slightly under the weight of his scarily muscular arm.

He's lying next to me, on his side, I can see him staring at me out of the corner of my eye. He isn't holding me; he's holding me down.

'*I know,*' he says again.

The light from the flickering candles creates creepy little shadows that dance on the walls. It's distracting, watching them, my eyes playing tricks on me as I try to make sense of the shapes.

I try to ignore it. I need to focus. He knows...

'Ed, my love, I don't know what you mean,' I start. 'I'm just—'

'Spare me your false protests,' he snaps.

He sits up in bed, lifting himself onto his elbows as his biceps bulge and his abs ripple – he *has* to be doing that on purpose.

'I swear to you...'

I try to sit up too, but he pushes me down flat on my back.

'Did you ever love me, Adelina?' he asks. 'Or was it all a lie? I knew in the depths of my stomach that I shouldn't trust you, but you convinced me that you loved me and I fell for it.'

'Ed, of course I love you,' I insist. 'I never thought I would find love, but love found me, *you* found me. When we happened upon each other in the forest, and we knew it was wrong, but we knew we were meant to be...'

'But it was all an act, wasn't it?' he says angrily. 'To infiltrate my family, to do what? How far would you go? Would you—? No... no...'

The realisation hits him hard, like a ton of bricks, and you can really see it on his face. He almost looks constipated.

'Ed...'

'It was you,' he says. 'My brother... you were the one who...'

'Ed, I love you,' I say again – like I mean it this time. 'Make love to me again, right now, and tell me you don't feel it.'

I roll my eyes, but only in my head, careful not to let my face slip, not even for a second.

He whips the covers from me and presses his naked body down on top of mine. Christ, he's heavy. Like lying underneath a Ford Fiesta. It's about as thrilling too. It's not that he isn't gorgeous. He's practically an Adonis. Perfectly chiselled muscles, big dark eyes permanently fixed in a brooding stare, a jaw so tight it's almost painful to look at. He just isn't my type at all. I'm definitely not going to miss kissing him.

He moves me to the edge of the bed, dangling my head off the side as he kisses my neck. He moves up to my lips where he promptly slips his tongue in my mouth. I just need to act like I'm enjoying it for a few more seconds until…

'This is for Varitan,' he announces solemnly.

Tears flood his eyes as he reaches under the bed and grabs a small axe. He raises it up above his head, gathering strength, ready to chop my head clean off.

I stare at it, frozen in horror like a rabbit in the headlights, as he swings the axe down towards my face.

'And *cut*,' a voice calls out.

Everyone springs to action on the set around us. A young woman runs towards me with a dressing gown, to cover my nearly naked body. For the sex scenes, I get a skin-coloured modesty patch and a genital guard, which is sort of like a big plastic shoehorn that they attach to you with latex glue. But it never really feels like they do all that much to actually protect your modesty.

Alex Forbes, the actor who plays Edrym opposite me, pretty much just wears a sock fixed in place with some wig tape, but let's just say he overacts his sex scenes just as much as he does his regular scenes, and it usually slips straight off. I'd say *thankfully* we have a closed set for scenes like this, but Alex clearly doesn't mind. Right now, he's just standing there, talking to the director, as naked as the day he was born.

Jane, my agent, is the next person to approach me. It isn't usual to have your agent on set with you, but today isn't a normal day.

'Is that it?' I ask her.

'That's it,' she replies with a big smile. 'Your final scene. There's just one thing left to do.'

'God, they don't need me to do any reshoots with him, do they?' I reply, nodding towards Alex, who appears to have found a reason to flex a bicep as he watches the scene back on one of the monitors. He's pointing something out to the director, probably just to use his arm.

'Nope, no more reshoots,' Jane says. 'They've got everything they need for your brutal murder.'

'Fab,' I say sarcastically.

'You just need to shoot your exit interview,' she reminds me.

Ah, that's right. When anyone dies in this show they interview them for the discussion show that airs after each episode. They have a live studio audience for the discussion, but not for the interview, not since someone threw an egg at an especially mean elf from Season Two. *Bragadon Forrest* fans are nothing if not passionate.

'Ergh, fine, let's get it over with,' I say.

'Just one thing,' she starts.

I can tell from the look on her face that I'm not going to like it. And then I notice the make-up girl hovering close by with the fake blood.

'Oh, seriously?' I moan.

'You're supposed to look fresh from filming your final moments,' Jane reminds me. 'And you have just had your head chopped off.'

'The fans do know this is a TV show, right?' I say. 'I mean, they must, if they're watching me do my exit interview.'

I sigh. It's almost all over with.

'Fine, cover me in blood.'

Just another day at the office.

I should just be grateful I'm allowed to wear a dressing gown for the interview. But it wouldn't be unlike the show to have me do it in the nip. After all, they do love their sexposition scenes, where they'll shoehorn in shagging and nudity just to keep the viewers' attention, while they explain the more boring aspects of a plot about fairies and elves fighting for the throne of Bragadon Forrest. Take it from someone who played a fairy princess – it's astounding how little they wanted me to wear and how often. Fairies are all small, slim, pretty and always scantily clad creatures. The elves are all big, muscular types – the men *and* the women – and they're always flashing their muscles, *at the least*. I never knew fantasy was so sexy, until I joined the cast of one of the biggest shows on TV.

After six seasons, it feels like forever ago since I started. And now I'm on my way out.

I'm ushered from one set to another, where a makeshift stage is set up with two chairs facing each other. Mikey King, the host of the *Bragadon*

Forrest Talk Show, is waiting for me with a big smile on his face.

'Hey Emmy, fresh from filming your final scene?' Mikey asks me as I sit down opposite him.

'I just felt the fake blood drip down from my neck into the piece of plastic glued to my crotch,' I say, like it's the most casual thing in the world. 'I couldn't be fresher.'

Mikey laughs.

'Great, let's get straight on, shall we?' he says.

Mikey makes the introductions while I shift awkwardly in my seat. I wasn't lying about that fake blood.

'So, here I am with Emmy Palmer aka Princess Adelina. Emmy, how are you feeling?' he asks.

Obviously, I'm not going to answer that completely honestly.

'Erm, yeah, just kind of weird,' I reply. 'To have been doing this for six seasons, and playing such an important character in the show, *Bragadon Forrest* has been a huge part of my life. I'll always have fond memories of my time on set.'

'Obviously yours and Alex Forbes' characters,

Adelina and Edrym, were sort of like the Romeo and Juliet of the series. Do you think it was always bound to end in tragedy for those two?' Mikey asks curiously.

Another question I don't think I should answer in too much detail. Well, the reality is that it's more a case of *me* having some personal issues with the showrunner – who unfortunately is the person who is pretty much in charge of everything – and *him* having me killed off prematurely. The character arc doesn't really come into it in that case, does it? But I can't say that.

'I guess when you have two people from warring families trying to make it work in the crossfire then someone is bound to get hurt,' I say.

'Well, then fans will be shocked, I'm sure,' Mikey says. 'You were the show's true hero. Do you think this signals the start of a difficult time?'

'Oh, absolutely,' I reply. Now that is an honest answer – both on and off screen.

'I imagine Edrym will miss Adelina, even though it was him who killed her,' Mikey continues. 'And I'll bet you're going to miss working with

Alex, huh? I bet there are plenty of people out there who would have killed you sooner to roll round in the sheets with Alex.'

Mikey laughs. I cringe a little but smile politely. I can't let my game face slip yet.

'Oh, those scenes are nowhere near as sexy to shoot as they appear when you watch them back,' I insist. 'They're so carefully choreographed and, to be honest, more like exercise than anything else. My core has never been stronger.'

Mikey laughs that same laugh again, right on cue.

Sometimes, I get this feeling we're all just wearing our game faces, going through the motions.

'I guess the question on everyone's lips is this: what is next for Emmy Palmer?' Mikey asks finally.

I smile as I stall for time, searching my brain for a few words to throw together, but the truth is that I don't know. I have absolutely no idea what I'm going to do now.

2

There are two types of northerners: those who think London is amazing and those who think it's a shithole.

My uncle, for example, always talks about how he'll only be happy when we hack England off just below Sheffield and 'send the rest of 'em off to France'. I don't think it's a trait exclusive to York-shire men, or even northerners, it seems as though lots of people outside London think it's the pol-luted, rat-infested, overrun heart of capitalism where people in the street wouldn't pee on you if you were on fire, never mind say hello. Not like up north where, by the time you've tipped your flat cap to someone they've already folded your ironing and popped an apple pie in your oven, obviously.

The people who are not like my uncle are more like me. The kind of person who sees London as a city of opportunity. I'm not saying nothing else happens anywhere else ever, but when you grow up in a small coastal town in Yorkshire, dreaming of being an actress, you can't aim much higher than Emmerdale if you plan on staying local, so you don't really have much choice but to move, and everything that's anything happens in London.

I moved to London right after I finished sixth form, working various jobs here and there, until I got my first big break – the role of Adelina. I don't think anyone knew at the time just how big the show was going to be, but as shows like *Game of Thrones* grew in popularity, people's appetite for fantasy grew until our show was huge as well.

Of course, the lifestyle appeals to me too. I love the bars, the shops – the Tube is incredible. And then there's my apartment...

I have a two-bed, two-bath duplex in Soho. The front of the building looks quite traditional, boasting huge sash windows that let in tons of light, and on the other side of the building, I have floor-to-ceiling windows and bi-folding doors that open out on to my teeny-tiny terrace. The period façade balances Edwardian character with a contemporary approach to light and space, and the ultra-modern interior gives me the best of urban loft living. Maybe I know what I'm talking about, or maybe that's the pitch the sales girl gave me, but the beautiful thing about acting is that, if your delivery is right, no one really knows when you're faking it. Well, that's what I like to think, at least, because as good as I may be at pretending, I do often find it hard to hide what I'm feeling if I feel strongly enough about something.

God, it's good to be home. After washing off all the fake blood, hopping into my own clothes, and having those impossibly heavy, long blonde hair extensions removed, I left the set finally feeling like myself again, whoever that is. I've been playing Adelina for so long now and the show is so big I haven't been able to escape it for a minute. I can't even buy milk without someone yelling one of my fake names at me. And by fake names, I mean either Adelina, my character name, or Emmy Palmer, which is actually my stage name.

To make a long story short, no two actors can have the same working name, so when you come to register your name if someone else is already working under that name, you have to come up with something else. Well, I was born Emma Watson, and despite being four years older than her, *the* Emma Watson got quite the head start on me on screen, so I had to improvise. I figured, my family and friends always called me Emmy growing up, and I just liked the sound of Palmer, so that was that. Emmy Palmer was born.

I ditch my keys in the bowl I keep on the chest of drawers just through my apartment front door. A mirror hangs above it and the sight of my hair causes me to double take. I wear my insanely long blonde hair extensions for extended periods of time, so by the time I have them taken out, I can never quite get over how different I look. I find it fascinating when people crave super-long hair because I can never get rid of it quick enough. With my fairy hair gone, I have a stylish blonde lob, just a little bit past shoulder length, and that suits me just fine. I ditch the oversized sunglasses I hid behind on the way home to reveal my tired eyes.

I finally feel as though I can relax. I know it sounds like I complain a lot, but it's not all bad, playing a fairy princess for so many years did buy me this apartment.

I kick off my shoes, let my coat fall to the floor and slip off my jeans, making it look a little bit like I've just vanished into thin air leaving nothing but a pile of clothes behind. I flop down onto the sofa, letting the large, soft cushions swallow me whole. I close my eyes. It's so quiet here. I can't hear the city outside, nothing in my apartment is making a noise – the only thing I can hear is the sound of my own breath, which seems to get louder the more I focus on it, and now I'm doing that my heartbeat has joined the party, thudding in my ears.

Suddenly, I don't feel so good. My breathing changes, it's as though I'm no longer doing it on autopilot, I'm having to think about each breath, my brain telling my body to take in oxygen and push it out again. As a funny feeling in my stomach kicks in and I wonder what on earth could be wrong with me, it makes sense all of a sudden. I'm having an anxiety attack. I think now that I'm home, now that I'm me again, now that my crazy world seems to have calmed, the reality of the situation has finally hit me. I no longer work on *Bragadon Forrest*. And without *Bragadon Forrest*, my life feels sort of empty.

My agent has been trying for months, ever since I found out I was being killed off, to find me some work, but I've wound up frustratingly typecast after being in a fantasy show for so long, so the good roles aren't exactly coming in thick and fast. As Jane keeps reminding me, the moves I make now will define my career. She says that if I accept the crappy sci-fi and fantasy gigs I'm being offered, that will be it, that's all I'll ever get. I'm not saying I won't accept less than a Marvel movie or to be main cast on the next Netflix drama that makes it big, but I can't imagine spending the rest of my days wearing next to no clothing and getting my head chopped off. I don't want that to be my thing.

The peace and quiet is interrupted by my phone ringing. Refusing to get up from my 'relaxing' spot, I dangle my upper body off the sofa and walk my hands a little across the floor, managing to reach my jeans with my little finger, pull them close and retrieve my phone from the pocket.

It's my friend Laura – Laura Jade, yes *the* Laura Jade, the one who hosts *You Should Meet*, the dating TV show where single contestants meet potential matches on behalf of their single friends, but if they want them for themselves they can steal them. It's so simple but it's so explosive *every* single week. It's amazing how willing people are to ditch their friends for someone hot whom they met half an hour ago. Recently Laura has been trying to get me to sign up for the celebrity version, but it sounds like my worst nightmare. I'm happy being single but, even if I weren't, a reality TV show is not the way I'd go about finding a meaningful relationship.

'How is my favourite fairy princess?' Laura asks when I finally answer.

Everyone who works on the show has to sign a strict confidentiality agreement. Other than my agent, I'm not allowed to tell anyone that I've been killed off.

'Can't complain,' I lie. 'How are you?'

'Yeah, I'm great, just finished filming some promos for *Celeb YSM*,' she replies. 'We've got Fabrizio Napoletano on board – are you sure I can't tempt you into taking part?'

Fabrizio Napoletano was one of the winners of *Love Island* a couple of years ago (you won't be shocked to hear that he didn't stay with his partner for much longer than it took them to bank the prize money) and has been on the romance reality TV circuit ever since. He's good looking – of course he is, or he wouldn't be a popular regular on all of these shows – but he's not exactly a catch in my eyes, not only because of the sheer volume of women I've watched him plough his way through on various TV shows, but also because just like I've been typecast as a fantasy princess, Fabrizio's entire identity is dating TV shows. Once he finds love, that's it, his career is over, and with so many girls throwing themselves at him regardless, he'd be crazy to cash out now.

'Oh, so tempting,' I reply sarcastically. 'But no thanks.'

'OK, big shot,' she teases. 'But, you never know, one day you might be begging to be on my show. Until then... fancy drinks tonight?'

I feel so emotionally and physically drained (getting beheaded will do that to a girl) and, in a way, the last thing I want to do is go out on the town. On the other hand, my celebrity stock is sure to plummet once people realise I've been killed off, so it makes sense to keep my face out there. Every now and then there is a member of the paparazzi lingering around outside my building. I once made the showbiz pages for walking home with two take-away coffees instead of one, which resulted in the headline: *'Does Emmy Palmer have a secret fairy prince?'* when, in reality, I was only carrying two cups because they gave me a free sample of some coffee beans to try at home, in my fancy new machine, which I still haven't used. In my line of work, when you're at home and bored during the day, sometimes walking for that takeaway coffee is the only way you'll see signs of life. It's all or nothing. Manic days on set and celebrity parties, or days home alone filled with nothing other than what you can think to fill them with, which for me is shopping and coffee.

'Sure, why not?' I reply. 'Where did you have in mind?'

'There's a new restaurant, Encounter, throwing a swanky launch party tonight, and we're on the list,' she says excitedly. 'So, go get tarted up, I'll text you the address, and I'll see you there, yeah?'

'Yeah, OK, sounds good,' I reply, trying to match her enthusiasm. 'How long have I got?'

'Not long, actually,' she replies. 'I said we'd be there early, to pose in some of the promo shots. All exposure is good exposure. But, yeah, I'd probably start getting ready now. And make sure you get yourself in the party mood, will you? You sound miserable.'

Aww, isn't it nice to have friends who care?

Sometimes – and it is only sometimes – I feel like I'm working when I go out with Laura. Well, it almost sounds like she's booked us a gig, having us turn up at Encounter before the launch to take pictures that will be plastered all over social media. Still, it's a reason to get dressed up and have fun, which beats a night of sitting on the sofa, trying to figure out what I'm going to do with my life, and eating every beige food I can get my hands on, because now I don't need to worry about being nearly naked for the camera for large chunks of the year, all I can think about is making the most of all the things I've been denying myself for the past six seasons. Actually, I can think of no better place to do that than a restaurant.

We've no sooner said goodbye and I've dragged myself to my bathroom when I hear my phone ringing again. I dash back to the coffee table where I left it.

'Hello,' I say, after answering the number I don't recognise.

'Hello, it's your Amazon delivery, I'm knocking on the door but no one is in,' a voice on the other end of the phone says.

'You're at my door?' I say.

'Yeah, with the green garden gate,' he replies.

I'm confused for about four seconds.

'Oh, right, yes, sorry,' I babble. 'It's a gift for my granddad. Is he not in?'

'No one is answering but it says I need to see some ID, so I can't just leave it,' he explains.

My granddad, Tony, is without a doubt my favourite family member. I know, you're not supposed to have favourites, but in my family the competition isn't all that stiff. Don't get me wrong, they're my family, and I love them all, but Granddad is the only one who gives me absolutely zero hassle. I miss him so much, living in London, when he's back home in Yorkshire. I don't get to see him as much as I would like so the least I can do is make sure he always has plenty of his favourite tipple – Glenmorangie whisky.

'Could you leave it with the neighbour?' I say, offering my best solution, but I can't help but think about how unusual it is that Granddad isn't home.

'Sorry, love, I can't, not if I need to see ID. We can try again tomorrow,' he replies.

I always have Granddad tell me when he's running low, so that I can get a bottle to him before he completely runs out, so I'm sure he'll be fine waiting another day. He's not dependent on it but with his arthritis being really bad these days he doesn't get out of the house much, so if he likes to spend his evenings having a glass of whisky and watching episodes of old sitcoms like *Fawlty Towers* and *Only Fools and Horses*, then I'm happy to oblige. While eighty-eight might be a 'good age' (whatever the hell that is), it doesn't mean he's on the scrapheap just because his knees and his wrists don't work as well as they used to.

It is odd, that he isn't in, given how little he goes out. Perhaps my mum has taken him to a doctor's appointment or something. I drop her a quick message, asking her to give me a ring when she's got a minute, just to make sure everything is OK there. It would be nice to hear her voice today, even if I can't tell her why.

My heart feels a little heavy, thinking about my granddad. He's not only the greatest granddad in the world (I'm sure everyone says that, but in my case, it's true) but he was more of a dad to me than mine ever was.

Ha! So much for getting myself in the party mood, I've wandered down a path that is growing increasingly dark, haven't I?

Showering away any remnants of my beheading makes me feel a little better and as I begin to style my newly shortened hair and paint on my game face, I feel much better and, dare I say it, excited about a night out with Laura.

As if my hair didn't suddenly feel short enough, wrapping it around the large barrel of my curling tongs has only made it seem shorter still, but at least it doesn't take half as long to style as the long extensions did. By the time I've slipped on a pair of black trousers, over-the-knee black boots, a bright red silk vest, my trusty leather jacket, some silver accessories and my Alexander McQueen black, white and red skull scarf I actually look like myself again. Adelina has left the building.

I'll head out into the cold November air, book myself an Uber, and then enjoy my last few moments of calm on the drive there, because these things are usually pretty non-stop all evening.

I can't really say why, but I get this sense of something not being quite right the second I step outside my building. My uneasy feeling is soon explained by the paparazzi waiting outside for me. Not one – the usual one – not two, but *five*. Five photographers all shouting my name, trying to take my photo, barking questions at me but I can't pick one whole question out of the chaos. The explosion of noise makes my ears ring, blocking out almost all other sound, and I feel so overwhelmed by the giant camera lenses, the big dark eyes hiding the photographer behind them, that for a moment, my eyes just dart back and forth between them, almost as though I'm posing on autopilot.

I might have been doing this job for a while now, but let's face it, I'm not that famous, that I should have five photographers waiting for me.

Something must have happened. Could news have leaked about me being killed off? They wouldn't put that in the news though, would they? A spoiler like that and the fans would destroy whichever news outlet leaked it.

I don't know what else to do other than quickly lift my clutch bag up to hide my face while I fiddle with my door fob, trying to get back inside my building. I'm safe as soon as the external door closes, but I don't slow for a second until I'm in my own apartment with the door closed and locked behind me.

I shrug off my jacket and whip off my scarf, suddenly roasting hot, before taking out my phone. I've typed my own name into Google before my bum has touched the sofa. As soon as I see the headlines, I slump down in my seat, wishing once again that it would just swallow me up, eat me alive, or at least let me hide inside it for the foreseeable future.

I'm in the news. I'm in the *fucking* news. And it is absolutely mortifying.

I need to call my agent, but first I need to call Laura, tell her I'm not going to be able to make it tonight. She'll be annoyed, unless she's seen the news, in which case she probably won't mind. I have a strong feeling no one is going to want to be seen with me for the foreseeable, not now I've been branded a homewrecker.

3

You can't beat a big bath and a glass of wine, can you? Whether you're celebrating or sulking, a glass of something and some beautiful-smelling bubbles is always the way to go. Well, I say you can't beat it, but given that I'm currently sulking, I wouldn't mind the water-to-wine ratio being reversed.

I've been lying here for two hours now – I've had to warm the water up so many times I think I'm technically in a different bath to the one I started with. Each time I let out the cold water and replace it with warm, I throw in a different bath bomb, and the only ones I have to hand are these Essential

Mood Melters that I got sent by a PR company. Each one has different ingredients and promises to deliver a different mood boost with it. I started with 'Calm Your Mind', moved on to 'De-Stress Bomb', and I think the scent of 'Sleepy Vibes' is just starting to fade away now. Though none of these bath bombs have done anything close to what the box promised. Perhaps I had too much faith in them, especially given everything that's going on tonight.

I'm at that point in my bath where I have two choices. Both my bath and my glass need replenishing, so I could soak in here a while longer, or I could get out and try to sort my life out, but if I do that then I have to face up to the fact that I am *fucked*. I'm not prepared to do that yet.

Jane says I've to hang in there. That I should keep my head down for a few days and wait for things to blow over while she starts formulating a plan and puts it into action. She says it's all going to be fine. That's easy for her to say. She isn't reading headlines about herself such as: *'Emmy Palmer has married boss under her spell'* or *'Emmy Palmer takes married showrunner to fairy land*', although I'm sure reading lines like: '*Do you think fairy princess Emmy Palmer can foretell her own career's death?*' might give her pause for thought. My problems are her problems and, boy, do I have a problem now.

I always worried about how the press would handle my abrupt departure from the show. Well, Adelina and Edrym were supposed to be endgame, everyone knows that. I had hoped that by the time my final episodes had aired that I would already have my next big gig lined up, that I would be able to style it out as personal choice, rather than because I was pushed out.

Well, so much for that plan, after the story that has hit the news today. Nothing gets you killed off a TV show like having an affair with the married showrunner. Well, except one other thing, the truth. But while the truth may be the truth, the rumours don't exactly do me any favours, and they definitely don't make me seem very professional, which is unfortunate when you're looking for a new job. I know, I shouldn't worry what people think as long as *I* know the truth, but there are certain people who I desperately don't want to read these headlines: my family.

The last thing I want to do right now is call my mum and tell her all about it, but better she hears the truth from me than reads a horrible version of events in the news.

I eyeball another 'De-Stress Bomb' on the side of the bath as the phone rings. I consider whether it might live to see another day, if I can just nip these horrible rumours in the bud, at least as far as my family is concerned, but the phone seems to ring for ages – does it usually ring this long, or am I just feeling extra paranoid today?

'Hello Emmy,' my mum eventually answers. Does she... does she sound upset? Shit, I should have called sooner.

'Hello, Mum, how are you?' I ask, testing the waters.

'Oh, you know,' she replies. 'How are you?'

I just can't read her. Perhaps she hasn't seen the news yet. It might not be too late to limit the damage.

'Yeah, yeah, I'm OK,' I start. 'Erm... have you seen the news this evening?'

'I haven't actually had a minute to myself today,' she says, in quite a casual way, given her usual workload. My mum is always running around after someone, either my stepdad and half-siblings or my granddad, or she's shopping or cleaning or *something*. 'Is it something good?'

Oh, her hopeful tone makes this suddenly feel even harder. How do I spin this? They say all publicity is good publicity, right? But they also say no news is good news, so...

'Erm, not great,' I reply. 'The press are running some horrible rumour, and it's completely untrue, there's no truth in it.'

I'm babbling, and repeating myself, and it's not entirely true that there's no truth in it, but it's certainly not true-true. I pause and take a deep breath.

'They're saying I had an affair with Danny Terrence, the showrunner from *Bragadon Forrest*, which I'm absolutely not, and I never have, it's just a rumour and my agent is going to shut it down. I just wanted to tell you, before you read it, even though I knew you'd know it was all rubbish.'

I finally exhale. I hope that, somewhere in that mess of dialogue, my mum got the message.

'Oh, love, I'm sorry,' she says. 'That's just awful but, no, of course we know it's not true, and I'll make sure the family knows. I'm with the aunties now, actually.'

The aunties, as we call them in our house, are my mum's older sisters, Vera and Beverly (Vee and Bev to their friends). They're quite the double act, and almost completely identical, with the exception of Vee having bright red hair, whereas Bev has gone gracefully grey. They're in their late sixties, but while Bev is on her second husband, Vee never married. She gets her fair share of action though, and don't we all know it, because they both have what I can only describe as Samantha Jones from *Sex and the City* energy.

'Say hi from me,' I say. 'Is everything OK? You sounded a little off when I called, I thought it was because you'd seen the headlines.'

'Oh no, nothing like that,' she says. 'Your, erm... your granddad died.'

Mum delivers this line in such a matter-of-fact way, for a second, it hardly registers.

The words sink in so slowly. They echo around inside my head as my brain tries to make sense of them, because they can't possibly mean what they sound like they mean, I spoke to him on the phone yesterday and he was fine.

'What?' I say weakly.

My mum doesn't say anything for a few seconds – or maybe I don't give her time to talk – before a surge of questions pour out of me.

'What happened? When did it happen? Why are you telling me at the tail end of a different conversation? Why didn't you call me, Mum?'

'They think he had a heart attack,' she says. 'I found him in his bed at lunchtime. I called an ambulance, they did everything they could but, by the time they got him to the hospital...'

Oh my God, how horrible that must have been for her. I can't even begin to imagine – and the fact she's able to talk to me so calmly now just goes to show how strong she is in times of crisis. Then again, she has been through a lot.

My gut reaction is to be upset, to have a go at her for not telling me immediately, to cry and cry, but I can't do that to her right now. She's going to need me to be strong.

'Mum, I'm so sorry,' I say. 'Are you OK?'

'Oh, you know,' she says again.

'Why didn't you call me?' I ask.

'I didn't want to bother you with it,' she says, before reconsidering her words and quickly back-tracking. 'I mean, I knew you were working, and you've got a lot on, and I didn't want to drop it on you in the middle of the day, if there was nothing you could do.'

'But there *is* absolutely something I can do,' I insist softly. 'I'm going to pack a bag, I'm going to get a train ticket booked, and I'll be there as early as humanly possible tomorrow.'

'Oh, love, you...' I can hear the aunties bickering about something in the background. 'You don't know what that would mean to me. I...'

The sound of the aunties fades as it sounds like my mum moves into a different room.

'I'd really appreciate it,' she says in hushed tones. 'They're driving me mad.'

'Of course,' I reply. 'Is Gracie there?'

Gracie is my sister. At thirty-six, she's two years older than me, but that's actual years, maturity-wise she's miles ahead of me. She lives down the road from my mum with her husband, Carl, and their kids, Darcy and Oscar. She's got a family home, a family car – and a family, obviously, which isn't the route I have taken. I can't help but feel like a big kid when I compare myself to her. She has it all figured out. I'm sure she'll be forcefully proactive in helping my mum with whatever needs doing right now, steering her through the motions in a very pragmatic way, but pragmatism isn't all you need at a time like this.

'She had to go,' my mum says, rather simply. I suspect there's more to it than that.

'OK,' I reply. We'll get into that later. 'Well, I'll see you in the morning.'

'OK, darling,' she replies. 'It might do you good,

to come here for a break, if you've got a lot going on there.'

'Yeah, you're right,' I reply. 'I just wish it were under better circumstances. We can take care of each other.'

'We certainly can,' she says with a big sigh. 'See you tomorrow.'

It's only the second after I hang up the phone that I allow myself to cry. Isn't it interesting how, when we lose a family member, we do our best to stay strong for the people we think need it? I don't want to cry in front of my mum because she just lost her dad. When she isn't crying she doesn't need me crying too, setting her off again – of course, she'd be furious if she knew that was the way I was looking at it.

I just... I can't believe he's gone. I only spoke to him yesterday and he sounded absolutely fine. Better than fine. He told me he wasn't in as much pain as usual with his arthritis.

My granddad was more to me than just a granddad and I can't even begin to consider the hole that this is going to leave in my heart right now because I have to be strong. I have to. I have to be there for my mum.

I wipe my tears with the backs of my hands, lean forward, grab another 'De-Stress Bomb' and drop it in the water. It makes a loud splosh as it plummets to the bottom of the bath before rising to the top and fizzling away. If only the smooth scent of lavender could cut through the overwhelming feelings of stress I'm feeling, melting away the grief as fast as the bath bomb disappears into the water, but when the fizzing has stopped and the water has settled, I feel no different. Well, that's not true, I don't give a shit about my incredibly small-time, crappy tabloid scandal right now. All I want is to get home to my family.

But, as for what lies ahead of me back home, let's just say I'm going to need to pack a lot of bath bombs to deal with all that.

4

There is a silver lining, when it comes to only being famous for playing a character in a popular TV show and nothing else.

Bragadon Forrest is watched all over the world. It's the ultimate water-cooler TV discussion when a new season is on air. It's one of those shows where you can pretty much guarantee someone, at some point, will ask you if you watch it, and while not everyone will say yes, to those who do, the characters are pretty iconic. But that's my point: the characters are iconic.

Princess Adelina, with her almost-white blonde

hair that goes down past her hips, in one of her infamous, barely there fairy outfits, her pointy ears and her spectacular iridescent wings – all of which mean that, in real life, I look absolutely nothing like her. The ears and the wings are a combination of costume and post-production, so obviously I don't have those, and now that my hair extensions are gone, I've been able to tone my white hair into a honey blonde, which makes me look more human. You'd also never catch me in one of Adelina's teeny-tiny, sparkly outfits either. In real life, I much prefer to wear dark colours (with the occasional burst of red or pink to match my lips if I'm dressing up), and given that it's November, my day-to-day involves varying pairs of skinny jeans and jumpers with extra-long sleeves.

Basically, when I'm looking like me, I look nothing like Adelina, so the silver lining is that, to a degree, if I stick on a pair of sunglasses, I don't get mobbed in the street. I've had glimpses of the suffocating fame that comes with having a recognisable look, at events like Comic Cons, or in the middle of shooting when my extensions have to stay in, and it's safe to say, I hate it. It really is a blessing, that only die-hard fans or people who follow me on Instagram would recognise me popping into the local M&S for a bag of Percy Pigs, but the downside to this, of course, is the old typecast problem I'm having to contend with now I need a new job. People in the industry only see me as a fantasy star and, after doing it for so long, it's the last thing I want to do next, never mind *forever*.

I am grateful that no one noticed me on my journey home today because I'm really not in the mood to talk to anyone. I had to catch two trains to even get close to my home town, so lots of lingering in stations, grabbing coffees from packed coffee shops, and I was basically a sitting duck on the train, but no one noticed me. Regular Emmy blends right in.

Now that I'm finally here, my train pulling into the station, it all feels real.

Getting ready last night, packing my bag, letting my agent know (she was very sympathetic, especially with the backdrop of all the bad press I'm having to contend with too), and then getting up early this morning to catch the train – it all just felt like going through the motions, motions that were mind-numbingly distracting, but there's nothing like your home town slowly revealing itself to you through the window of a taxi, to give you the harsh reality check you need. I've popped back now and then, for a couple of days, for birthdays and Christmases, but never under circumstances like these.

I grew up in Marram Bay, a tiny tourist hotspot on the Yorkshire coast. The place is perfectly picturesque. Every direction you glance in is like something fresh off a postcard. We're famous for a lot of things, here in Marram Bay. Officially, it's for things like our amazing tidal island, and all the weird and wonderful annual festivals we throw. Off the record, it's one of those places where everybody knows everything about everyone. No matter how quick you are to clean your dirty laundry, there will always be a gaggle of locals who remember the stink, and you can see the repulsion on their faces.

I remember, when everything happened between my mum and dad, when they separated, it was like this huge scandal. I was only six at the time, but I remember feeling this sense of shame, like I'd done something wrong, when neighbours gave me their dirty looks, but even more so, when they turned up at the door with casseroles. Like, *hey, heard the husband's gone, no sense in starving you and your two kids to death.* Not that my mum was ever anything other than amazing. She was always more than enough of everything to fill the roles of both mum and dad, but my gran and granddad certainly played a huge part in raising me too. When my gran passed away, back when I was fifteen, I was heartbroken, but it only strengthened the bond I shared with my granddad. I still can't believe he's gone. Ordinarily, he's the first person I would rush to visit, and even though I would always tell him not to, he would have tea and biscuits laid out for my arrival. I wonder what will be waiting for me at my mum's house, but I don't have to wonder for long.

Outside the front door of my mum and step-dad's detached house is my sister, Gracie, who is actually glaring at her watch with a ticked-off look, as though I'm late for something. Gracie and I

somehow look really similar *and* completely different. There's an obvious family resemblance, but we
just give off completely different vibes. Gracie has
always been the sensible one and I think I'm re-
garded as somewhat of a wild card these days, but
mostly just because I haven't conformed – not that I
see Gracie getting married and starting a family as
conforming, but the fact I haven't hit those mile-
stones yet tends to make older relatives especially
assume it's from a place of aggressive feminism or
an inability to grow up, or something similar. On
the flip side, whereas I tend to dress like a shy goth
in a bad mood, Gracie's colour palette is softer, and
more welcoming.

'There you are,' she says as I step out of the car.
She hurries down the driveway to help me out with
my case, but she quickly pushes it to one side so
that she can wrap her arms around me and squeeze
me tightly.

As I hug her back, I feel the stiffness leave her
body, even if it's only a little, as she relaxes in my
arms. God, it's good to see her. I'll bet she's glad I'm
here too – perhaps more so than anyone else – be-

cause with Mum and the aunties all sitting north of sixty, and our half-siblings still being at school, I'm the only person she has of her generation. Unless you count her husband, Carl, but he's always been one of those strong, silent Yorkshire men.

That said, Gracie can be a closed book herself, but even just being silent with someone who gets it is enough to make you feel better sometimes.

'How are things in there?' I ask, because if she's waiting for me outside in the cold, things must be bad in the nice, warm house.

'Mum and the aunties are talking funeral arrangements,' she tells me. 'It's absolute mayhem. Honestly, there is just no defusing them, if I had a gun with two bullets my only option would be to shoot myself twice. The last woman standing would probably argue with herself.'

Oh boy, things are bad. I had a feeling they would be, not just because a death in the family is a difficult time for even the strongest family unit, but because my lot can be kind of chaotic at the best of times.

'Remember when we had Ernie, before we had

him fixed, if there was another dog on the street who was in season, he would just hump the air?' I say with a laugh, in an attempt to cheer her up.

'Exactly like that,' she says, her face softening into a smile. 'I'm just so glad you're here.'

'Where are the kids?' I ask.

'At home with Carl,' she says. 'And Roy is out with Louis and Megan.'

Roy is our stepdad and Louis and Megan are our half-siblings. I love Roy. Pretty much from the moment we met, even though I was only eight, I knew that he was going to be good for my mum, and for me and Gracie too, and he was. They say it takes a village to raise kids. Well, with my dad off the scene, our village was a combination of my mum, Roy, gran and granddad, and the aunties, and do you know what? It worked. We all turned out just fine.

Sadly, my relationship with Louis and Megan isn't what I'd like it to be, which is not only a shame but really annoying, because you would at least think the fact I'm on TV might make them think I'm cool (even if I'm not). They're my mum and

Roy's kids, and this is their family home. They're seventeen now, and with me moving away over a decade ago, and with the age gap, we never really bonded. Gracie has always been around, so she's developed an enviable relationship with them, just like 'real' siblings, whereas I always feel like they keep me at arm's length.

'Shall we go inside?' I suggest as the cold November air manages to find its way inside my coat.

Gracie takes one final deep breath of fresh air, savouring the peace and quiet for a few seconds, before allowing her shoulders to fall heavily.

'OK, fine,' she says. 'But don't say I didn't warn you.'

Once inside, I follow raised female voices and the heat from the fireplace until I'm in the lounge where I find my mum and the aunties sitting around a table laid with one of my mum's signature afternoon teas.

'"If I Had a Hammer"!' Auntie Bev exclaims, somewhat violently.

Wow, things really are kicking off.

'No, that was Mum's favourite song, you daft old bat,' Auntie Vee corrects her.

'Hey, I'm the same age as you,' Bev replies.

'You're nine minutes older than me, thank you,' Vee corrects her. 'And we played it at Mum's funeral.'

I'm relieved Auntie Bev was referring to the song, and not just threatening her sisters with violence, but things really do seem tense in here.

'Actually, we played it at her wake,' my mum corrects them both. Then she notices me in the doorway.

'Oh, Emmy,' she says as she jumps to her feet.

Mum hurries across the room and hugs me, squeezing me even tighter than Gracie did, for even longer. She looks stressed out, and absolutely knackered, but she always has a big smile for me.

'Perfect timing, love,' she starts. 'We've just put lunch out, sit down, help yourself.'

I can think of nothing better right now than sitting by the fire with my mum, eating finger sandwiches and cakes, and reminiscing about Granddad, because that's the only thing you can do when you lose someone, right? Just focus on all the good they brought to the world and relive all your happy memories together.

Or, you know, arguing about funeral music is cool too, I guess.

I take a seat on one of the sofas around the coffee table, next to where Mum is sitting, opposite the aunties. Gracie sits in Roy's armchair.

'We were just discussing what music your granddad might like at his funeral,' my mum tells me rather tactfully. 'We all have different ideas about what he said he fancied, over the years.'

'Oh, I actually know one song he really wanted,' I say cautiously, bracing ever so slightly, just in case I get my head bitten off.

'Oh?' Vee says. 'And how do you know?'

'We were talking about it, only a few months ago, actually,' I reply.

'Why were you talking about his funeral a few months ago?' Bev asks, with a level of suspicion you would offer to someone you thought might actually have murdered the person in question.

'We just used to chat,' I say. 'About anything and everything.'

Granddad and I used to have long phone calls, all the time, just chatting, covering a bizarrely varied list of topics. One minute we would be talking about the state of the government, then it would be about how to eat less meat. We could move seamlessly from 'Do aliens exist?' (probably, but not like they do in the movies) to 'What was the name of that robotic dog I had when I was a kid?' (it was called a Poo-Chi and, Ernie, our actual dog *hated* it).

I remember the day we spoke about funerals vividly because it stuck in my head for a few reasons. First of all because, when I told him I didn't want a funeral, because I didn't like them, he told me that it didn't matter; that my funeral was never going to be for me; it would be for the people I left behind; my parting gift to them; to help them say goodbye and feel like they were doing something to honour my life. I'd never really thought about it like that. I'd always thought of funerals as depressing ordeals. Because, after you lose someone, just as you start to try get your head around the fact that they're gone and try and make peace with them not being around any more, then the funeral comes along and takes you back to how you were feeling on day one – if not slightly worse because, even though death feels so final, having a funeral really does feel like drawing a line under it all. I suppose that was Granddad's point though, that you need it for closure. You need to give your loved ones that day to make peace with it.

The other reason chatting funerals with Granddad stuck in my mind so firmly was because, at the time, I remember feeling really freaked out. Even though he was eighty-eight and struggled with his joints, he was otherwise fit as a fiddle. It wasn't so much that I was worried about why he was bringing the subject up, more that I didn't want to consider the fact that one day he wouldn't be around any more. When you're young, death seems almost abstract. Something so far down the line there's no point thinking about it. I know that I'm not exactly old, given that I'm only in my thirties, but the older I get, the longer it takes to push it out of my mind again.

'Ooh, go on then,' my mum prompts me. At least she's finding my presence helpful.

'"Can't Take My Eyes Off You",' I tell them. 'Specifically the Engelbert Humperdinck version. He said it was perfect, because not only was it a happy, upbeat song, but it always made him think of Gran, and that huge, lifelong crush she had on him.'

Engelbert Humperdinck, Cliff Richard, Des O'-Connor – it's incredible how different my gran's pin-ups were from mine. Even when I look at photos of those guys when they were younger, they look too old for me. I wonder if girls today look at the heart-throbs I had on my walls like they're old geezers. David Beckham, Leonardo DiCaprio and Nick Carter. Wow, I clearly had a thing for curtains.

'That's perfect,' my mum says. 'You walked in at just the right time.'

Deana Holme, my mum, is so different from her sisters, in all ways possible, you would never guess they were related. She's tall and enviably slim. She doesn't go to the gym or anything, and she doesn't live on a diet. She must just have something in her DNA that skipped her sisters – and me too. My diet and exercise regime for keeping in shape for playing Adelina was *the worst*. Well, I'm not playing her any more, am I? Which means I can get to work on these sandwiches and cakes without worrying about any especially snooty women in wardrobe prodding at my monthly bloated tummy and sighing heavily.

My mum is definitely putting on a brave face. The aunties are wearing it on their sleeves a little more, but I can see it in my mum's eyes. I guess I know where to look.

'Granddad wouldn't want us bickering over music,' Gracie chimes in.

'It's not the music that's the problem,' Vee tells her. 'It's Dad's house.'

'*We* want to sell it,' Bev adds. 'Your mum doesn't want to rush into it.'

'Why would you rush into it?' I ask curiously.

'Your uncle Richard has a gambling problem,' Vee announces. Bev doesn't flinch at this revelation about her husband. Neither does my mum, which makes me think this must be pretty common knowledge in the family. 'He's only ever a bad day away from getting in with the wrong sorts of people.'

I'm sure she's exaggerating. Probably just to get her hands on some cash, even if it means throwing her brother-in-law under the bus.

'And I need emergency surgery,' she adds, somewhat casually.

Now I really hope she's exaggerating.

'Is everything OK?' I ask, the sudden thought of another family member being ill making me feel like my jumper is trying to strangle me.

'Emergency *plastic* surgery,' Bev adds reassuringly with a roll of her eyes.

'I'm not sure cosmetic surgery constitutes an emergency,' my mum adds delicately. She's always been the diplomatic one.

'You don't know what it's like, being single at my age,' Vee insists. 'With all the divorces and premature deaths these days, there's just too much competition out there for a woman...'

I get the feeling she was about to say her age but then she backed out, as though her sisters (most notably her twin) and her nieces wouldn't know that her turning seventy isn't a million miles away.

'What do you think you need?' I ask curiously.

'Nothing vulgar, like what you're thinking,' she ticks me off. Oh, wow, believe me, my brain definitely wasn't going there. 'I'm like a teenager down there, thanks to never having any bloody kids.'

There are more people in this room who have had kids than who haven't and the ones who have scoff and roll their eyes at Vee.

'I need a little eye lift,' she says. 'Just a tweak. So I can compete with the other ladies on Matcher – how's the app dating scene in London?'

Oh, God, she's talking to me. The last thing I want right now is for this to turn into an analysis of my love life. I'm definitely not swapping dating horror stories with my auntie.

'I can't say I've tried app dating,' I say, hoping that will be an end to it.

'Right, no, don't suppose you need it, being on

the telly,' Vee replies. 'I imagine you can just steal any man you—'

Vee's sentence is cut short when a loud bang, originating under the coffee table, makes her jump.

'Oh, right, yes,' she says, as though she's suddenly remembered something.

I'm guessing, given the recent press about me, Bev probably tried to kick Vee under the table and missed. Now they're trying to style it out.

Everyone reads the tabloids then.

'Basically, we both need the money,' Bev says. 'And your mum, because she's got her Toy Roy, doesn't, so she's holding out on us.'

As much as we all love Roy, the aunties love to tease my mum over the fact he's five years younger than her, not that the age gap is even detectable, given that they're both in their sixties.

'That's not it,' my mum insists. 'It's dad's home. The thought of just... of just selling it off to strangers, right away. Of having to go over there with boxes and clear out all of his things, his entire life...'

I wrap an arm around my mum as she starts to

cry. This is horrendous. When someone dies, someone important, it's like a vital piece of the puzzle is ripped away, and it's so hard to see the bigger picture without it. I really, really wish there was something I could do to help her.

'I'm sorry,' Bev says, softening a little. 'It's just... the money really would help.'

I feel for my aunties too – perhaps Bev, slightly more than Vee – but this is just an impossible situation. Unless...

'I'll buy it,' I say, without really thinking it through.

'What?' my mum replies as she wipes her eyes.

'Yeah,' I say, figuring it out as I go. 'I'll buy it. I can do it up, modernise it, sell it later on, at some point, but this way you all get your money and there's no rush to empty it.'

'Love, you don't have to do that,' my mum insists.

'It will be a good investment,' I say. At least, I think it will.

Well, I've got the money, and I can't see me getting any more until I get some more work lined up, so it makes sense to invest in property, and my granddad's house is amazing, it just needs updating. I was thinking I may as well stick around up here, support my mum, at least until after Christmas. I can do some of the work myself, it will give me something to focus on.

'Can she do that?' Vee asks Gracie.

'How should I know?' she replies.

'Ask Carl, he works in conveyancing, doesn't he?' Vee replies.

'Right, yeah,' Gracie replies, then she realises the aunties are staring at her. 'What, right now?'

She seems a little taken aback by the aunties' eagerness to get their inheritance.

'OK, I'll go give him a call,' she says before heading into the kitchen, closing the door behind her.

'Oh, this would be perfect,' Bev says, before she and Vee switch to talking between themselves about how they're going to spend their money. The aunties have always been on the selfish side. My mum says it's an eldest-child thing – although she probably doesn't say it in front of Gracie, given that she's her eldest.

'Are you sure about this?' my mum asks me. 'It's a big thing to do, to buy a house...'

'It is, but I really want to,' I reply. 'I have so many memories attached to the place, it will be nice to spend some time there, and I really could do with a fun project.'

'It's a five-bedroom house,' she reminds me. 'That hasn't been decorated since *I* was in nappies.'

Mum may be exaggerating, ever so slightly, but Granddad's house is quite outdated now. He absolutely loved it the way it was, and something about changing it into something he would probably hate feels rotten, but I know he'd understand. He would never want it preserving as some sort of strange museum, dedicated to the life of Anthony Grant, the little-known-but-absolute-best granddad in the world.

'It will be fun,' I insist before lowering my voice. 'And it means you can empty it in your own time.'

My mum wells up again.

'Are you doing OK?' she asks me.

'Oh, you know,' I say, which is such a *my mum* thing to say.

'You don't have to put on a brave face here,' she insists.

'Does it look better like this?' I ask, using my index fingers to shift my eyebrows as far up my forehead as they'll budge, careful to glance over and make sure neither of the aunties clocks me making fun of Vee.

My mum erupts with laughter so I quickly let them go.

'Oh, love, I haven't laughed like that in days,' she says, squeezing my hand. 'Thank you.'

It's good to see her smile, even if it's only for a few seconds. I do need to put a brave face on it though, because my mum will find it easier to be strong if I do, so will Gracie. At a time like this it really is strength in numbers.

'OK, spoke to Carl,' Gracie announces as she joins us again. 'Yeah, he said that's all quite easy. Get it valued, agree a sale price, get the sale documents and deeds drawn up, or something to that effect.'

'Did he say how long it takes?' Vee asks, her eyes not getting any younger.

'He said he can turn it around in no time for you – maybe a couple of weeks or so, if Emmy doesn't need a mortgage. But he did say only one party can use him for the conveyancing.'

'Bagsy Carl, for legal services,' Vee says quickly.

'Sure, you can have him,' I say with a chuckle. 'I can find my own.'

'Yeah, well, that's that then,' Gracie says. 'He made it sound easy.'

'Let's shake on it,' Vee says.

She extends a hand in my direction. Her insanely long nails reach me about ten seconds before the rest of her hand.

'Wow, those are some nails,' I say, careful not to get stabbed by one of them.

'I'm doing nails now,' she tells me. 'You'll have to let me put a set on you, I'm practising for my business.'

I smile and nod. We'll see about that.

'So, I'm buying a house,' I say, like it's the most normal thing to say.

'You're buying a house,' Gracie replies before pursing her lips and telling me very clearly with her eyes that this may not be such a good idea.

Who knows if it is a good or bad idea – all I know is that it's going to make a very difficult time much easier for my family and it's going to give me a fun distraction, and lord knows I need one of those right now.

5

There's something magical about visiting your childhood bedroom, isn't there? *Is* there? I wouldn't actually know, because the house my mum and Roy share with their kids is not the house I grew up in.

I grew up with my mum, dad and Gracie in a modest semi-detached house at the other side of town. We stayed there for a while after my dad left, but then we moved in with Roy, and shortly after I moved away, my mum and Roy bought somewhere new together. So now they live here, in this beautiful four-bed detached, which is perfectly picturesque, and I'm staying in their guest room, which is gorgeous too – show-home worthy – but I feel no connection to it.

I feel a million miles from my life in London right now, which is preferable. I have defaulted to my personal phone number, leaving my work SIM at home. Well, everyone who knows me, who I can trust, has this number. None of my friends reached out to me when the news hit and when I called Laura to explain why I wasn't heading out, she was kind of cold with me, almost scared my bad press might be catching, until she asked me to be on her TV show again, as though I might suddenly be desperate enough to say yes. I don't need people like that right now. I'm happy only being contactable by my family and my agent.

There's a knock on the guest room door.

'Come in,' I call out.

I'm currently sitting on the bed, sorting through the limited clothing I brought with me, wishing I'd brought more because, truthfully, I didn't realise I was planning on staying until after Christmas until the thought popped into my head earlier.

'Hello, duck,' Roy says.

'Hey,' I say, jumping up from my bed, hurrying over to give him a hug.

Roy has always called me duck. I can't remember exactly why, it's just one of those silly childhood stories where, I think because he's always called Gracie goose, I must have felt left out, or something like that... I can't quite remember, but it still makes me smile.

Roy is technically my stepdad, but to be honest I just consider him my dad. Growing up, I would always tell my friends that Roy was my dad, no one needed to know any different, but when I think back to who played the 'dad roles' in my life I can't neglect to give my granddad an honourable mention. Before Roy was on the scene, he was always there – even before my dad left, to be honest. My granddad bought me everything I needed, he taught me to swim, to ride a bike, he attended every single parents' evening with my mum. After my dad left, despite a few forced visits at the start, I eventually stopped spending time with him. Especially as I grew older, and better understood what he had done to our family and why. My mum is an angel who has always encouraged me to have a relationship with my dad, but when she knew I was old enough to make up my own mind she let me and didn't say anything more about it, other than the occasional encouragement to reach out to him. Granddad could never forgive him either. No one hated my dad for what he did to our family more than my granddad. He never spoke a word to him, after the day he left.

'So good to see you, duck,' he says. 'How have you been? How's tricks in the forest? Still dominating, I hope?'

'You're never going to get spoilers out of me, so quit trying,' I say with a laugh, trying to push to the back of my mind the fact that I've been killed off. 'You'd be gutted if I ruined it for you anyway.'

It's always awkward when people push me for spoilers, given the fact I have a strict confidentiality agreement and couldn't tell them if I wanted to, but it's even more unpleasant now, especially because I can't tell them about my exit.

'You're probably right,' he replies. 'But I do still

need vengeance, after Shirley in accounts spoiled the death of Arancha for me, because she watched it *illegally* on the internet while her son was home from university. My kids don't pirate TV shows for me.'

'What was the point in having them then?' I joke.

'I ask myself the same thing,' he says with a chuckle. 'Moody little buggers, not like you and your sister.'

'Are they downstairs?' I ask.

'Yes, and dinner is ready, your mum said to tell you,' he replies. 'Bangers and mash. I've asked them to be nice.'

'The bangers and mash?' I quip.

'The horrible teenagers,' he replies. 'The bangers and mash are always lovely.'

'OK, let's go then,' I reply. 'I'm starving.'

'You're back to eating meat then?' he asks as we head downstairs.

'I never really stopped,' I reply. 'It was just the diet they keep me on for the role, so obviously I don't need to worry about that now.'

Shit.

'Ooh, why, is Adelina going to turn into a huge elf?' he asks curiously.

Incredible, that I've almost let slip already, after years of never leaking a word of what happens in the show. I guess this time it's different.

'I've filmed all my scenes for the season,' I reply. 'Had a few reshoots yesterday but that was it. I figured I can let my hair down and have what I like – it is Christmas after all.'

'A very valid point,' Roy replies. 'I've been going to the gym recently, can you tell?'

You can't.

'You can,' I reply.

'I've been working on my muscles,' he says proudly.

Roy is a small, skinny man with a shiny bald head. If he got buff he would look terrifying.

'Good for you,' I tell him.

'Better for you that you're having a break from it,' he replies as we approach the dining room.

He pauses in the doorway for a second.

'Ladies and gentlemen,' he starts, in a ring announcer-style voice, as though I'm about to take part in WrestleMania. 'Emmy Palmer!'

'Hello, love,' my mum says cheerily but calmly.

The twins react even less to the playful hype.

Louis and Megan are a matter of days away from their eighteenth birthday, which means they'll legally be adults soon, but they're still very teenagery teenagers. I imagine we all feel like we were more grown-up at certain ages than those who come after us. They still look like kids to me, although Megan definitely looks more grown-up than her twin brother, with her face full of make-up and her poker-straight brown hair. Louis still looks like a scruffy kid, with his messy brown curls and his baby face.

'Hey,' Louis says with a nod.

'Hi,' Megan adds, only looking up from her phone for long enough to make obligatory eye contact with me.

Generally speaking, people think I have a pretty cool job, to the point where it doesn't seem to matter what kind of person I am, people will tend to be friendly with me. Not Louis and Megan though. I not only do not impress them in the slightest, it's almost as though they have a negative opinion of me.

'Emmy, can you help me carry dinner through, or maybe sort some drinks?' my mum asks.

I absolutely love that, when I'm home, I'm just like anyone else visiting home.

'Sure,' I reply.

'Can I have a beer?' Louis asks.

'Of course, you can, lad,' Roy replies. Louis' face lights up. 'When you're eighteen.'

Louis sulks dramatically, like Kevin the moody teenager played by Harry Enfield – a reference that I'm sure would only make me seem a million years old, if I made it.

'I am literally days away from being eighteen,' Louis reminds him.

'Well, I'll be the first one to wish you happy birthday,' Roy says through a smile he can't quite hide. 'But until then best I can do is a J2O.'

'We'll be right back,' Mum says.

She hooks her arm with mine as we walk to the kitchen.

'You doing OK?' I ask her.

'Hanging in there,' she says. 'Keeping the brave face on for the kids. I worry about how they're handling it.'

'Ah, they seem fine – hostile as ever,' I joke.

'They do love you, you know,' Mum tells me.

I make a nondescript noise and pull a face to convey just how much I doubt that.

'They do,' she insists.

'Their faces, voices and general demeanours must have missed the memo,' I say with a shrug. 'It's fine, they're teenagers.'

'I think now that they're a bit older – and don't say anything, will you? – that your job is starting to make things a bit difficult for them at school,' she says in hushed tones as she dollops mashed potato into a serving bowl.

'Oh?' is about all I can think to say.

'Yes, well, all their school friends watch you and, you know, lots of sex, lots of nudity. It isn't easy being a teenager – especially a teenage boy – when it's your sister, and your mates are teasing you.'

'Oh,' I say again, still not really knowing how to

reply. 'I don't suppose I'd thought about it like that.'

I feel a bit icky suddenly.

My granddad's voice pops into my head, because he always used to tell me not to give a shit about what anyone thought, so long as I was happy.

'That's a big smile,' Mum points out.

'Just thinking about Granddad,' I tell her. 'And the things he would say.'

'Yes, he keeps popping into my head too,' she replies. 'I'm taking comfort in it though. It's as though he'll never really be gone.'

Mum's voice crackles a little on those last few words. I briefly remove the spoon from her hand and give her a hug.

'It's going to be OK,' I tell her.

'It is,' she replies. 'The funeral will be hard, and I might kill an auntie in the meantime, but I'm so just so happy you're here.'

'How are the plans going?' I ask.

'The aunties are overwhelmed,' she replies. 'And they have no idea what he would want. I need to go to his house tomorrow, pick out a suit for him... the aunties thought it might be too hard.'

'As though we get a choice,' I say with a sigh. 'Would you like me to come with you? I can help you choose something, and it would be good to see the place, see what I'm getting myself into.'

I laugh playfully but, you know, that's a good point. What am I getting myself into?

'I haven't been there since the day I... found him,' she says. 'I'd really appreciate you coming with me.'

'No trouble at all,' I reply. 'It's just so nice to spend time with you.'

'It really is,' she replies. 'I do miss you.'

'I miss your cooking,' I tell her, lightening the mood. 'Come on, let's get this stuff through before it goes cold. It smells amazing.'

I help Mum carry the food through before popping back to grab a round of soft drinks and a beer for Roy, which he seems to delight in drinking in front of his underage son, before taking my seat at the table.

Dinner is amazing, and Mum and Roy's house is so lovely, and warm, and homely but, I don't know, I do feel like a guest here. I mind my manners, I ask for things you wouldn't usually ask for in your family home, and I feel a little self-conscious in front of the twins now, knowing that I'm apparently ruining their street cred.

But all of that considered, I'm happy to be sticking around for the rest of the year, mostly just so that I can be here to support my mum. Well, the aunties are useless, and I'm hearing Gracie's name being mentioned less that I usually would, she's normally the first person to step up and help. Perhaps she thinks she gets a break now that I'm here. Perhaps she deserves one.

It's going to be hard, going to Granddad's house tomorrow, knowing he isn't going to be here, but I'll do it for my mum.

Strength in numbers. We all just need to help each other through this next week, through the funeral, and then that's the hardest part over. I hope. But I just can't seem to fully acknowledge the feeling that Granddad is gone and he isn't coming back. Not because I'm in denial but because I just can't imagine a world without him in it.

6

It's been almost a year since the last time I visited 29 Mulberry Crescent, my gran and granddad's large detached house, but standing outside it over the years never felt any different. Until today.

It has never mattered how old I was – four, fourteen, thirty-four – I would always take a moment to stand outside and stare up at the place.

It's an old, stone-built Victorian house. They all are on this cul-de-sac. All perfectly picturesque, in their own way, but with some big differences.

It's quite helpful, having Gracie's husband Carl on the case, because not only does he work in conveyancing, but he knows everyone else in the area who does too. He's sending someone over to do an official valuation, but he has some insider knowledge, having recently sold another house on the street.

Mulberry Crescent, while still tastefully sympathetic to its origins, is a real mixture of old and new. There are twelve houses on this street, not identical properties, but all from a similar time and of a similar size. Carl has informed me that this street is fast becoming the place to be, and property on it is rapidly increasing in value, because people are slowly buying up these tired old houses and turning them into modern mansions. With the addition of large extensions to create modern open-plan living spaces, bi-folding doors, double-height windows that allow light to pour into the main hallways (I always remember Granddad's seeming so dark, especially with the dark, wood-panelled walls and the banister to match), it's a fusion of old and new that is really quite attractive. But what Carl told me about the most recent fixer-upper property that was sold on the street, and the sheer volume of ever-increasing offers over the asking price, tells me that buying this house is actually a really smart investment for me, even if I don't really know what I'm doing. I'd imagine, if my own family weren't selling it, there would be a bidding war, even if it is tired and very old-fashioned. I suppose I'm lucky (in a very weird sort of way) that I have one auntie who doesn't want her husband to lose his kneecaps to a gang of men and another auntie who wants to lose some of her eyelids so she can attract similar.

The nostalgia hit that was missing when I was at Mum and Roy's house is more than compensated for, just by standing in this garden now. All my favourite childhood memories are of things that happened in this house. I'm sure Mum feels the same way.

She hesitates at the door for a second. I don't know if she's messing with the keys to buy herself a little more time or if she just can't get her hands to work. She must be casting her mind back to the day she found him here. Poor Granddad. I can't stand the thought that he was all alone.

'Hey, let me go in first,' I suggest. 'I just want to, kind of, cast my eye over the hallway, seeing it for the first time in ages, to see if any inspiration hits for doing the place up in the future.'

That makes absolutely no sense. None at all. Obviously, I'm just trying to save her from retracing her steps from a couple of days ago and, thankfully, she doesn't question my shaky logic.

'Yes, OK,' she says, stepping to one side. 'I'm glad you're keeping it, if only for a little while. Granddad would be so happy if he knew.'

I step inside first with my mum close behind me. I turn to look at her and catch her staring up the stairs.

'Put the kettle on,' I say. 'I'll just nip to the loo.'

'OK, love,' she says with a heavy sigh.

I watch Mum head for the kitchen before dashing upstairs.

Even though I've visited my granddad countless times across the years, I haven't actually been up these stairs in forever. I used to love charging up them when I was a kid, before sliding back down the shiny, wooden banister.

I head for my granddad's bedroom to make sure there's nothing in there that will upset my mum, and thank God that I do. The paramedics, understandably in such a rush to get my granddad to the hospital, have left a few random things scattered around the messy bed. I quickly straighten his bed covers, to make it look less like he was just ripped out of it, and kick the rubbish under the bed. One of the things the paramedics left behind is what I'd guess is a bag of saline, just lying there on the floor. I can't help but imagine being in my mum's shoes, watching them fight to save him, trying and abandoning different things before hurrying him into an ambulance. This stuff is the last thing she needs to see.

I find Mum sitting at the wooden table in the centre of the kitchen. It's a massive kitchen – it would most certainly have an island at its heart, if you were redesigning it. All of the rooms here are a generous size, in a way that you just don't seem to find these days. I know property in London is entirely its own thing, so not really comparable to houses up here, but I know that when I was apartment hunting, I just couldn't get over how tiny the rooms were in most places.

Similarly, Gracie recently bought a new build here and, while they're beautiful houses, the rooms don't compare to these ones as far as the size goes. Of course, Gracie's place is tastefully modern, but here things are positively not. Take Granddad's open-plan lounge and dining room, for example. Such a large space but so cluttered with old chairs and chests of drawers – he even has an old box-shaped TV, rather than a flat modern one. He was more than happy with it and didn't want to change it, so there was no sense in forcing a new one on him. Gracie bought him a digital radio to replace the old one on his bedside table – it's probably still brand new in its box in a cupboard somewhere.

'He spent so much time in this house, especially in recent months, that it just feels so peculiar to be in here without him,' Mum says. 'More so because it feels like he's still here.'

She nods towards an almost-empty teacup, I'd imagine from the night before he died, sitting on the table. As I take the seat next to Mum, I notice a worn pair of slippers sticking out from under one of the other chairs. It really is like he's still here, pottering around somewhere, and I'm just waiting for him to walk in and ask me if I've got the 'good stuff' – he always called his favourite whisky 'the good stuff' – and he'd always pour me a small glass, safe in the knowledge I hated it, before shrugging, smiling, and topping up his own glass with it.

'Let me make the tea,' I insist, swiping the old teacup away, placing it in the sink and putting the kettle on.

'Thanks, love,' she replies. 'I still can't believe it. That we're here, and he isn't, and we're picking out an outfit for him to be cremated in.'

And this is why I don't like funerals. What a thing to have to get your head around, to have to pick out an outfit, knowing what it's for, what's going to happen.

'I know, it's awful, I'm so sorry,' I say as I wrap my arms around her, standing behind her chair, resting my chin on her shoulder. 'But I'll help you through it.'

My mum holds my hands and squeezes them in acknowledgement.

'Let's talk about something good,' she insists. 'This will be your house soon. Well, I know you're not going to live in it, but it will be your project, I suppose.'

'I don't have to rush to do anything, you know,' I say, worried my mum might find it upsetting to see the house slowly changing. 'We could just lock the place up and leave it for a while.'

'Oh no, love, don't worry,' she insists. 'It has to happen eventually and the thought of you doing it is a lovely one. Have you thought about what you're going to do?'

'Well, I remember how enormous the attic is, so plenty of storage for things you and the aunties don't want or don't want yet, no rush to move anything out. I thought I might just start emptying rooms and get straight on with the decorating... renovating... decorating?'

It's just occurred to me that I don't fully know what I'm doing.

'Vee can't stop raving about the young man who did her facias,' Mum says.

'I bet she can't,' I say through a snigger. 'I have no idea what that means.'

'He's done a few odd jobs for her,' Mum continues, not picking up on my amusement.

If he's a young man alone in Vee's house with her, I'll bet she had him doing some *seriously* odd jobs.

'He's really good, and well connected – shall I ask him to pop around?' she asks.

'Yeah, that would be great,' I reply. 'Maybe he can help me formulate some kind of plan.'

'I do think it's nice, that you've bought the place, your granddad really would be so happy.'

You can tell she means that. She has such a peaceful smile. It's so nice, to be able to do this for her.

But then her smile falls.

'Let's go pick out a suit,' she says. 'I just want to get it over with and have a rest before the aunties and Gracie come over later. Your sister is insisting on saying a few words at the service. That's fine by me, of course, but she isn't good at public speaking at the best of times, never mind when she's upset. But you can't tell Gracie anything, can you?'

'You certainly can't,' I say with a smile. 'But at least you've got me here to help you now. I actually think I might be the normal one.'

Mum just laughs.

'Thanks again for coming,' she says. 'And for helping. And for buying an actual house to save me a few tears.'

'I'll always be here when you need me,' I tell her. 'And I definitely need a break from London right now.'

'Do you want-to-slash-need-to talk about what's going on with you?' she asks.

'Definitely not,' I reply. 'But, thank you.'

'Maybe once all this is over,' she says before quickly changing the subject. 'Right, you finish making those cups of tea, I'll see you upstairs and we'll try and find a suit your granddad wouldn't hate wearing, because he did hate wearing all suits.'

'I'd think he'd be furious, if you choose any-thing other than a clip-on tie,' I say with a chuckle.

'Oh, Bev and Vee will be furious if I do, but you're right, it's what he would have wanted,' she says before sighing deeply and heading upstairs.

I hurriedly finish making the cups of tea. I'll have a word with Vee's 'lovely young man' builder and see what he has to say. I'm nervous, and kind of excited, but mostly, just so happy I'm going to have a distraction, from losing Granddad, and from work drama. Mostly, I am secretly delighted I'm going to have a hiding place. I can't imagine showing my face in London again for a while.

7

What's the worst first date you've ever been on?

I imagine there are two kinds of answers to that question. I reckon most of us have a few tales of first dates that ranged from crap to mediocre. I fall into this category. My mediocre dates are the ones where things have been fine, but there just hasn't been a spark or I didn't have much fun. As for crappy dates, I'd say my weirdest experience was the guy who took me to Five Guys because I'd said I liked it there, but because he was 'clean eating' he just watched me eat, but that was just awkward (yes, I did have a burger anyway) and kind of dull. Not exactly a nightmare.

But then there's the other kind of worst first date. The one where, if you ask the question, the person responding has this one big, awful, epic nightmare of a first date, so awful it's the only one they mention. All the crap and mediocre ones have faded from their memory, to make way for a monumental stinker of a date to haunt them forever.

A date at a wake has to fall into that category, without a doubt.

'That's a really nice dress,' Dave tells me. 'Really nice. Quite tight.'

I awkwardly tug at my dress ever so slightly, as though that's going to make my 'tight' dress (that isn't actually *that* tight) able to cloak my body from his gaze.

'Thanks,' I say. I need to change the subject because I'm feeling so awkward right now. 'So, what do you do?'

I can hear muffled voices coming from upstairs. I can't quite tell if they're raised, like in an argument, or just loud, as is often the case in this family.

The only noise in this room, other than the intermittent conversation between Dave and me, is the sound of the clock on top of the fireplace ticking – and I swear it sounds much slower than usual.

'I work at Barton's cider brewery,' he says before pausing to eyeball the living room. Then he turns back to me. 'You?'

'I'm an actress,' I say.

I think we'll leave it at that. I don't mind telling people I'm an actress when they don't know who I am because usually they just give me a polite smile and tell me 'That's nice', but I can see behind their smile and behind their eyes that they feel sorry for me, that they think I'm some poor jobbing actress struggling to get gigs. I like it that way though.

'I do know who you are,' Dave tells me, looking me up and down. 'I've seen a bit of your stuff... I've seen, you know... bits on the internet.'

Dave must be in his late fifties. He looks like he should be working in a brewery – or hanging around one, at the least. He has a long beard, a ZZ Top style one, with longish messy hair to match. It's a sort of a sandy-yellow kind of grey. His fingers have yellow staining, as do his teeth, and the culprit is no surprise. Not only does he smell like cigarettes, but he has one, pre-rolled, behind his ear, poking out through his hair.

'You've seen something I've been in?' I reply.

'I've seen... a scene or two,' he says, widening his eyes for effect.

I roll my eyes. Is he trying to suggest he's seen one of my romantic scenes or something? These scenes are always carefully shot and, while we might be nearly naked when we film them, they're edited in a way that means no one has ever actually seen me naked... but people like this always make me feel like they have, and like I didn't exactly get a say in the matter, which I *hate.*

I look over at the fireplace, at the slow-ticking clock, then at the framed photo next to it of my mum and Roy, smiling widely, almost like they're laughing at the weird situation I've found myself in. I imagine I'll see the funny side of it later.

'Erm, OK,' I reply.

I take my phone from my bag and do that thing we're all guilty of when we're sitting in a waiting room or avoiding someone in the street. I aimlessly switch from app to app, looking at nothing in particular, just to busy my eyes.

'Nothing funny,' Dave says quickly. 'Just when I saw your photo on Matcher, I was curious, so I looked you up.'

He has my attention now.

'What?' I say. 'You saw *my* photo on a dating app?'

Oh boy, I hope my photos aren't being used for catfishing, that's the last thing I need.

'Yes, well, a photo of you with Vera,' he says.

My eyebrows shoot up just as Auntie Vee walks in the room.

'Can I use the bog?' he asks in his super-strong Yorkshire accent.

'Of course,' Vee replies. 'Little room under the stairs.'

Once it's just the two of us in the living room she sits down next to me.

'Thanks ever so much for keeping him company while I was upstairs,' Vee says. 'You doing OK, chick?'

She gives me a sort of concerned smile and a squeeze of my leg. Things that would be perfectly normal, and appreciated on the day of my grand-dad's funeral, except...

'I'm just trying to work out what's weirder,' I start. 'The fact that you're using a photo of me on your dating app profile, or that you're bringing a date to a *wake*.'

'Well, first of all, it's a picture *with* you, not *of* you, I am a proud auntie – is that a crime?' she demands to know. 'And you're not the only one who gets to be sad today, you know, he was my dad. Of all the days for me to be alone, and all the shitty family events we all have to turn up to, this is the one I do not want to go to alone, OK?'

I suppose she has a point. Kind of. I get why she wouldn't want to be alone but, still, who brings a plus-one to a funeral?

It was my mum and Bev dragging Vee upstairs to 'help with my mum's dress' that landed me alone in the living room with Dave. Obviously, they were taking her up there to ask her what the hell she was thinking bringing him here, and my mum insisted I stayed downstairs with him, to keep an eye on him, although it felt more like he was keeping an eye on me.

'Much better,' Dave announces as he rejoins us. 'Are the funeral cars here yet?'

I raise an eyebrow.

'You'll need to drive behind us in your own car, like we said,' Vee reminds him.

Oh, thank God for that, mum would have hit the roof.

The front door opens and closes.

'Hello,' Gracie calls out.

'We're in here,' I call back.

Gracie looks great in a black skirt, black coat and a white blouse, but I can see her dark circles and her tired eyes, no matter how much make-up she's wearing to try and conceal it. She looks like she's been up all night crying her eyes out.

She looks at Dave, then at me, for an explanation.

'Auntie Vee's date,' I tell her casually.

Gracie just shakes her head and bats her hand

dismissively, as though she isn't surprised, nor is she all that bothered.

'Can I see you in the kitchen?' she asks.

'Yes, of course,' I reply.

'You two are sisters?' Dave double-checks as we're about to leave the room.

'We are,' I reply.

'You talk different,' he says, in such a way that makes it obvious he isn't a fan of my particular accent, because he scrunches his nose up at me.

'Emmy lives down south,' Gracie tells him politely as we shuffle past.

'There's nowt wrong with where you come from,' Dave calls after me as we leave the room.

'Oh, I can think of one or two things,' I reply, under my breath, just loud enough for Gracie to hear me.

Once inside the kitchen we both take a seat at the breakfast bar, where Mum has laid out tea, coffee and pastries. It all looks amazing but I couldn't eat a thing. It doesn't look like anyone else is hungry either, because it all remains perfectly untouched.

'Can I get you anything?' I offer.

'Oh, God, no thanks,' Gracie says, practically gagging at the suggestion. 'I just thought I'd save you from the random man in the living room.'

'You're not knocked up again, are you?' I ask.

'Emmy, of course not,' she snaps back. 'What's *your* excuse? Do you have an eating disorder?'

I can tell from the look on her face that she immediately regrets her outburst.

'Sorry,' she says softly.

'No, I'm sorry,' I say. 'I only meant that, you used to make that face at food when you were first pregnant, that's all.'

'I get it,' she says. 'I'm just so stressed out.'

Gracie clocks my hands.

'Oh, God, did Vee get you with a set of her hideous fake nails?' she asks, already knowing the answer.

'Oh yeah, big time,' I reply, admiring the Tanya Turner-style talons glued to my finger ends. 'She was starting to wind Mum up last night with, you know, just her general personality, so I mentioned it to distract her. Turns out she had her kit in the car.'

'Oh, lucky you,' she jokes sarcastically.

I decide to pour us cups of tea. To be honest, I think we need it. It's going to be a long day.

'Where are Carl and the kids?' I ask.

'They went ahead to the church,' she replies.

'Yeah, so did Roy and the twins, help get things ready – there's going to be a sort of slide-show type thing, apparently,' I say, with all the importance you'd afford a rocket that had landed on Mars.

'Fancy,' she replies sarcastically.

I smile as she eagerly takes the teacup from me.

'Do you think your eulogy is a good idea?' I ask softly. 'If you're not feeling great.'

'I'm doing it, Emmy,' she insists. 'I *can* do it. And it's all planned and written down, so I only have to read the damn thing.'

'OK, I was just checking,' I say. 'Because I don't think I could stand up there and do that today.'

We're interrupted by Dave who coughs loudly as he enters the room. I'm not sure if this is to alert us to his presence or if it's just because he smokes too much. We both stare at him.

'Just came to see if I could cadge a brew,' he says. His eyes light up. 'Ooh, croissants!'

The way he pronounces croissants – exactly as you would guess, going off the spelling alone – makes me cringe.

'Should put me on until the funeral scran,' he tells us.

I force a smile and give him a nod of acknowledgement. Dave is so Yorkshire it hurts. He eventually leaves the room with what he came for.

'No matter what happens, we just need to keep him away from Mum,' I tell Gracie. 'The last thing we need is for this funeral to go the way of basically all of our family events.'

'Remember at Great Auntie Joan's funeral, when Uncle Richard showed everyone the scar on his arse "from the Falklands"?' Gracie says, somehow smiling *and* grimacing.

'Ergh, I can still see it when I close my eyes,' I say with a shudder. 'Funny how he never mentions that it was nothing to do with the war, and that he actually hurt himself chasing a penguin when he was pissed-up on holiday.'

Gracie snorts.

Seeing the scar on Uncle Richard's aggressively ageing buttock was an ordeal, but seeing him fall over in the first place would definitely be something I would have enjoyed, if I were there.

'Today is going to be horrible, isn't it?' Gracie says with a sigh.

'We'll get through it together,' I tell her. 'Strength in numbers.'

'Yeah, that's true,' she says, squeezing my hand. 'I don't know if anyone has told you, but Dad is going to be there.'

'What?' I shriek. 'Oh, God. As if I don't have e-bloody-nough to deal with today.'

'Come on, we'll get through it together,' Gracie reminds me, in her most soothing voice.

'Hmm,' I say, unconvinced.

Today is going to be hard enough. The last thing I need is my absent bloody father turning up for once – who my granddad *hated*, by the way – it just feels like such a double slap in the face.

It's fine. It's going to be fine. I just need to make sure Gracie doesn't unravel, make sure Dave doesn't talk to my mum, make sure my dad doesn't talk to me...

It's a distraction from grieving, sure, but today is going to be hard enough.

I knock back my tea as I hear my mum coming down the stairs.

'The cars are here,' she shouts from the hallway.

I take a deep breath. OK, here we go. It's just this one day and then that's the funeral done.

Why do I feel like it's going to be one hell of a long one?

8

The last time I was in this church was for Great Auntie Joan's funeral. I brought my then-boyfriend (note: boyfriend, not date) and Auntie Bev introduced him to the vicar as 'Emmy's *friend,* Will' – extra emphasis on friend, because God forbid the vicar know I fraternise with boys. I'm sure Reverend John will be pleased to see I'm solo at this one.

Not much at all has changed here since the last time I visited – not that it ever does in churches. The only thing I've spotted so far is the 'modern' new sign they've had placed in the doorway. It says:

Christ Church

They've somewhat creatively made the 't' into a cross. I say somewhat because they haven't done a very good job. It looks like it says Chris Church, which really amuses me for some reason.

'Anthony "Tony" Grant,' Reverend John says, kicking things off.

I glance around the church, which is absolutely packed, but I expected no less. My granddad was an amazing man, everyone loved him.

I really, really wish we could overhaul the whole funeral system, because seeing his coffin in the car – and now at the front of the church – is something I'm struggling with. This isn't how I want to remember him. I want to remember him as he was the last time I saw him, through all the memories I had of him growing up, and all the wonderful things people are saying about him today.

'And now one of Tony's granddaughters would like to say a few words,' John announces. 'Grace, if you would like to join me.'

Gracie jumps, as though she wasn't expecting it. She flashes me a worried look before removing a folded piece of paper from her handbag and heading towards the front of the church.

'You'll do great,' I whisper after her.

Gracie stands in front of a microphone set up for the occasion. She leans forward to speak into it and, as she says 'hello', her voice booms around the room. She flinches. She seems so unbearably nervous; I wish I could help her.

'When we were planning Granddad's funeral, I knew I wanted to get up here and talk about him – even though public speaking isn't really something I'm good at – because I wanted the world to know just how important he was to all of us,' she starts.

I glance over at my mum, who is sitting one seat away from me, and smile. She dabs her cheeks lightly with a tissue. She's smiling at Gracie, nodding along with her speech, which she must have practised for my mum a million times. I just kept out of it. I could tell it was something Gracie really wanted to do on her own – she's always been so painfully independent – and that was fine by me. I would never sign up to do something like this. I just don't think I'd be able to pour out my heart in front of an audience – not with my actual feelings, obviously. What I'll *pretend* to do in front of an audience clearly knows no bounds.

'...and then he met my gran, Annie, and they got married, and then had their twins, Vera and Beverly, and then my mum, Deana,' Gracie continues. 'And when it... and when it came to family... When my granddad would talk about my gran, he would always... he would always say...'

Oh, God. Gracie is struggling. She's really struggling. It's hurting my heart, watching her, there's an actual pain in my chest.

'He used to say...'

Gracie hits her limit. She's had enough. She doesn't think she can do it. She hurries from the stage and takes her seat back in between Mum and me.

Reverend John hovers somewhere between where he was standing and the microphone. I don't think he knows what to say or do.

Gracie sits with her face in her hands. I look

over at my mum, who is pleading at me with her eyes, asking me to do *something.*

I widen my eyes at her. Isn't it funny, how you can have full conversations, without saying a word, with those closest to you?

I don't know whether it's something Mum tells me with her eyes, or if it's just something stupid I decide to do on the spot, but before I know it, I am hurrying to take Gracie's place, standing in front of the microphone, at the front of the church, in front of all these people, and I don't even have her speech to finish reading it, because she took her piece of paper with her.

Right, OK, I just need to think...

'Hello, I'm Emmy, one of Tony's other grand-children, I'm just going to pick up where my sister left off,' I say, hopefully loud enough to hide the rumbling in my stomach. Wow, it's been a long time since I had stage fright. Even the last time I was on this stage, when I was probably only ten or twelve, I stood here and sang 'Tomorrow' from *Annie* – I don't even remember why, it was a primary school thing – and I felt more confident than I do now. I daren't make eye contact with anyone. I just need to look through the audience and get this over with.

'Granddad always used to repeat one quote about family – in fact, he even had a magnet on his fridge with it on. It was: "Family is a gift that lasts forever",' I start.

I dare to glance at my audience, the sad faces, the encouraging smiles. I even hear a few 'aww's. There's a huge tear lurking in my right eye but I can't let it slip out. I need to keep my brave face on.

'But then he would quickly tell us it was bullsh... errr...' Oh boy, perhaps I shouldn't quote Granddad word perfect in church. I laugh awkwardly. 'He would tell us that quote was rubbish. He actually really hated it because he always felt like it suggested family was something everyone just had. As though it just ticks along in the background for our entire lives, with no maintenance or effort. Granddad knew better than that. He said families were hard work. That every single member was actively choosing to be there, playing their part, keeping things running smoothly. If someone didn't want to be a part of a family any more and removed themselves from the machine, well, other members would have to step in and replace the missing parts. Granddad didn't think family was a gift, he thought it was an honour. And, while I agree with him wholeheartedly, at the same time I always knew that he was a gift. That I was lucky enough to have wound up with the world's best... not just granddad, but the world's best human. If he were here, I think he'd tell you to hug your loved ones extra tightly tonight, and if there's one thing I've learned from him, it is to absolutely worship those who love you. And bull to those who don't.'

I can't help but smile on those last few words. Granddad was (what my gran used to call) a 'mouth' because of his colourful language. He wouldn't have said 'bull', he would have said something far worse, but we are in a church.

'Anyway... thanks,' I say, providing a rather awkward finish to a speech I was otherwise pretty happy with, especially given the fact I improvised it.

'Absolutely beautiful,' John says as he takes my place, front and centre. 'Thank you, Emmy.'

I'm over the moon to see that, as I glance around the church, most people are smiling, giving me little waves or nods of acknowledgement. My mum is a heartbreaking mixture of a big smile and eyes full of tears. I'm taken aback as I sit back down next to Gracie though. She is scowling at me.

'Are you OK?' I whisper to her as John sets us all up for yet another hymn. I suppose, in a church, you have to have hymns at a funeral, right? Granddad would have *hated* it though. Hymns like this, at funerals, are a guaranteed source of tears. Each deep breath, before you push out each line of sadness, is like a kick to the stomach. As though any of us need help extracting tears right now.

'I can't believe you did that,' Gracie replies through gritted teeth.

'Did what?' I reply.

'Stole the show,' she replies.

We're all instructed to stand up to sing.

'Abide With Me'. Christ, does it get more depressing than that? (Also, can I say 'Christ' like that here?)

I give Gracie a playful nudge with my elbow.

She ignores me. Wow, she really is mad at me. It's times like these I wish I had an older brother, instead of an older sister, because Gracie does have a flare for the dramatic (although she'd swear the same was actually more true of me).

How on earth can she accuse me of trying to steal the show? She bailed on her speech – and I don't blame her, because I have insisted all along that getting up and saying a few words at a funeral sounds like torture, and something I would never do – and the only way I found the strength (or at least pretended I did) to take her place was to fill the sudden silence, the pause in the programme, because I didn't want her to feel embarrassed, or like she'd let anyone down.

As the service draws to an end, and it's time for the family to leave the church first, Engelbert Humperdinck's 'Can't Take My Eyes Off You' plays – the one part of this whole thing (except maybe my impromptu almost-swearing) that Granddad would be happy with. It's such a happy song. I can't help but smile – subtly, of course, this is a funeral after all – as I walk down the aisle. I think about him and my gran, playing the song on their record player, dancing together in the dining room while Gracie and I sat at the table, watching, giggling. We absolutely loved sleepovers at their house when we were kids. This song will always be my lasting memory of those good times.

You know when you can just feel someone's eyes on you? I mean, obviously lots of people are looking at us, offering us sympathetic glances as we make our way out of the church, but it's not that. I feel uncomfortable, like someone is staring at me. On the occasions someone clocks me on the Tube or shopping, I get this same feeling.

I don't need to look for long before I realise. That's when I spot him. The last person I want to see right now. It isn't an ex, or anything that could be remotely amusing – this isn't a movie meet-cute – it's (for lack of a better term) my dad.

He smiles at me and all I can think to do is look away, pretending I didn't see him, although we both know I did. Genuinely, the only thing that could make this day worse is my bloody dad being here. I glance at Gracie, hoping she's noticed, hoping for a little support, but she's so mad at me she can't even hold eye contact.

Great. Great, great, great. I was worried this wake was going to be boring, I'm *soooo* happy to have all these avenues of tension now. This is *just* what I needed today.

9

I should probably preface what I'm about to say with the fact that I don't know whether this applies to everyone, or just my family, but I like to think it isn't just an 'us' thing.

Why is it that funerals are always so much fun? When I think of funerals I've been to – every single one – while the service is always a serious, respectful affair, the wake is usually a party. I suppose you need one, to offset the tragedy of the day, and how often is it that you get everyone in one room like this?

I don't know why it is, but I can't say I've ever

had a bad time at a wake (although today is shaping up to be an exception). I feel so odd saying it, I really do, but I think it's that strength-in-numbers thing, everyone spending time together, trying to focus on the good memories and the good times again. It's a big, warm hug on an otherwise horrible day.

It's a little different today though, because today I am trying to avoid my dad. Eric Watson. It's hard to decide if he was a worse dad or husband – I like to think he excelled at being the absolute worst at both. Looking back, I don't suppose I do have any happy memories with him, or whether perhaps his finale in our family was enough to cancel out everything that came before it. Well, when you find out your dad is cheating on your mum, and then he leaves you all to start a new family with his new girlfriend, it kind of takes the shine off the fact that he taught you how to ride a bike (although incidentally he didn't teach me how to ride my bike, my granddad did). Dad ditched us when we needed him the most and, not only did he obviously not come back, but for some reason he decided his best course of action was to stay away. It was only in more recent years (coincidentally, when I'd finally landed a big TV show) that he started really sniffing round again. I couldn't be less interested in a relationship with him but he doesn't seem to take the hint.

The wake is being held at The Anchor, one of the only pubs in Marram Bay that is actually a pub. All we really have here these days are fancy bars or stylish pubs, but The Anchor has a real working-men's club vibe. Granddad used to come here every weekend, back when he could get around on his own.

It's a dark place, literally speaking, thanks to all the dark wood and dull-green soft furnishings, that aren't all that soft any more. We've got the private function room for the wake to ourselves. Sort of like at a wedding, there are far more people here at the wake than there were at the church, but unlike weddings or funerals, the evening do tends to be a family-only thing.

I spy Gracie over at the buffet table so I make my way over there. She's taking sandwich requests from her kids, Darcy and Oscar. Darcy is seven and Oscar is five, and it sounds like they're both about as fussy when it comes to eating as Gracie was when she was a kid. My mum always tells stories about that one year when all Gracie was willing to eat was ketchup, which Gracie always denies. She finds her childhood stories embarrassing whereas I tend to lean into them. Then again, I probably have far more to feel embarrassed about these days.

I pick up a white paper napkin from the table and wave it in front of her.

'Hello,' I say cautiously. 'Please don't stab me with a breadstick.'

Gracie's tight jaw suddenly relaxes.

'I'm sorry,' she says. 'I'm a mental B.'

She lowers her voice, just in case the kids have suddenly cracked her system where she replaces swear words with letters.

'A raging, F-ing B,' I reply quietly through a smile. 'But seriously, I'm sorry if I did the wrong thing.'

'You didn't do the wrong thing,' she insists. 'I just bottled it, thanks for picking up the pieces.'

'My agent will send you my bill,' I say with a bat of my hand.

'Are you going to eat something?' she asks.

'Erm, yes,' I reply.

Everything looks absolutely amazing, but the more you love the person whose funeral it is, the harder it can be to eat.

Gracie spots something over my shoulder. I look behind me but I can't work out what it is.

'Can you watch the kids for a minute?' she asks.

'Erm...'

'Thanks,' she says, not waiting for a reply before she dashes off.

'Right,' I say to myself.

All of the food is from M&S and I don't think I ever met a version of a Colin the Caterpillar cake I didn't like – Colin is a British icon, and a chocolate caterpillar cake is a staple at any party, no matter how old you are. I pick up a plate of mini Colins before popping a whole one in my mouth, much to the amusement of my niece and nephew.

'You want one instead of those sandwiches?' I ask them through a mouthful of chocolate cake.

They both nod. Well, come on, they just lost their great-granddad, if a little cake makes them smile, then why not?

'Cheers,' I say, holding one up for them to 'clink' theirs with. Mine looks so funny, in between my fingers, with my comedically long nails. I should have just used a nail to skewer one, it would have been easier.

'I always knew you'd be good with kids,' I hear a voice behind me say. It's my dad.

'I guess I take after my mum then,' I reply, unable to resist taking a swipe, I hate it when he pretends he knows me. He left when I was six so he hasn't exactly featured in my life all that much. He's barely a guest star.

'It's good to see you,' he says, sort of sheepishly. I always feel this awkward undertone of something from him. Embarrassment, I think, but I'm never sure if it's for everything he's done over the years, or if it's just from the immediate discomfort of being face to face with me. 'How have you been?'

'Better,' I reply, full of my usual angst. It turns out, when you have daddy issues, you harbour that typical teenage resentment into your adult life. 'Fine,' I add, softening ever so slightly. 'You?'

'Can't complain,' he says as he scratches his beard.

Dad isn't much taller than me – I'd swear he's shrinking as he's getting older, because he can't be more than five foot eight, but I didn't used to think of him as being on the shorter side for a man. He has curly dark-brown hair with an enviably low number of grey hairs for someone in their sixties. He has a bend in his nose, about halfway down, from a time when I was only a baby, and he started a fight down the pub and got punched in the face. I guess it just never set properly. He looks quite smart in his suit, if I'm being honest, not that I'd ever tell him that.

'I was sorry to hear about Tony,' he says, filling the silence.

I just nod.

'Look, I know you probably wish it was me in there, instead of him,' Dad starts.

I feel my jaw drop.

'What an awful thing to say,' I reply, suddenly

finding my voice. 'Today is a horrible day as it is. I can do without your pity party, thanks.'

'I just meant—'

'I don't care what you meant,' I snap. 'To even suggest I'd wish anyone was dead today is just unreal. Today isn't about us, it's about paying our respects, and everyone else is managing it.'

'Duck, Mum said you might want your name putting down for the pool tournament,' Roy interrupts. He's all smiles, until he clocks who I'm talking to, and how tense it is. 'I'll come back in a bit.'

'You were saying,' Dad says, the smarmiest grin plastered across his face. 'This is a time for paying respects—'

'Don't give me that look,' I reply. 'You obviously don't remember much about *our* family. Granddad loved pool – he played on the team they had here. He was so good they have his team's cues on display in the pool room. A few people thought it might be a nice tribute, to play in his honour.'

'I just meant that you really would be partying, if it were me, instead of him,' Dad says, in a way that suggests it means something different to what he said before, when in fact, he's really just doubling down.

'No one parties at funerals,' I insist.

Right on cue, the disco ball that hangs above the function room springs into action. So do all the lights dotted around the room. Colourful, dancing lights, bouncing around, illuminating the faces of the suddenly confused mourners. The next thing I notice is the sound of feedback, like when a microphone gets too close to a speaker. I instinctively glance at the small stage but the curtains are closed, apart from a small gap in the centre.

Then I hear a familiar voice – unmistakably my niece, Darcy – bellowing out a far from perfect rendition of 'Let It Go' from *Frozen* into the microphone at point-blank range. For a few moments no one moves, no one says or does anything.

'Shit, shit, shit...' Gracie mutters to herself as she practically flies across the function room. I can't hear her saying it, but I can tell from the way her lips are moving. I guess she abandons her swearing system in an emergency.

Gracie disappears behind the curtain for a few seconds. Then her voice booms through the PA system.

'What on earth do you think you are do—'

The audio cuts off.

Shit, this one is on me.

'Were you supposed to be watching them?' Dad unhelpfully asks.

I've inadvertently caused enough of a scene already, I'm not about to cause another one.

'I should go make sure she's OK,' I say. 'See you.'

'OK, see you later,' he says.

He's doing that thing he does where he just looks so impossibly sad. It's almost hard not to feel sorry for him, which makes me even angrier at him, because you don't get to just ditch your family for a new one and come out of it unscathed.

I notice Gracie exiting stage left with Darcy and Oscar, practically dragging them off the stage, one in each hand.

I hurry over, through a room full of people who have quickly moved on from the musical interlude

– I actually think it may have been a rather welcomed dose of comic relief.

'I'm so sorry,' I insist when I reach her.

Oh boy, is her face red. So red and puffed up it's as though I can hear the blood boiling underneath her skin. The kids are just paralysed with fear, they know they're in big trouble for this.

'I ask you to watch them for a few minutes,' she says. 'A few minutes!'

'I got collared by Dad,' I tell her.

'Just be civil with him, that's what I do,' she says.

'But I don't want to be civil with him,' I reply. 'He doesn't deserve civil.'

'And you don't deserve to carry around baggage that should rightfully be his,' she says, putting the conversation to bed. 'I just really, really didn't want this funeral to be as crazy as the rest, just for once. I'm taking the kids over to Mum, some of the extended family want to see them. Well, they did, before the floor show. You coming?'

'I think Roy is waiting for me,' I say.

'For?' she asks curiously.

'There's a pool tournament in the other room,' I tell her.

Three... two... one...

'*A pool tournament?*' she shrieks.

'Everyone thinks Granddad would have loved it – it's just a bit of fun,' I say.

'JFC,' she exclaims. So, we're back to kid-friendly swearing and blaspheming. 'Just, keep things on track, OK? Don't let it get crazy. You watch things in there, I'll keep the peace in here.'

'That seems fair,' I reply. 'You've got the kids and Vee's date *du jour* to contend with. I've got the competitive sports and the heavy-drinking relatives.'

Gracie looks her kids up and down, softening towards them again. She licks a finger before using it to remove the remains of the chocolate cake from around Oscar's mouth.

'Where's Carl?' I ask her.

'He had to go,' she tells me plainly. 'Let's just get this day over with.'

'OK,' I say, puffing air from my cheeks.

I leave Gracie to go and play nice while I go into the other room to play pool.

A pool tournament at a wake feels very on-brand for this family but it's probably an accident waiting to happen.

So much for this wake being a normal one.

10

When I was at school I was not what you would call a cool kid. Not at all.

The drama club was basically made up of two types of people. First of all, you had the cool kids, the ones absolutely bursting with confidence, the beautiful creatures born to be on the stage. Then you had the kids like me. The theatre nerds. The ones reading *A Midsummer Night's Dream* for fun on a Saturday night. The ones fascinated by the craft of acting. I can't think of many hobbies where you can be both cool and uncool for being into it.

Needless to say, with great nerdy interests comes

a low level of athleticism, so I was always terrible at PE, and always picked last. Unsurprisingly, despite all of my training for my work on *Bragadon Forrest*, and the frankly uncomfortable level of fitness I had to maintain (until I came home and started shovelling mini Colins into my face), this is something that has followed me into adulthood. Even with sports that don't require much athleticism, like pool.

I'm in the pool room next to the function room where teams are currently being chosen for the tournament. To be honest, this is the last thing I want to do, but it's not only a decent distraction from why we're really here, but if I keep busy then I can avoid my dad too.

To make the process as fair as possible (although in my opinion picking teams for games is never fair) Roy, who appears to be managing the tournament, has divided us into two groups, with one group being instructed to pick their partner from the other. That's right, I didn't even get picked for the team who gets to pick teams.

I'm not massively bothered because, first of all,

this is just a bit of fun. Second of all, there's an even number of people, so everyone is getting picked by someone. Or so I thought.

At some point in proceedings someone from the group of people who gets to pick their partner has decided that they'd probably rather not play, and instead of saying anything they've just wandered off, leaving us with an odd number.

So, here we are, just me and Dave, Auntie Vee's wake date who must have decided the fun was in this room and strolled through (fine by me, I just want him keeping out of Mum and Bev's sight, because they're still not happy about him being here), waiting to be picked by Louis. You would think this would be a no-brainer. Louis is my brother. My half-brother, sure, but we're blood relatives. Dave is just someone trying to bang our auntie. There's no way he's picking him over me.

'I'm going to go with this bloke,' Louis announces, pointing at Dave.

Dave punches the air proudly.

'What?' I can't help but blurt.

'He looks like he'd be good at pool,' Louis reasons, implying I don't.

'Never played in my life,' Dave confesses proudly with an excitable clap of his hands.

I'm not sure if Louis not picking me is because he really doesn't like me or if it's just good old-fashioned sexism. Either way, it's not great, is it?

There are four large pool tables spread out in the heart of the room. They're tired-looking things, like they've been here forever. I'll bet my granddad played on each one.

Now that there are only fifteen of us, that still means two teams on each table, it's just that I'll be playing alone. Fine. Who cares? It's just a bit of fun.

'I'll just be on my own team,' I announce. 'It's no big deal.'

'Princess Adelina could kill us all with a cue and take the trophy in the blink of an eye,' a participant, who I don't recognise, offers up.

I laugh politely.

'I'm sure we can find someone to play with you, duck,' Roy says kindly, although this makes the situation seem all the more tragic.

'I'll play with her,' a voice announces, almost heroically.

Of course, it's my dad.

'Oh, great, OK,' Roy says. He's well aware of our history and our current strained relationship. He doesn't get involved but not in a dismissive way. I think he knows that this is a very delicate situation and that he's in a very awkward position. He's never ever tried to take the place of my dad in title, he's just always been there to fill the gaps when I've needed him. I have so much respect for Roy for that. Of course, this also means he's too much of a good guy to tell my dad to piss off. And because I always feel like I'm the only one going out on a limb to make my dad feel the consequences of his actions, I don't really feel like I can make a scene now.

'Great,' I echo.

We all make our way to our tables. Dad and I are playing Roy and Megan. Megan has never actually played pool before so Roy is doing the dad thing, showing her how to take her shot, celebrating with her when she does a good job. When it's my turn to step up, as I fidget with whatever the stick thing is that helps you reach the white ball when it's hard to get to (not a clue) I notice my dad take a couple of steps forward. I shoot him a look that tells him to back off.

'Ah, crap, am I missing it?' a voice says. 'Just nipped out for a sandwich.'

It's Sam, who is my mum's cousin's son, so whatever type of cousin that makes him to me, he's that.

He's holding a plate in front of him with a small mountain of sandwiches on it in one hand and a cheese and pickle sandwich in the other. His grip isn't great so the grated cheese is raining down onto his plate. It actually looks really good. I could be tempted to try and coerce my appetite into coming back with one of those if it wasn't for the huge knot in my stomach, caused by this impromptu, unwanted father-daughter bonding session.

'I'll tell you what, Sam, you can take my place,' I say, placing the cue down, making moves back towards the function room.

'What?' my dad says.

'You don't have to do that,' Sam says through a mouthful at the same time.

'No, no, it's fine,' I insist. 'You've just reminded me that I haven't really eaten today. Best I don't play sports on an empty stomach.'

'Going to nip outside and eat a frog?' the un-known participant jokes from the next table – another reference to my TV show. Sorry, former TV show. Genuinely, it's such a huge part of my iden-tity, especially to other people and how they look at me, that the thought of suddenly not being a part of it makes me feel even sicker.

'Very good,' I say, pointing at the man, acknowl-edging his very clever joke. 'But, yeah, go for it, Sam. I'll go grab some food.'

I don't wait for a response, I just dash off to the function room, but I'm no sooner through the door when I notice that, on the table in front of my mum and the aunties, where they are surrounded by mourners all wanting to show their support, there are two *Bragadon Forrest* box sets. As I get a bit closer, I notice the Sharpie sitting next to them and, oh my God, had someone genuinely brought something for me to sign at a funeral? I quickly put the brakes on and make a play to leave the room before anyone sees me.

I hurry through the corridor heading towards the door to step outside for a bit. I just need a minute away from it all. As I reach the door, the main room of the pub catches my eye. I can see a fireplace with a real fire burning away inside. Music is playing, but only quietly, and it's not too busy. It actually looks kind of inviting and, most importantly, it has a bar with none of my relatives or my relatives' friends anywhere near it.

I pull up a stool at the bar – a bar that feels a million miles away from the ones I'm used to in London – and order myself a cranberry and lemonade with a shot of vodka in it. Well, it's the closest thing I'm going to get to a cocktail here. I was tempted to get a Kapop, just because I didn't realise they still existed. You know the crappy alcopops you exclusively drank when you were a teenager? Turns out they're still a thing, and in more ridiculously bright colours than ever. I'm a classy grown-up woman so I decide to order a classy-ish grown-up drink. The man behind the bar serves it with a straw, which I appreciate, even if it is a plastic one. So it turns out I'm a classy grown-up woman who drinks through a straw.

I notice two men sitting over by the fireplace getting up, as though they're about to leave. It looks like a beautiful spot to sit, and there are even a few random old hardback books on the coffee table, which I can't resist having a flick through, so I make my way over there, ready to dive into their spot before anyone else does. It looks like the best seat in the house.

I hover patiently, only for the man with his back to me to turn around and walk straight into me, knocking my drink all over me.

'Oh, shit. I'm so sorry,' the man mumbles.

'No worries,' I reply, because I was probably standing a bit too close to the back of his chair, but then I clock the blood trickling down his hand. 'Oh, erm...'

'Shit,' he says again.

I lead him over towards the bar. On my way there, I notice that one of my nails has come off –

just the one. I didn't think anything could look worse than a full set but I was wrong.

'I'm so sorry, I think I caught you with my nail,' I tell him once we are back over at the bar.

I ask the barman for some paper towels.

'You know, I don't usually come here,' the man explains, 'and when my mate suggested a drink here I made a joke about getting stabbed.'

I laugh, but I do feel awful. I hand the man a paper towel from on top of the bar so he can soak up the blood. The cut isn't that bad, but it could have been a lot worse considering the length of these nails.

'I'm sorry about your drink, let me replace it,' the man offers.

'No, you don't have to do that. I can't replace your skin.'

'It looks like I might have ruined your shirt,' he says, nodding down at the cranberry stains on my white shirt. 'Is that my blood or your drink?'

'Oh, it's just my drink,' I reassure him.

'Then you definitely have to let me buy you a drink,' he insists with a smile. 'Come on. This was my fault, and I'll feel bad all night if you don't let me.'

'Well, OK, thank you,' I say. 'I can't have you feeling bad all night as well as bleeding out.'

'That's more like it,' he says. 'Same again?'

'Actually, can I have a green Kapop, please?' I say. I do kind of wish I'd got one before, for old times, so this is my chance.

He pulls a face at my request and laughs.

'My God, I really am too old to be here.'

I'm not entirely sure how old he is – early forties maybe? He certainly isn't too old to be here though.

'Erm,' I say before glancing around the room, pointing out with my eyes the fact that everyone here is older than us – some of them older than us put together, I'll bet.

'OK, point taken,' he says. 'Too old to be on a bar crawl with my mate then.'

His mate who is currently sitting over by the fire on his own, staring down at his phone, waiting for his friend to return.

'I'm sure you're not,' I reply.

He's actually quite handsome, now that we're chatting face to face, with his chiselled features, his piercing green eyes and his short, dark hair.

'I'm Mike,' he says, offering me his bloody right hand first before swapping it for his left.

'I'm Emmy.'

I shake Mike's hand before getting the barman's attention to see if he has any plasters. He goes off to find me one.

'So, what's a nice girl like you doing in a dump like this?' he asks.

I pull a face.

'Wow, really? That old line?' I chuckle.

'Oh, shit, sorry, that wasn't a line,' he insists. 'I mean it quite literally. You genuinely seem too nice to be in a dump like this. *I'm* almost too nice to be in a dump like this. Almost.'

Mike has a nice smile. Warm and friendly.

'I'm, er... actually supposed to be next door, at the wake,' I tell him.

'Oh, I'm sorry to hear that,' he says. 'Did you lose someone close to you?'

'My granddad,' I reply. 'I'm sure you know what families are like. I just needed a breather.'

'I understand,' he replies. 'Believe me, I do. Take my family – please, take them.'

I laugh. I love corny jokes.

'Emmy, there you are.' I hear my auntie Vee's voice from behind me.

I close my eyes for a second, as though that's going to make her disappear.

'Here I am,' I say.

'Can I borrow you for a moment?' she asks.

Her eyebrows are raised so high she might not need that eye lift after all.

'Back in a sec,' I tell Mike.

I follow Vee into the doorway.

'So, who the hell is that?' she asks me, cutting to the chase.

'That's Mike,' I tell her. 'We bumped into each other.'

'You know him?' she replies.

'No, I mean... I... we literally bumped into each other. He's just replacing my drink and I'm making sure he doesn't bleed to death.'

I flash my finger with the nail missing at her.

'Well, there's no need for that,' she laughs, and I realise it's my middle finger I'm waggling at her. 'Is he not a bit old for you though? How old *is* he?'

We all glance over at Mike and he gives us a wave before pointing at the green Kapop waiting for me on the bar.

'He's just buying me a drink, Vee. Chill out,' I insist.

'You'd better go and get it then,' she says with a knowing grin. 'And I thought everything printed in the papers was a lie.'

I bite my lip to hold my tongue. That was an obvious swipe about the married showrunner I supposedly had a thing with being older than me. I'm going to ignore that.

I head back over to Mike and thank him for my drink.

'Listen, I'm here with my mate and he's boring me senseless,' Mike tells me. 'Do you girls want to join us for a chat?'

'Girls?' I say. Then I realise Vee has followed me back in and is lingering close beside me.

'You have to say yes,' Mike insists, 'because if I bleed to death my mate will be able to tell the police it was you, if you're still here. At the very least he'll get a good enough look at you to give them a useful description.'

I laugh.

'One little drink can't hurt,' Auntie Vee says in, yep, that's her flirtatious voice.

'This is Ken,' Mike tells us as we take a seat at a table with him. Ken looks a bit older than Mike, he's probably in his early fifties, at least, and although he has short, dark hair, his is flecked with grey. He's wearing black thick-rimmed glasses and is swigging from a bottle of beer Mike has just handed him. He puts it down on the table to shake hands with us.

'You two aren't regulars in here, are you?' Vee asks curiously.

'We're not,' Mike replies. 'It was Ken who dragged me in here, I think he's trying to find me a woman.'

Ken looks embarrassed.

'I'm only trying to do you a favour, mate, I'm sick of you being a grumpy bachelor,' Ken reasons.

'So, what do you do?' I ask Mike, changing the subject, hopefully dispelling some of the awkwardness.

'I make the little things count,' he replies.

'Mate,' Karl interrupts. 'That is so cheesy. He's a maths tutor for kids.'

We all laugh. That was actually quite cute.

'We're both tutors,' Mike continues.

'You know, I am just so thirsty,' Vee says, inspecting her already empty glass.

'I think I'll join you,' Ken chirps up, giving Mike an obvious nudge. 'I fancy something with more of a kick.'

I don't know if he's talking about getting another drink or he's referring to Vee. Either way, it checks out.

'I am so sorry about him,' Mike apologises when we're finally alone.

'I *stabbed* you,' I remind him. 'I think we're even. How is your hand?'

'I think I'm going to make it,' he says with a

smile. 'Oh, back in a second, Ken's left his wallet on his chair.'

I watch Mike as he heads over to the bar. So, he's a little bit older than me, he's still gorgeous, and really, really nice. Most importantly he's someone to talk to who makes this horrible day feel a little easier. Unlike some people...

Vee sidles up to me.

'So, what do you think?' she asks.

'He's nice, isn't he?' I reply.

'Yeah, but his friend seems like a little bit of a wet blanket,' she replies. 'Not too bad-looking though. Are you going to make a move?'

'Vee, we're at a funeral,' I remind her. 'And is *he* not a bit young for you?'

'You have to get back on the horse sometime,' she tells me. 'If today tells us anything it's that life is short. This Mike could be the perfect horse for you to, you know, get back on. You know what I mean?'

'I do and I wish I didn't,' I say through an awkward laugh.

Mike sits back down next to us.

'... you wish you didn't?' he prompts, catching the tail end of our conversation.

'Oh, just family stuff,' I reply.

'Are you two related?' Mike asks, sounding surprised.

'Sisters,' Vee tells him.

He chokes on his drink, just a little, but styles it out. The way he's looking at us, I can't tell if he's thinking Vee must look really old or I must look really young for my age.

'So sorry to hear about your granddad passing,' Mike tells her.

Vee places a hand on her chest.

'Thank you,' she says solemnly. An Oscar-worthy performance.

'Drinks,' Ken calls out.

The smile returns to Vee's face immediately.

'Coming,' she practically sings.

'Your sister seems great,' Mike says once we're alone again.

'Yeah, I think it's pretty safe to say no one has a sister quite like mine,' I reply, amusing myself.

I sip my green drink, which tastes just as toxic

as I remember them tasting, but the nostalgia that comes with it tastes great. Oddly, yet another thing that reminds me of my granddad and how fantastic he was. I remember drinking too many of these at a party when I was sixteen. I can't have had more than three, but I felt hammered. I was too scared to call my mum because I knew she would go mad, so I called Granddad instead and he picked me up – and he never breathed a word of it to my mum.

'What do you do, Emmy?' Mike asks me.

Something has just occurred to me. I think there's something about being back here in the home bubble and not just being geographically far away from my 'real life' that makes me feel like I've travelled back in time too. I can't believe I've only just twigged, but Mike so very clearly has absolutely no idea who I am and, wow, what a treat. That's why it feels so great hanging out with him, because he's just treating me like a random person he met in the pub.

'I'm an actress,' I tell him, because I don't really want to lie, and hopefully he won't want to get into the details.

'Oh, that's fascinating,' he says. 'Do you do anything else or...?'

'Just the acting,' I tell him.

'That's great,' he replies. 'There can't be much acting to do around here though?'

'I actually live in London,' I reply. 'I'm just here for the funeral. Well, I'm sticking around until after Christmas, *if* I can stick it out.'

'Family really driving you mad?' he says through a sympathetic smile.

'You've met my sister,' I remind him.

He nods knowingly.

'I'm really appreciating hanging out with someone who isn't one of them, so thank you,' I tell him.

Mike thinks for a second.

'Listen, this might seem a bit odd, or a bit forward but, well, would you like to go for dinner with me sometime?' he asks.

I laugh a little. Not at his suggestion, mostly just enough to convey my awkwardness.

'Oh, I don't know about that,' I start. 'I don't

usually go for dinner with random men I meet in pubs...'

'Something else we have in common,' he says with a smile. 'Neither do I.'

'She'd love to,' Vee chimes in from behind me. 'It will do her good to socialise.'

'Well, no pressure,' Mike insists.

He grabs a pen that's been left lying around on the coffee table and writes his number on a beer mat.

'Just let me know if you fancy it,' he says. 'And I'll let you get back to your wake.'

I take the mat from him and smile at it.

'Thanks,' I say.

'Maybe see you later, Emmy,' Mike says as he puts on his coat.

'Maybe,' I reply, still smiling.

He heads to the bar where he picks up Ken before the two of them head for the door. Vee sits down next to me. She notices the beer mat in my hand and shakes her head.

'*You're* judging *me*, sis?' I say in disbelief. 'You were the one who told me to get back on the horse.'

'I am judging you but that's not why,' she replies as she pulls a paper towel from her pocket. I notice it has a phone number on there. 'I'm just amazed that I managed to get his mate's number before you got his.'

I don't point out to Vee that she's in here flirting up a storm with a younger man she just met when she has a date in the other room – mostly because that will just prove her point. Auntie Vee has men coming out of her... wait, scrap that, I need to re-think that statement. What I mean is that Vee has more than her fair share of men interested in her – more than me, that's for sure. Perhaps I could learn a thing or two from her, ideally sooner rather than later, before I have to start lying about my age.

One thing she is absolutely right about though is that life is short and today I feel that burden more than ever. I'm just not quite sure it's have-din-ner-with-a-man-I-just-met short though. Perhaps I'll see how brave I'm feeling tomorrow.

11

I jolt awake all of a sudden and, oh my God, I've gone blind. I know the term 'blind drunk' but I didn't think it was quite so literal.

I reach up to rub my eyes only to realise I'm wearing some sort of eye mask – no idea where I found it – so I quickly remove it. The first thing I notice is all the black eye make-up on the inside of it. The next is the fact that Megan is sitting on the end of the bed.

'Oh, good morning,' I blurt.

'Dad said to wake you and tell you your breakfast is going cold,' she informs me. 'And I'd dress nice if I were you.'

'Why, do we have company?' I reply, rubbing at my tired eyes, only to cover my hands in black eye make-up too.

'No,' she replies. 'You just look really bad.'

I glare at her. Well, I sort of squint at her, through one eye, because I haven't quite adjusted to the light in the room yet.

Megan heads downstairs so I nip into the bathroom to wash my face and brush my teeth before throwing on a tracksuit and heading for the kitchen.

There should be some sort of hangover loophole that dictates that the one you get after a funeral should be as gentle as possible – if not non-existent. Well, come on, it's a funeral, an incredibly tough day for all involved, and not only do lots of people drink to help them through it but people around them buy them drinks too, and then there's all the toasting...

It doesn't really matter how I try and justify it. I

drank too much yesterday and now I'm feeling the consequences.

'And this is why I don't let you kids drink,' Roy jokes to the twins across the breakfast table.

'She's definitely an advert for not drinking,' Megan teases, although it feels a little more mean-spirited than Roy intended his joke.

I just shrug my shoulders as I take my seat at the table, where my mum has left a full English in my place, that I absolutely cannot face eating.

'You say that now but at least a third of yesterday was like a fever dream,' I point out. 'And then maybe another third of it, I don't even remember. Whereas you had to be present for every last second of it.'

I try to keep my smugness playful. Obviously, I'm not advocating drinking to blot out the days when life is hard, but I hate the way Megan makes me feel, like she's always looking down on me. I'm telling you, if she isn't her school year's bully, I'll eat my breakfast (which I still can hardly look at right now).

'What's everyone up to today?' Roy asks before sipping his coffee.

'*We're* booking our birthday party,' Louis says, reminding his dad.

'Oh, right, yes, so we are,' Roy says. He meaningfully takes a bite out of a sausage before he continues speaking with his mouth full. 'Bloody heck, eighteen years old. Do you remember your eighteenth, Emmy?'

'Were there dinosaurs there?' Megan teases.

I can't even pretend to laugh at that one.

'I certainly do,' I reply. 'You and Mum took me to the West End to see a show, we went out for dinner, stayed in that gorgeous hotel.'

It really was an absolutely truly perfect eighteenth birthday celebration – to me, at least. Not only was it exactly what I wanted but, because the twins were only two, they stayed with Auntie Bev, so I got to enjoy a whole weekend with my mum and Roy.

'Didn't you have a big party?' Megan asks curiously.

'Nope,' I reply.

Even though she asked the question I don't think she was expecting to hear that answer.

'What, no party at all?' Louis chimes in.

'Emmy has always preferred to keep things low-key,' Roy says in my defence, with a big smile and a reassuring wink. 'You're very subtle, aren't you, Emmy?'

'Didn't I see you literally murder an actual baby on your show?' Megan says, with all the disgust you'd feel if I had *literally* murdered an *actual* baby. I know what scene she's referring to but, even in the show, I don't *murder a baby*. Instead of getting into that, I take a different approach.

'Ah, you watch my show, do you?' I ask through a slight grin.

'Not really,' she quickly insists. 'But everyone at school talks about it, so I hear loads, and it sounds horrible.'

I glance at Louis.

'I don't watch it,' he says. 'But my friends do. Dean Barnes has a huge poster of you on his wall. I can't go over to his house, it's so weird, seeing my half-sister on the wall.'

Louis hangs his head and goes back to staring at his plate.

I consider his words. Yes, I would refer to Megan and Louis as my half-siblings, if it were relevant, but sitting here at this table, where everyone knows the family tree well, I can't imagine going out of my way to use the word 'half'. I don't know why, but it wounds me a little.

'I think your show is great, duck,' Roy says. 'If you're not football or Made in Essex Island on the Beach these two won't be interested.'

My mum enters the room, returns the phone to its holster, sits down next to me and grins the grin of a thousand secrets. Either she knows something or she's up to something. Either way, I need my poker face firmly on right now.

'You have a date,' she says.

Oh, God, she knows something.

'Wh-ha-hat?' I laugh, in no way successfully styling it out.

'You have a date,' she says again.

No one else seems to know what she's talking about. How on earth could she know?

'Good morning, campers,' Auntie Vee announces as she enters the kitchen. 'Deana, I love that new scent in your downstairs lav, what is it?'

'I don't think—'

'Ah, that would be me,' Roy says, cutting my mum off. 'I sprayed some of that Joan Malone stuff Deana keeps on the windowsill. It didn't smell too great before that.'

He laughs. Louis sniggers. No one else is impressed. Mum is positively fuming.

'You sprayed *Jo* Malone in the downstairs toilet?' Mum asks in a combination of horror and disbelief.

Roy just finds this even funnier now.

'What? What did I do?' he laughs. 'It's a spray, it's the toilet – what?'

'Emmy bought me that,' Mum tells him. 'It's worth more than you. It's just for show.'

'Why would you buy her a present she can't use?' Megan asks. 'That sucks.'

Why do teenage girls have a permanently disgusted look on their face? Surely not everything *sucks*?

'Mum, I bought you it to use, you should use it,' I insist. 'That way I can buy you more.'

'I'm not wasting Jo Malone on this lot,' she insists. 'Anyway, back to what I was saying. You've got a date.'

'I've got a date with who?' I ask curiously, doing everything I can to avoid my auntie's gaze. I can't believe she told her.

'With... wait for it... Kay and Billy, your old best friends,' she says excitedly. 'I arranged a mate date for you.'

Oh wow, that's the last thing I was expecting her to say. I haven't seen them in years!

'A play date for someone who is nearly forty is kind of tragic,' Megan says.

'Tragic is expecting your mum and dad to pay for your birthday party when you legally become responsible for yourself,' Roy chimes in. 'When I was eighteen, I already had a job and I was paying my parents keep.'

I'm pretty sure he's joking about the tragic part, just to make me feel better.

'I told you, if I wanted to *pay* to live somewhere,

it wouldn't be here,' Megan insists. 'Your parents charging you for being born – when they made you be born – infringes human rights or something.'

'Ooh, Emmy, love, are you going to eat that hash brown?' Auntie Vee asks me.

'Go ahead,' I say, pushing my plate away a little.

'Normally, I'd insist you eat something but Billy and Kay said they'd meet you at the deli on Main Street in an hour, so you'd better go get ready,' Mum says. They were so keen to see you when they heard you were in town.'

She looks so pleased with herself. Like she's arranged a lovely surprise for me. I haven't seen Billy and Kay in years, so it will be nice to see them, I'd just rather do it without a hangover, and without my mum arranging it for me.

'Wow, OK, I'd better go get ready,' I reply.

'That's not all,' Mum says. 'Vee and I are going over to your granddad's – I mean, *your* place – to let Vee's builder friend in, see about getting some of the jobs done, get some quotes. He's only free in half an hour, but Vee and I can let him in, he lives in the area.'

'Ooh, is this the *lovely young man* you were telling me about?' I ask, saying the words my mum used to describe him in her voice.

'He is lovely,' Vee says. 'Fit accent.'

'Cringe,' Megan says at our sixty-something auntie's use of the word fit. She will most definitely have heard that on some reality TV show.

'Don't you say fit?' Vee asks her.

'Yeah, but I'm not, like, eighty,' she replies.

'This is why I didn't have children,' Vee says, directly to me for some reason. 'Don't fall for it, you'll get no joy from them.'

'Got it,' I reply. 'Right, I'll go get ready, then head to the deli.'

'Bring us back some of them cannoli,' Roy says. 'As many as you can carry.'

I nod.

'I will do,' I reply.

I pour myself a cup of tea from the pot.

'Erm, you might want to go get ready now,' my mum says.

She points subtly at her hair in a way that is supposed to alert me to my own.

'Yeah, without my heavy extensions, my own hair does this while I sleep,' I say with a shrug.

I feel like everyone is staring at me.

'Obviously, I'll fix it before I leave the house,' I say. 'Bloody hell, fine, I'll go get ready.'

'And don't forget the cannoli,' Roy calls after me in a terrible Italian-American accent. I wonder if he's referencing *The Godfather* or if he just really wants some cannoli.

The last thing I thought I'd be doing today is seeing my old friends. Friends I've only briefly seen once or twice since I left school. I'm weirdly excited about it. A little nervous though too. No matter where I go and whom I see, I can't shake this feeling that they've seen the headlines about me recently. Even though most people are too polite to mention it, I wouldn't be surprised if Kay and Billy want to talk about my job, they were my old drama club buddies after all.

I'm still technically under contract, and sworn to secrecy, so I couldn't tell them I'd lost my job even if I wanted to. But this is all the more reason I need to line up some new work now, before people know I've been given the boot, because no one wants you if they think no one else wants you. I'll schedule a call with my agent, see if she's got anything for me. In fact, I'll do it on my walk to the deli, just in case she gives me good news. Otherwise, my only forthcoming acting job will be pretending to my old friends that everything is fine. I'm good, but I doubt I'm that good.

12

Kay, Billy and I were an inseparable trio when we were at school. We were so close, in fact, that one of the horrible girls in our year started a rumour that we were some sort of throuple (thankfully she wasn't armed with that word at the time). There was never anything romantic between any of us though, we were just close friends, all equally obsessed with the drama club.

Sadly, as so often happens when someone moves away, we sort of lost touch. We're still Facebook friends (not that I use it), it's not like we fell out, but we did grow up and move in different directions and gradually stop interacting regularly. A big leap from being joint at the hips but it did happen slowly over the course of over a decade.

Walking into the deli to see the two of them sitting at a table together, eagerly thumbing through a script, pointing things out, looks of absolute concentration on their faces – my God, I feel like I'm sixteen again. Sure, they look older. Maybe Billy's dark-brown hairline is creeping back, ever so slightly, and Kay's round cheeks have matured into the face of a grown woman. They look like adults, but I still see the kids I used to know.

Kay glances up for a moment and spots me lingering in the doorway.

'Emmy Palmer – *the* Emmy Palmer – oh my God,' she practically squeals.

She jumps from her seat and hurries over to me. Billy isn't far behind her.

'Look at you,' she says. 'Look. At. You.'

'Look at *you*,' I reply. 'You look gorgeous!'

Kay has always had natural honey-blonde Goldilocks hair. She still does, almost down to her waist, only now, instead of the centre parting she used to have, she has it all swept over to one side. She has a sort of boho look going on that feels genuine.

'Hey, Emmy,' Billy says from behind her.

Billy is a jarring combination of shy and theatrical. He's so animated and over the top and somehow so unsure of himself and slightly timid.

'Hello, you,' I say, extending my arms to give him a hug.

'It's been a long time,' he says as he squeezes me back.

'Don't hog her, Billy,' Kay insists playfully, cutting in. She somehow squeezes me even tighter.

'It's been *forever*,' I say as she finally releases me.

'And – oh boy – have you been busy,' Kay says excitedly, like she can't wait to hear all about it. 'Let's get you a drink – do you still drink tea? Or it is green chai lavender detox tea for you now?'

If anyone else said that to me I'd think they were making fun of me, but I don't get that vibe from Kay at all. She's always been so sweet. I genuinely think she believes a good old cuppa might not be what I drink these days.

'Still tea,' I say with a laugh.

'Channy, can we get the biggest pot of tea you have for my friend?' Kay asks the girl behind the counter.

'Yeah, all right,' Channy replies. She looks me up and down. 'Do we know each other?'

Channy looks like she might be in her mid-twenties. She has kind of a punk-rock look. The left half of her hair is jet black while the other side is peroxide blonde. She has winged eyeliner to die for and blood-red lips. The fact she's dressed entirely in black makes me feel better about the fact that I'm wearing black skinny jeans and a grey off-the-shoulder jumper – because Kay and Billy are both wearing a mixture of colours, I would have felt kind of drab without Channy here.

'Have I seen you on the gig scene?' she asks curiously.

'Wow, Marram Bay has a gig scene now?' I blurt.

'It's not really a scene,' Billy chimes in. 'We do

have a few good local bands who play at the pubs and the festivals.'

'One of which he plays drums in,' Kay adds. 'He's so modest.'

'You always were,' I tell him with a smile. I swear this makes him blush a little.

'Chan, Emmy is a famous actress,' Kay tells her.

She sounds almost offended on my behalf that Channy doesn't recognise me.

'Oh, I'm not famous-famous,' I insist. 'I'm in a fantasy show. I don't even look like me when I'm on TV.'

I actually see the look on Channy's face change as she recognises me.

'Holy fuck, you're Princess Adelina,' she blurts. 'I'm making a cup of tea for Princess Adelina. Oh my God.'

Channy is practically cackling with delight.

'We never get anyone famous here. Never, ever,' she says. 'Apparently, we had some well-known photographer but who even knows who photographers are, right? Princess Adelina! Oh my God! Can I take a selfie with you?'

'Of course,' I reply with a smile.

Thank God I made an effort today.

'I'll take a picture for you,' Kay offers.

Channy ditches her apron and hurries round from behind the counter. She wraps both her arms around me, so we're in a kind of hug, like we've been best friends for years.

Kay takes the photo then offers Channy her phone back.

'Could we do one more?' she asks.

'Yeah, sure,' I reply.

'This time could you, like, pretend to strangle me?' she asks, like it's the most normal thing in the world.

'Strangle you?' Billy says, as though he might have misheard her.

'Yeah, like, hook your arm around my neck, like you did with Lamruim in Season Two, when you killed him,' she says enthusiastically.

I just laugh.

'Don't worry, I get that a lot,' I say. 'Of course, I'll strangle you.'

I basically spend every Comic Con I attend pretending to murder people for photos.

'Right, sit down,' Channy insists, rather firmly. 'I'll bring you your tea and a bunch of goodies. All on the house.'

'Oh, you don't have to do that,' I insist.

'It's my pleasure,' she replies.

I take my seat at the table with Kay and Billy.

'That must be so bizarre,' Kay says.

'It was bizarre to start with,' I reply. 'I suppose I'm used to it now.'

'We always used to fantasise about what it would be like, if one of us made it,' she says. 'I always knew it would be you. Remember your performance in *Romeo and Juliet* in Year 11? You were phenomenal!'

I remember that Scott, the coolest, hottest lad in our year was playing Romeo, and that I was gutted when I found out we had to pretend to kiss, because the teachers said it would be inappropriate to tell us to kiss for real. I suppose I had it in my head that the only way a geek like me was going to get the hottest lad in the school to fall for me was if he had to kiss me for some other reason (granted, I can't think of many others) but in doing so, he would realise he was madly in love with me. What we had to do instead was sort of link our hands together, as though we were about to arm-wrestle, change the angle and then essentially suck our own thumbs. It was really, really weird, but somehow set me up for a career filled with filming awkward sex scenes.

'Are you guys still acting?' I ask, nodding towards the script in front of them.

'Oh no, not really, this is nothing,' Kay babbles. 'Well, sort of. We're a part of the local theatre group. You'd love it. And we've recently signed up a bunch of great people, some familiar faces. You should absolutely join, just for old times, if you're not rushing off back to London – your mum said you bought a house!'

'I'm only staying until just after Christmas,' I reply.

'That's a shame,' Kay says. 'Well, we are having a fundraiser for the theatre tomorrow, so you could come to that?'

'Yeah, of course, message me the details,' I reply. 'I'm just going to get things moving with the house renovations, do as much as possible, then go back home. I wouldn't have bought it if it wasn't my granddad's place.'

'We were so sorry to hear about your granddad,' Kay says.

'Yeah, we have such fond memories of spending time at Tony's,' Billy adds.

'Thanks,' I reply.

It's so weird, the way the two of them talk, saying 'we' instead of 'I', like they're an actual couple, although they haven't mentioned anything to me about them being together. Perhaps this is what it was like, looking at the three of us, back in the day. No wonder people thought there was something romantic going on.

'Here we are,' Channy says, placing the biggest plate of sweet treats I have ever seen down in front of us. 'Enjoy. Sorry, we were out of frogs.'

I laugh politely. You eat one frog on TV and no one ever lets you forget about it.

'These look amazing,' I say, my hand hovering

over the plate as I work out what to eat first. After what Roy said about the cannoli, I'm very tempted to try one.

'Oh, Emmy, there you are,' I hear my auntie Vee say as she runs through the door.

I spin around in my seat.

'Is everything all right? Is Mum OK?' I ask quickly.

'Your mum is fine, there's just a problem with the house,' she says. 'Tel, the lovely young man who did my facias, was measuring up and he's hit a water pipe, the house is flooding!'

'Oh my God,' I blurt.

'I thought I'd better come get you, with it almost being your house now, so quick, come on, let's go,' she insists.

'I'm so sorry,' I tell Kay and Billy. 'I'd better go.'

'God, yeah, go,' Kay insists. 'We'll message you about the fundraiser.'

'Thank you, sorry again,' I insist. 'See you tomorrow.'

To be honest, the last thing I want to do is attend a fundraiser for the local theatre club. They are my old friends though, and I did just rush out on them, albeit for a good reason. Shit, it's so like me to buy a house that immediately gets destroyed in a flood.

I hurriedly follow Vee outside but, instead of walking in the direction of the house, she heads down Main Street. The only thing this way is shops and then the seafront.

'So, tell me again what happened,' I say, sick to my stomach. I have no idea what I'm supposed to do. The house isn't even legally mine yet.

'Oh, the house is fine,' Vee says with a bat of her hand.

'What?' I reply. 'You said...'

'I made that up,' she tells me. 'Come on, I'm taking you to Pandora's Boutique, and I'm picking you out a dress.'

I notice she says 'picking out' and not 'buying'.

'Why?' I can't help but ask bluntly.

'Your old auntie needs a favour,' she tells me.

It must be a big favour, if she's using the term old, because Vee goes above and beyond to pretend she is younger than she is, even to me. She only uses the term old when she wants to tug on your heartstrings, reminding you that she won't be around forever.

'Oh, God, what?' I reply.

'Do you remember yesterday, at my dad's funeral,' she starts. She's already laying it on pretty thick. I dread to think what's coming.

'Just about,' I reply.

'And those two lovely young men we met,' she continues.

'Those two older men,' I reply, highlighting the fact that they were older than me. 'Yes...'

I'm certain I know where this is going and I don't like it at all.

'Well, Ken has asked me out on a date this evening,' she tells me.

'Good for you,' I reply.

'But he wants you to come too, for Mike,' she says. 'And, I can tell from the look on your face that you're going to say no, but, please, do it for me?' Vee pouts like a child.

'Come on, Auntie Vee, don't make me go on a

double date with you,' I plead. 'That's so weird, and I'm not even interested in Mike.'

'But he's gorgeous,' she insists.

'So date them both,' I reply.

'Believe me, I did float the idea,' she replies.

I believe her.

'So, the house is fine?' I double-check.

'Yes, absolutely fine,' she replies.

I did wonder how a tradesman managed to hit a water pipe by 'measuring up' but I never questioned whether or not my auntie might be lying to me to get me on a double date with her.

She pouts again.

'OK, fine, I'll come with you tonight,' I give in.

I can't even hide the fact that I'm not happy about it.

'You're an angel,' she tells me. 'Easily my favourite niece.'

'Today, I'm sure I am,' I reply.

'Right, come inside, let's pick out some dresses,' she says excitedly.

'I do have some dresses at my mum's,' I tell her.

She pulls a face.

'What?' I ask.

'We could get you something brighter – friend-lier – than your usual style,' she says. 'Oh my gosh, we could get matching dresses!'

'Absolutely not,' I say.

'Coordinated then,' she replies. 'Oh, this is going to be so much fun. I'm so excited. You won't regret this, Emmy.'

She's so wrong about so many things. There's no way I'm coordinating outfits, that would be so weird; it's absolutely *not* going to be fun; and the thing I am most sure I regret already is a double date with my sixty-something auntie.

13

The last few times I've visited home it's only been for Christmas and birthdays, so either we've celebrated in various family homes or, a couple of times, I've arranged for us to go to restaurants in Leeds, which is our nearest big city.

What this means is that I have rarely had time to explore Marram Bay and Hope Island, our gorgeous tidal island.

I'm over on Hope Island this evening and I'm totally at the mercy of Auntie Vee. I'm cutting her some slack because however I'm feeling since losing my granddad, well, it must be so much harder for her. She lost her dad. She's my auntie and I love her so if that means I have to eat dinner with a middle-aged man and his slightly younger friend then so be it.

The fact that we're going to a restaurant over on the tidal island has its pros and cons, but in situations like tonight, when I'll most certainly want the night to end, there is actually a timer on it – definitely a pro, because it means it can only go on for so long. Twice a day, when the tide comes in, the road that connects Hope Island to the mainland is temporarily covered by the North Sea, isolating the island about a mile offshore. Then, when the tide goes back out, and the road beneath re-emerges, the island reconnects with the mainland. This means that there are times when it is safe to drive or walk across the mile-long road, and times when you are absolutely not allowed to even try, even if you can still see the road. For the most part, if you grew up here, or if you've lived here for a while, you know how long you've got to drive across the road, either side of the buffer, as the tide starts coming in. You also know just how quickly that water does actually creep up over the road and, believe me, it is fast. Locals know not to chance it, lest their car get swept out to sea with them in it, but many a tourist has required a sea or even an air rescue over the years.

So, you know, with it being best not to take any chances, we will absolutely be crossing the causeway home while it is safe to do so. Auntie Vee has assured me that, with the road closing at 11 p.m., we will most definitely be leaving in time to get a taxi home, so I will be doing that with or without her, come hell or highish water.

The other silver lining this evening is that we're eating in a place that is new to me. I think one of the coolest things about a tourist hotspot like Marram Bay and Hope Island is the fact that while, at times, everything seems really traditional, business owners are actually working overtime to innovate and bring the tourists something unique.

For example, tonight we are Yorkzzia, a bar and restaurant specialising in a pizza with a Yorkshire twist. The pizzas must be good because the place is absolutely rammed. Even the bar is teeming with people. I'm especially excited to try the pizza: I have been staring at the one I fancy on the menu the whole time we've been here (wensleydale and locally made cider chutney), which is over an hour now, and I am positively starving. Well, I never got to eat my cannoli, and I never actually went back to my mum's (I got ready at Vee's) because I was too embarrassed for Mum to find out what I was doing with Vee.

Ken and Vee are really into each other. Uncomfortably so. They're flirting so fiercely I swear there is heat coming off them. Ken is wearing a smart pair of chinos and a white shirt – he looks way smarter than he did the other evening, which makes me think he's made an extra effort for Vee. As for Vee, when we were in Pandora's Boutique, the fancy clothes shop on Main Street, I picked up a black dress with subtle flecks of silver in the material. Vee came over and asked me if it was the dress I was planning on wearing and, when I said I was considering it, she decided that was the dress for her. Rather than wear the exact same dress as my (non) sister, I searched for something else. I'm glad I did because I found the dark-green, silky, floor-length, long-sleeve dress I'm wearing now. Vee scoffed at it, asking who on earth covered so much skin on a date. I didn't waste my breath repeating the fact that, for me, this is not a date. I picked this dress because I liked it, I'm not out to impress anyone else tonight.

Mike has scrubbed up well too. He's wearing a very neat pair of blue jeans (so neat they must have been ironed) and a long-sleeved black top. Vee and Ken have been pretty much completely ignoring us, so we're talking between ourselves.

I'm not all that keen on Ken but I do quite like Mike. And it's not because he's clearly never heard of me, or because he doesn't have his hand on my auntie's thigh (although they are clearly huge bonuses). It's because he just seems like a nice man. He's friendly, polite, and quite charming really. It might not make much sense but there's something about his eyes, something that feels so familiar. Something about Mike just makes me feel like I know him.

I pick up the menu *again* and read the list of pizzas for the millionth time.

'Even the menus themselves are starting to look delicious,' Mike jokes.

'They really are,' I say with a sigh. 'I know they're really busy, but this wait for a table is ridiculous.'

We briefly catch Vee's attention.

'We should probably tell them we're here,' she says before immediately turning back to Ken. 'So, as I was saying—'

'Hang on a sec,' I interrupt. She reluctantly turns back to me. 'You haven't told them we're here? We might have lost our booking.'

'Oh, should I have booked?' Ken asks causally. 'I didn't actually book a table. Maybe you should tell them we're waiting.'

I look at Mike and widen my eyes.

'I'll go see if they can fit us in,' Mike says with a frustrated laugh.

'So, as I was saying,' Vee starts again, and suddenly it's like it's only her and Ken in the room again.

I watch Mike chatting with a rather frazzled hostess and I can tell from their body language it's not good news.

I leave the two lovebirds alone and make my way over to meet Mike.

'Fully booked,' he announces. I'm not surprised.

'Right, OK,' I say with a sigh. 'So, we need to find something else to eat.'

I am beyond disappointed I'm not getting my pizza now.

'Looks like they already have,' Mike says, nodding towards Ken and Vee.

'Oh God,' I blurt.

They're kissing so passionately I can see their tongues moving in a piston-like manner, in and out of each other's mouth. No one wants to see their auntie Frenching a practical stranger.

'Shall we just get out of here?' I ask him.

'You read my mind,' he replies. From the look on his face, I can tell he's finding this as disturbing as I am.

'I'll just go tell her we're going,' I say. 'In case she worries about me.'

Ha! She won't even notice I'm gone, but I should tell her anyway.

I head over and tap Vee on the shoulder a few times to get her attention. Just touching her while she's kissing Ken makes me feel ridiculously uncomfortable, like I'm a participant in... whatever this is.

'Vee... Vee... Mike and I are going to leave,' I tell her.

'Just a second, babe,' she tells Ken.

Babe. Oh my God.

Vee walks me maybe two or three steps away from where she was sitting.

'You're going with Mike?' she says.

'Yes,' I reply. 'We're going—'

'Do you have protection?' she asks as she fidgets with her handbag.

Oh... my... God.

'I can just punch him in the throat or kick him in the balls,' I tell her. 'No weapon needed.'

'That's not what I meant,' she says seriously.

'I *know* what you meant,' I tell her. 'And just having this conversation kind of makes me welcome a kidnapping. No protection of any kind needed.'

She opens her mouth to speak.

'Because I'm *not on a date*,' I remind her. 'We're just going to grab something to eat. Meet you back here at 10.45, so we can get across the causeway before it closes, OK?'

'OK, fine, fine,' she says.

'Your sister seems like a handful,' Mike says as we push our way through the crowd to leave.

'You don't really believe she's my sister, do you?' I ask.

'When it comes to women, I believe what I'm told,' he replies. 'Like most men, I excel at saying the wrong thing.'

'But *really*?' I say with a raised eyebrow.

'No, not at all,' he replies through a playful scoff. 'Is she your friend? Your mum?'

'Close,' I reply. 'My auntie. She has a twin sister.'

'Oh my God, there's two of them?' he jokes.

'You're safe,' I reply. 'The other one is married. OK, so, where can we get some food?'

We glance up and down the busy street, where most of the restaurants on Hope Island are, but it's not looking good.

'It's the Christmas season,' he tells me – of course, I already knew that. 'It's impossible to get a table without a booking.'

'I don't think I've ever been hungrier,' I say with a sigh.

I'm so hungry I'd actually go to the corner shop, buy a bag of crisps, and sit and eat them in the abbey ruins.

'How thick is that coat?' Mike asks me.

Can he read my mind or something?

'Fairly,' I reply through a nervous laugh. 'Why?'

'I spent this summer doing up my garden,' he tells me. 'Every last inch of it. I wanted to make the ultimate summer party garden. Problem is, I didn't finish it until October, so I didn't exactly get the summer parties I wanted. But I have bought some fancy outdoor heaters and, most importantly, I have my own outdoor pizza oven. I could make you that pizza. What do you say?'

'Wow, that sounds amazing, and it's such a generous offer,' I say genuinely. 'But – and I hope you don't take offence from this – I'm not sure about going to the house of a man I just met.'

'Not house,' he corrects me with a cheeky smile. 'Garden. Anyway, it was just a thought. A means to get you a pizza in matter of minutes.'

'Minutes?' I reply. 'Where do you live?'

'Here on the island,' he replies. 'Only a couple of streets away, in one of the old Victorian stone terraces. Look, I know you're only here supporting your auntie, and that I don't stand a chance with you, and that's fine by me.'

I think for a second.

'Pizza oven, you say?' I reply, biting my lip thoughtfully.

'I know, this has a sort of *Chitty Chitty Bang Bang* feel to it, but I'm not trying to kidnap you with the promise of pizza – much as you just made it sound like that would work,' he says with a laugh.

'It's 2021,' I reply with a shrug of my shoulders.

'The burden is on you, to convince me you're not going to put *me* in your pizza oven.'

'That's a fair point,' he replies. 'What about if I give you my address right now, and you go give it to your auntie? That way, if you don't turn up, she'll know where to find you.'

I think about seeing my auntie and Ken kissing again.

'I think I'd rather take my chances,' I joke. 'OK, fine, let's go. Let's see this pizza oven in action.'

'Great,' Mike says with a clap of his hands. 'Let's do this.'

'Great,' I echo.

All jokes aside, I do feel safe going to Mike's garden for a pizza, I'm not just blinded by the hunger, and I'm certainly not naïve. I've handled myself before and I could do it again. And there's plenty of time to go there, have a pizza and a bit of a chat with Mike, and then met Vee back here to get our taxi before the causeway closes. If I can pry her off Ken, that is.

14

When Mike described his garden, he really under-sold it. It's a work of art. It's like something out of a magazine or an episode of *Grand Designs*. It's the ultimate 'pull for a chat' space, exactly like the kind you see on *Love Island,* except we're in Yorkshire, in November, and the only actual romance is between me and the glorious pizza I just devoured. That said, there is something about Mike. He's still charming as ever, and I still can't shake the feeling that I know him, even though I know I don't.

I love the garden. I love the plants, the decking, the water feature. I love all the lights he has everywhere – and I was blown away when I realised they were smart lights. I'm getting lots of ideas for my own money pit, even though I don't plan on living in it. I guess I just hadn't entertained having a house or a garden for a while and now my imagination is running away with me.

We've been sitting out here for a little while now. It's nice, drinking wine, enjoying the soothing warmth of the patio heaters. And Mike is great to chat to. He's intelligent, funny and very charming – for a non-date, of course, which is a shame really, because on paper it sure does feel like a date.

Mike also has outdoor Bluetooth speakers that are pumping out smooth classical music. As the track changes, I notice him smile.

'Ahh,' he says through a grin. '*This* song.'

'What's this?' I ask curiously, clocking his reaction.

'It's sort of embarrassing,' he replies. 'Years ago, when my brother got married, he made us all learn some truly terrible dance, to this song. I think he was embarrassed about doing his first dance on his own – well, with just his wife, obviously – so he decided to make it even more embarrassing and have us perform a dance. This was the song.'

'Oh, so you can dance?' I reply with a big smile.

'I can sort of dance to this one song,' he replies.

'You can't tell me that and not show me,' I say. 'You wouldn't have mentioned it, if you didn't want to show me.'

'The only bit I remember well is the dip,' he says, scratching his chin. 'Do you want me to dip you?'

'I think I do,' I reply with a laugh. 'Unless it's the wine talking. It is amazing wine, by the way.'

So amazing I think I might have had too much.

'Well, don't worry, I'll only tip you a bit,' he replies. 'Not so much I tip the wine back out.'

I stand up, ready to be dipped.

'I hope you know what you're doing,' I tell him.

'So do I,' he replies with a nervous smile. 'OK, so we just...'

I don't know why I was expecting this to go better than it does. As Mike dips me, he loses his balance and I tip back way further than I should. On my way down, I catch the tablecloth, and pull the contents down on top of me. Both glasses of white wine, plus the contents of our almost-full second bottle, cascade down on top of me. The garden has two water features now.

I quickly jump up and hurry off my coat, which is dry, but my dress is absolutely soaking wet, and it's freezing cold.

'Shit,' Mike says. 'Quick, come inside. We'll get you sorted out.'

I hurry in through the back door, a few paces behind Mike.

'I can give you some of my... balls!' he exclaims as he trips.

I stop abruptly, wondering if that was what he was actually going to say or if it was just because he was stumbling.

'It's all going wrong tonight. Sorry,' he chuckles. 'My son's balls... footballs are all over the floor, I'm always telling him not to leave them here.'

I hold the taken-aback position I assumed when he yelled 'balls'. He has a son?

'He's not here tonight,' he says, noticing what-ever look is on my face.

Poor bloke. I had considered that Mike could have been married before, but I never would have guessed he had a son. It must be awful for him, his kid probably lives with his mum, I'll bet Mike only sees him at weekends. It must be tough. Speaking as a child of divorce, I know how hard it is. In a weird way, I'm lucky that my parents didn't share custody of me, or that my dad never honoured whatever agreement they did have. It meant I never had to live between two houses like Mike's son must.

'This isn't a plot to get you into my bedroom,' Mike insists. He does actually seem embarrassed, and like he's worried I might be thinking that. 'But I have loads of tracksuits and T-shirts. If you want to take that wet dress off, you can borrow some of my clothes, until it dries.'

'That's really kind of you, thank you,' I reply.

If I had to try and imagine the bedroom of a divorced man living on his own, then this would be it. It's not exactly a lad-pad but you can tell that no woman had a hand in any of it. Apart from the big TV facing the king-sized bed, a wardrobe and a single chest of drawers, the room is pretty much empty.

Mike kicks a few random items of clothing out of his way as I follow him into his bedroom. You can tell he wasn't expecting company because he seems embarrassed by the mess. He grabs a clean pair of tracksuit bottoms and a zip-up hoodie from a drawer and hands them to me.

'Again, I'm so sorry,' he insists. 'I'll wait downstairs, in the lounge, while you get changed. And, again, so sorry.'

'Don't worry about it,' I say with a laugh, hopefully reassuring him I think it's funny. 'I did ask to be dipped.'

'I definitely mis-sold my dipping skills though,' he replies. He seems a bit more relaxed now he's sure I'm not angry. 'See you downstairs.'

Mike closes his bedroom door behind him. Well, I never thought I'd end up in a man's bedroom tonight, that's for sure. I might actually have beaten Vee to it. Once I'm certain I'm alone, I can't wait to get this cold, wet dress off. That's when I remember that my beautiful dark-green silky dress, that covers every inch of my body, has a long skinny zip all the way down the back and, try as I might, I just can't reach it. I try everything. Reaching for it, trying to pull it apart with pure strength – I even try grabbing a wire coat hanger from the wardrobe, to see if I can hook the zip, but it just won't work. There's only one thing for it.

I head downstairs and find Mike in the lounge.

'Was that stuff no good?' he asks, noticing I'm still in my dress.

'It's fine,' I reassure him. 'But how would you like to make this situation ten times more awkward?'

'Oh?'

'I need you to help me out of my dress,' I say plainly.

Mike's eyebrows shoot up.

'Well, well, well,' he replies with a slight laugh. 'Now who sounds like they're trying to manipulate the other?'

I can tell he's joking.

'I promise you, it's not a line,' I reply through a

big, dumb grin. 'I didn't realise I'd be needing to unzip it while I was out.'

'Yeah, yeah, I've heard it all before,' he jokes, lightening the mood, actually making this a lot less awkward than it could be. 'Go on then, come here.'

I walk over to Mike and turn around so he can get at my zip. My dress is quite delicate so he has to unzip it ever so slowly. As he does so I feel the backs of his fingers brush against the skin on my back. He hits a ticklish spot which sends a ripple of something through my body.

My dress loosens so I hold it in place at the front, because flashing this poor man is the last thing either of us needs tonight.

'Dad, what are my balls doing all over the floor?' I hear a man ask as he walks in the room. His voice sounds strangely familiar, but they all do up here, it's that friendly Yorkshire tone.

Thankfully, my back is to the door, so I can't see him, but then again, it's my back that is exposed.

'Son, what are you doing home?' Mike asks, sounding panicked.

Shit. I daren't turn around. I can tell from the

voice that Mike's son isn't a kid, but this is still so awkward.

'Oh my God, Dad, what the hell?' his son replies.

'Son, I've got company,' Mike says, in a way that is clearly designed to tell his son to clear off, but he doesn't take the hint.

'Yeah, I can see that,' he replies. 'You can't do this in your bedroom?'

'Come on, grow up,' Mike reasons.

'Grow up?' his son replies with a snort. 'I'm in my thirties and even I don't pull this stuff in the lounge.'

I don't know what it is that hits me first, the fact that Mike's son is in his thirties, like me, or the fact his voice sounds so familiar. I can't help but turn around and see who it is.

'Emma Watson?' he says, with a look of pure horror on his face.

Mike's son says my name and I react as though I've just met Henry Cavill. Actually, that's not true, because I have met Henry Cavill and I didn't freak out then like I am doing now. I'm in shock, frozen on the spot, I feel like I've just seen a ghost. I need to say something, anything...

'Hello, Scott,' I say, pretty casually (but completely forced), my hands cupping my breasts through my dress to ensure they stay covered now my zip is undone.

'Emma?' Mike says. 'Do you know her?'

'Do you not know her?' Scott says is disbelief. 'She's a pretty well-known actress.'

'Emma Watson,' Mike says out loud to himself as he racks his brains to see if the name rings a bell. 'Wait, what? From *Harry Potter*?'

He looks me up and down, as though he may not have realised he's been hanging out with *the* Emma Watson of *Harry Potter* fame all this time.

'My stage name is Emmy Palmer,' I tell him.

'So, how do you two know each other then?' Mike asks.

'I can clear that one up,' Scott says. 'We went to school together.'

15

With Scott storming off almost immediately after seeing his old school pal seemingly being un-dressed by his dad, suddenly it's just me and Mike.

I feel very naked, despite my dress only being unzipped. I quickly throw on Mike's hoodie, over my wet dress.

'Erm, how old are you?' I ask, probably a little too soon and a little more bluntly than I should.

'How old am I?' Mike replies. 'Who *are* you? How many identities do you have?'

Eesh. I remember my granddad's next-door neighbour, who was the same age as him, having this intense fear about identity theft. My mum always said it was an old-man thing to worry about.

'Just the two,' I reply. 'Both thirty-four years old.'

We look at each other for a moment before laughing.

'So that explains how you know Scott,' he replies, exhaling deeply before he speaks again. 'I'm fifty-four.'

Wow, this is awkward. Mike is old enough to be my dad, and I know this because I sat with (and had a huge crush on) his son through most of school. His son who just walked in on us looking like we were about to get it on.

The thing about Scott isn't just that we went to school together, I was practically in love with him. I used to spend hours wondering how I could get him to notice me – although I doubt teenage me would have gone the dad route, even if I had known how effective it's turned out to be.

'I should go,' I tell him.

'You don't have to go. It's late, stay the night.'

I flash him an oh-hell-no look.

'Not like that,' Mike insists. 'You've missed the causeway.'

'Vee said it was at 11,' I reply.

'Well, it's not, it's just before 2 a.m., I just checked,' he replies. 'Ken just texted me to say Vee has gone back to his place.'

'It's honestly like she doesn't care if I live or die,' I blurt, semi-amused.

'We have a spare room upstairs,' Mike tells me. 'Scott has probably gone to his mum's. He usually does when he's annoyed at me. So, if you want to stay in there for a bit? I'll set an alarm to sort you a taxi home the second the causeway opens.'

'That would be great, thank you,' I reply. 'Sorry for... something.'

I'm not really sure what.

Mike laughs.

'Me too,' he replies. 'Don't worry, Scott will calm down, and I'm sure he'll see the funny side too. When was the last time you saw him?'

'School,' I reply. 'Technically, just after sixth form. We almost went to the same uni.'

'Changed your mind about the uni?' he asks curiously.

'Changed my mind about going,' I reply. 'I moved to London instead, to see if I could make it as an actress.'

'It sounds like that was the right decision,' he says with a smile. 'I'd love to hear all about it but I'm going to leave you to get changed.'

'Thanks,' I say again.

Suddenly alone in my school crush's dad's lounge, half-undressed, soaked in wine, I can't help but laugh.

The next time I wonder whether or not it's a good idea to go home with a man, I'll know that I need to worry about far more than if the man has pure intentions or not. It turns out you never know who you'll bump into...

16

After hiding from Mike in his spare room, and then getting a taxi home, it was after 2 a.m. by the time I got back to my mum's.

I felt like a teenager again, sneaking in, trying not to wake Mum up so she didn't know what time I got home, and so I didn't have to explain to her where I'd been. Well, I think if she'd found out I'd been on a date and gone home with a man, no matter what I told her, she would have had me down to the GUM clinic faster than you can spell gonorrhoea.

When I got up this morning and Mum inevitably asked me where I'd been until late anyway, I told her I'd got carried away hanging out with Kay and Billy. Bless my mum, she said it was so nice to hear that the old gang was back together, and we were as solid as ever. She also said that we must be enjoying being around each other again, spending all day together, especially when I'd texted her to say I was going to the fundraiser today. That's when I remembered that I'd agreed to attend a fundraiser. It's not that I don't want to help, I'll gladly donate to their cause, whatever it actually is, but I'm really not in the mood to socialise today.

Still, I'm here now. It seems like it's been going on for a while, but I couldn't face coming any earlier. Luckily, it's not too cold today because it's an outdoor event, outside the old theatre down by the seafront. Now that I'm here, I'm realising this place is what they're raising money for. Wow. I used to come watch pantomimes here when I was a kid.

There's a board set out with information about the theatre on it. Apparently, it's a Renaissance Revival building, constructed back in 1931, designed by famous architect, Phillip Edwards, boasting iconic copper-covered cupolas on the corners that face out to sea. I just overheard someone saying the owner has spent a lot of money on things like structural work and removing asbestos, but the inside needs a complete makeover before it can be used again. So, I'm guessing that the theatre group Kay and Billy are part of is wanting to put on shows here. That's cool. It would be great to see the place back to how it used to be, especially given its history.

There's a large crowd of people gathered outside. There are tables set out with drinks and snacks, which look they have been provided by kind-hearted local businesses. I spot a plate of cannoli, just like the ones I didn't get to try yesterday, so I make it my first order of business to grab one. Then there's a table taking donations so the second thing I do is make my way over there and use the iPad available to donate money. I want to help my friends, of course I do, but I would really like to see the theatre back to its former glory as well.

'Excuse me,' a man says as he taps me on the shoulder. 'Would you mind taking a photo?'

He has a London accent that is just creeping into cockney territory. If we were actually in London it wouldn't be the strongest accent I'd heard, but up here it stands out a mile. I can tell, even through his big coat, that he's a tall, muscular man. His brown hair is super-short on the sides, but long and swept back on top, and he has a short, stubbly beard. All things considered, I would expect him to have brown eyes to match his hair but they're the brightest shade of blue and it takes me aback for a second.

'Oh, of course,' I reply.

I assume the position, sidling up to the man so he can snap a selfie of us together. I smile dutifully but he pulls away.

'Erm... sorry, love, I meant can you take a picture of us?' he replies, puzzled.

That's when I notice the woman standing next to him.

'Oh my God, yes, sorry,' I babble. 'Of course, sorry.'

I take his phone from him and take a photo of the two of them in front of the theatre.

'Sorry,' I say again as I hand them back the phone.

'No worries,' he replies with a laugh.

Well, at least I've managed to get embarrassing myself out of the way early, that's that box ticked. It's all uphill from here. At least it is until my gaze meets Scott's. He sees me too and, despite me mentally willing him to pretend he hasn't seen me, he makes his way over to talk to me.

'Emmy, hi,' he says, in a way that would be normal if last night hadn't happened, but still with a sort of unspoken awkwardness.

'Hey!' I reply brightly because it will only be weird if we make it weird.

'I wasn't expecting to see you here,' he says.

'Same,' I reply. 'You're still into drama?'

'I am,' he replies. 'And you obviously are...'

I don't *think* that was a dig.

The funny thing about me and Scott is that we've always had this sort of 'will they, won't they?' thing going on. It started in Reception (yes, Reception) when I had no less than three boys who I promised I would marry when I grew up. Matthew

F., Matthew C. and Scott. Obviously, I was a very conscientious *five-year-old* because I decided I needed to pick just one future husband, and in the end, I went for one of the Matthews.

The next time our paths crossed romantically was in middle school. We had a school disco once a month. They were genuinely amazing and I would absolutely attend one now if I could. I bet I'd have just as much fun as I did back then too. Imagine the scene: it's the 90s. We're in the school hall with flashy lights and a super-corny DJ. We're dancing to Steps, the 'Macarena', 'Saturday Night' by Whigfield, 'The Grease Megamix'. Trouser-skirts and pedal pushers were the height of fashion, along with those pointless headscarves Hannah from S Club 7 wore. The tuck shop sold Space Raiders, penny sweets, and the only drinks available were those cheap, kind of gross tasting ones in thin plastic cups with a plastid lid you were supposed to peel off (but if you were cool you made a hole in the bottom and sucked the drink out, because of course you did). At some point during each disco, the DJ would play something for the couples to slow-dance to, and it's odd when you're at middle school because only a really small number of people have boyfriends or girlfriends, and these relationships usually started because you were asked to dance at a disco.

One night Scott approached my group of friends and asked me to dance with him – and I know it was me he was talking to, but one of my friends thought he was asking her and she shouted at him, horrible pre-teen-girl style, telling him that she didn't fancy him, so he skulked off. I remember afterwards, when I was outside waiting for my granddad to pick me up, Scott came out to join me and we were both too embarrassed to mention it. It would have been the most perfect first-kiss moment because we sat in the school car park and watched the Hale-Bopp comet flying through the sky, but it wasn't to be.

It wasn't to be in Year 11 either. By that point, Scott was one of the cool kids and I was a well-established nerd. It was him who played the Romeo to my Juliet, who I didn't get to kiss. It really did finally seem like something was going to happen after our A levels though. Scott and I were planning on going to the same uni and we arranged a weekend away to visit the campus together. By this point the playground politics were long behind us, and it actually felt like we were going to finally, *finally* get together, it was obvious to both of us, one of just needed to make the first move. Unfortunately, I made the first move, *to London*, to chase my crazy dreams of being an actress. At the time it seemed like the deciding factor that called time on our 'will they, won't they?' It's funny, bumping into him again, after all these years, and all this stuff with his dad. It's nice to know I haven't lost my touch for making sure we never happen, just like I seemingly always have.

I suddenly realise why it was that Mike seemed so familiar, it's because he looks just like Scott, only a little shorter and, apparently, a lot older. I never would have guessed Mike was in his fifties.

'Darling,' I hear a woman's voice call out.

Scott and I turn to see a fast-approaching gang of fifty-something women. They have a clear leader, the one who called out to Scott. She's dressed head-to-toe in the kind of outfit you usually see people wearing when they're going for a hike, except her clothing looks so perfect I doubt she's used it to walk further than to the car. She's flanked by her friends who are all dressed similarly, but each of them wears a different colour, sort of like middle-aged, unmasked Power Rangers.

I'm guessing this is Scott's mum. I can't really remember her from back in the day either. I suppose Scott and I never really met each other's parents. I pretty much pretended I didn't know boys existed to my mum (other than Billy, but he didn't count as a boy-boy).

'So sorry we're late but we'll make big donations to make up for it. How are you today, darling?' she asks in that over-the-top, dramatic mumsy way. Sort of like if you were to ask a crying toddler how their non-existent injury was from landing on their bum.

'I'm OK,' he tells her. 'This is Emmy, by the way, the actress I was telling you about.'

Her eyebrows shoot up.

'Darling, can you fetch Mummy a drink, please?' she asks him, not taking her eyes off me.

Ergh, the way she talks to him makes me want to throw up.

'Of course,' he replies. 'Back in a sec.'

'I'm Valerie,' she tells me once Scott is out of earshot. 'Michael's ex-wife.'

'Lovely to meet you,' I reply – well, what the hell else can I say that doesn't make this very awkward very quickly?

'Ladies, this is Emma,' Valerie tells her friends. 'She went to school with Scott and now she's shagging my ex-husband.'

I'm momentarily taken aback by her use of the word 'shagging'. It's not an age thing. Auntie Vee says it all the time. I'd be shocked to my core if my mum said it though and I feel the same way about Valerie. Wow.

'How old are you?' one of her friends asks me, in the kind of patronising way you'd ask a four-year-old. Part of me doesn't want to give them the satisfaction of watching me plead my innocence.

'I'm thirty-four,' I tell her with a polite smile. 'How old are you?'

The friend clicks her tongue and rolls her eyes.

'Excuse Michelle,' Valerie tells me with faux sincerity, 'she just finds it hard to understand what a girl of thirty-four could possibly see in a man of Mike's age. I, on the other hand, read the papers.'

'Wow, you read the *Daily Scoop*?' I say. It's my turn to sound disapproving. Also, the term a 'girl of thirty-four' is genuinely hilarious.

'Is everything OK here?' Mike asks. Christ, where did he come from? Everyone is here.

'Can I, er, have a word with you?' I ask Mike, unable to hide my amusement at this entire thing that is absolutely not a thing.

'Why are you *all* here? This is an actual nightmare,' I tell him once we're alone.

'We're here to support Scott,' he replies. 'It's his theatre group. I keep telling him, it's a waste of time, this acting lark. No one makes it as an actor, do they?'

'Right,' I reply. I'm not getting into that one now. 'Sure. Anyway, the thing is, your ex-wife seems to think we're an item, and she's being absolutely awful. Scott seems really annoyed too.'

'Were Valerie and her friends unkind?' he says, wincing because I think he knows the answer.

'Have you seen desperate housewives?' I ask.

'That's not really my kind of TV show,' he says.

'I wasn't talking about the TV show,' I reply through gritted teeth. 'She and Scott both seem to think that you and I are sleeping together.'

'Oh, look, at that boat,' Mike says, pointing out to sea.

'Mike...'

'OK, you got me, I haven't exactly set them straight yet,' he says.

'You haven't exactly set them straight yet?' I reply.

'I'm sorry, I will do, it's just Val left me for someone ten years younger than me, and I'm still pretty bitter about it. You're twenty years younger than her, this will be torturing her.'

I glance back and notice Scott watching us like a hawk. He's standing with a group of women, maybe in their twenties, chatting. He's being fun and animated like he always is, just with one eye firmly on me and his dad.

'She does seem like she deserves to be tortured,' I reason. 'But I have enough going on, so can you please clear all of this up?'

'Fine, fine,' he replies. 'By the way, you left your dress at my place.'

As he says this an elderly couple walks past us, catching just enough of that sentence for it to sound bad.

'I was going to drop it at Ken's, see if Vee could get it back to you,' he tells me when we have a little privacy again.

'Oh, thanks,' I reply. 'I'd completely forgotten about that.'

'Come with me, I'll get you it now,' he replies.

Mike places a hand on the small of my back and leads me to the car park.

Sure enough, in the back of his car, in a bag for life that doesn't seem like it has long left, is my dress.

'I wasn't using you or anything, you know,' Mike

tells me. 'I did – do – really like you. I was just enjoying hanging out with you.'

'Oh, I know, don't worry about it,' I insist. 'You were right last night, I was only there in the first place to support Vee.'

'Ouch,' he replies through a semi-wounded laugh.

'Oh, nothing against you,' I quickly add. 'I just have a lot going on right now and a relationship is the last thing I need.'

'That's understandable,' he replies. 'But if you ever want a pizza, and you don't want to queue for it...'

I laugh.

'Would it be strange to hug?' Mike asks.

'Yeah, but we can do it anyway,' I reply.

'Hey, see you guys later,' a voice calls out.

It's Scott, getting into his car with one of the early-twenty-somethings before they drive off together.

'I think I'm going to head off too,' I tell him. 'I have an auntie to strangle for giving me one of the most awkward weeks of my life.'

'Give her one from me,' he replies before wincing at his careless choice of words.

After saying goodbye to Mike, I decide to head home, safe in the knowledge that I never want to see either of them again. The only thing I'm surer about than that is the fact that, a far as Scott is concerned, 'won't they' is finally set in stone, emphasis on the 'won't'. Oh, and I'm sure it goes without saying, but the same goes for his dad too.

17

'Your dad called while you were out,' my mum says casually.

'Yay,' I reply sarcastically. 'To apologise, I presume?'

Also sarcastic.

'Well, you never know,' she says. 'He wants you to go over to dinner tomorrow night, with him, Patsie and Katie.'

I'm so impressed by how unbothered Mum is, talking about Dad and his new family, when it still makes my blood boil to this day. It takes a big woman to go through what she did and still do her best not only to avoid bad-mouthing Dad, but to actively encourage me to maintain some sort of relationship with him.

'I'd rather go to dinner with...'

I was going to say Mike and Scott, but my mum isn't going to get that reference.

'Satan,' I say eventually. 'At least I know where I stand with him.'

'Saving you a seat, is he?' Mum teases. 'For what it's worth, I think you should go.'

'You do?'

I switch from staring at the lounge TV to staring at her. *Come Dine With Me* can wait.

'I do,' she says. 'You carry a lot of baggage around with you that most of us gave up hanging on to a while ago. Having dinner with him might help lighten the load.'

'Ergh, just, you know how he makes me feel,' I say, the anger prickling my skin, irritating me inside and out. 'And he's a coward, asking you to ask me.'

'I do think it's pretty brave of him to invite you to something that involves knives,' she says with a smile.

My dad might be rubbish but my mum is the ultimate role model. The way she's handled this – and everything – is spot on. I wish I could be more like her, so chilled out, but it seems like I've inherited my dad's temper instead, which makes me *really bloody angry*.

There's a knock at the door.

'I'll get it,' Roy calls out from another room.

'Will you go for me?' Mum asks.

'I will go for you,' I tell her.

Well, if I want to be more like her, there's no time like the present to start.

'Emmy, it's for you,' Roy announces, poking his head through the door.

I make my way to the front door where I find Kay and Billy.

'They want to know if you can play out,' Roy jokes.

I laugh.

'Hey guys, come in,' I insist. 'Come through to the kitchen.'

'We spotted you at the fundraiser earlier,' Kay says. 'But then we couldn't find you.'

'Yes, sorry, I had to rush off,' I reply. 'My agent called.'

Actually, technically, I called her on my way home, and as far as having any work for me goes, the answer is no (unless you count tell-all articles or a slot on my friend Laura's *You Should Meet* show, but I haven't heard from her myself since the scandal broke). I'm not exactly in demand for much else right now. Even the press are over my little scandal.

'No worries at all,' Kay says. 'We need a favour.'

'Oh yeah?' I say curiously. I have *no* idea what they're here to say.

'First of all, thank you for such a generous donation – we did see,' she tells me.

'Yeah, it means a lot,' Billy adds.

'It's no trouble at all,' I insist. 'It's such a stunning theatre, and I have such fond memories from my childhood, I'd love to see it restored for future generations.'

'Keep that in mind,' Kay says. 'So, the owner has done lots of the big jobs – like making the building safe, and it doesn't flood any more, which is fantastic – and the smaller auditorium is coming along, and we do have a brilliant local builder doing jobs for next to nothing, but the ballroom and the main, spectacular auditorium still need a lot of work. The fundraiser has helped a lot, but nowhere near enough, and the owner is starting to worry he might need to sell up, but no one will want to buy it – it's a whole thing.'

'Sounds like a nightmare,' I say.

'We've been at a loss, trying to think of ways to bring in the funds needed quickly,' Billy says.

'But then it hit us,' Kay adds, taking over the conversation again. 'It will be a lot of work, a lot of scrambling to sort things in time, lots of rehearsing. But, for one night only, we're going to put on a pantomime just before Christmas.'

'That's a fantastic idea,' I reply. 'It sounds great.

Save me a seat in the middle of the front row. I'm sure all my family will want to come too.'

'We need to charge top dollar-ish for tickets,' Kay says. 'So, if we're going to ask for the big bucks, we're going to need to give people a star. Plus, a big name will just help sell tickets generally.'

I am suddenly reminded of the fact that this conversation started with the phrase 'we need a favour' but I don't let it show on my face. I can't have more than a few seconds to get my excuse straight before they drop the favour bomb.

'We want you to be the star,' they both say, very excitedly, in perfect sync.

'Me?' I reply.

'No, the big fancy TV star behind you,' Kay jokes. 'Yes, you.'

'It will be great, getting some of the old drama group back together, for one big show,' Billy adds.

Oh, God. Things are bad but they're not panto-bad. There is no way I'm starring in a pantomime.

'Oh, you know I would be super down for this,' I start, serving up my half-cooked excuse. 'But my agent is really funny about stuff like this, she'd never agree.'

'Even if it's for a good cause?' Kay asks.

'*Especially* if it's for a good cause,' I reply. 'She's a nightmare, she won't do anything, if she thinks she isn't getting a cut for it.'

'Could you ask her?' Billy replies.

'Yeah, I'll definitely ask,' I say.

I won't.

'Can you ask her now?' Kay prompts.

'Right now?' I say. 'While you're still here?'

'We're desperate,' Kay replies. 'If this doesn't work, I don't know, it might be too late for the owner to sort things out.'

If I am sure of anything it is the fact that my agent will nip this in the bud before I have even finished asking her the question.

'OK, sure, I'll call her now,' I say.

As the phone rings, Kay and Billy just stare at me with big, dumb grins on their faces.

I do want to help, I really do, but that's why I donated. To star in a last-minute local pantomime in a theatre that is crumbling by the second would be career suicide.

'Emmy Palmer, twice in one day,' Jane says as she answers the phone. 'What can I do for you?'

I'm pretty sure there's a line in my contract that says she has to be overly enthusiastic whenever she talks to me. The glass is always half-full. Everything is always going to be fine, even when it isn't.

'I just had a quick question for you,' I start, flashing my friends a thumbs up. 'Where I grew up there's this gorgeous old theatre on the seafront.'

'Sounds positively idyllic,' Jane replies.

I tap the loudspeaker button so that Kay and Billy can hear what Jane has to say straight from the horse's mouth, which means I don't have to seem like the bad guy.

'Oh, it's amazing,' I tell her honestly. 'But it's actually in desperate need of some repair work so they're putting on a pantomime, for one night only, just before Christmas.'

'Well, that sounds like a fabulous idea,' she says.

'And they've asked me if I'll star in it,' I reply.

'Oh, wonderful,' Jane replies. 'What a brilliant idea. You should definitely do that.'

Huh?

Kay smiles even wider and silently claps her hands.

'It's a brilliant idea?' I say, double-checking I heard that right, because I can't have.

'What a fantastic opportunity for all involved,' she says.

'I'll just take her off speaker while we iron things out,' I whisper to Kay and Billy. 'Just in case she mentions any confidential contract details.'

Kay nods and Billy taps his nose.

'Fantastic,' I say to Jane, repeating her word back to her, reminding her what it was, because she can't have meant it, can she?

'I have to admit, I was expecting you to say no,' I reply with an awkward laugh, hoping she picks up on it, realises I want her to say no.

'To be honest, you need them as much as they need you,' she replies. 'After the bad press – true or not – your image needs a bit of a makeover.'

I am *so* glad I took my phone off speaker.

'I see,' I reply. 'And it's fine by you that is isn't a paying job?'

'Well, it is nearly Christmas after all,' she says. 'Have some fun, get people seeing you in a positive light again. Keep me posted but, otherwise, take it easy for the rest of the year, and we'll see about next steps in the new year.'

I take back everything I said about agents always being optimistic. That was definitely a shit sandwich, if ever I were served one. Positive, hopeful messages but the fact that I am not very popular dropped in the middle.

'OK, well, I'll speak to you soon,' I tell her.

'Speak to you soon, Emmy,' she replies.

'Well...' is about all I can say to Kay and Billy.

Kay runs around the table to hug me. Billy is close behind her, wrapping his arms around us both.

'Thank you, thank you, thank you,' Kay says. 'I'll schedule a meeting for tomorrow and send you deets.'

'This is going to be epic,' Billy says. 'Just like old times.'

Suddenly back home, with no real work, back with the old drama group, and my dad getting under my skin, wow, it really is just like old times. The only problem is that, this time, I don't have my granddad around to keep me sane.

'Can't wait,' I lie.

Truth is, I can't believe I've got myself into this mess.

18

I'm not saying the twins are creating a hostile living environment for me. I'm not *not* saying it either.

This morning, when I called through the bath-room door to ask Megan how long she thought she'd be, it was like she added every conceivable bathroom activity to her list of what she had origi-nally intended to do in there, because she took ab-solutely ages, despite her reply that she would be out 'in a minute'.

Then, when I went downstairs and mentioned that I fancied Frosties for breakfast, I'd no sooner grabbed my bowl when I noticed Louis pouring the last of the box out for himself.

Look, I get it, they find me embarrassing, but it's going to take a lot more than making me a bit late or forcing me to eat Fruit and Fibre as a plan B to run me out of town. As for running me out of the house, all of a sudden that actually seemed like quite a good idea.

I approached my mum cautiously.

'Mum, you know how I'm trying to do up Granddad's house ASAP, while I'm still in town,' I started after casually plonking myself down on the sofa next to her.

'Yes...' she replied cautiously.

'Well, I was thinking, maybe I should move in there now,' I replied. 'It's almost legally mine any-way, I can get started on some of the jobs, see what your highly praised handyman has done there al-ready. It makes sense, while I'm in town, to get as much of the work done as possible.'

'That's a great idea,' she replied with a big smile, not even taking her eyes off the TV to say it.

I was expecting her to be upset so this took me aback a little. I didn't say anything.

'You never know,' she started with a smile. 'If you move in there you might fall in love, and never want to leave.'

I just smiled in reply to that comment. It's a lovely thought, it's just not a very realistic one.

Satisfied my mum wasn't upset at me moving out, I gathered up my things and I'm heading over to Granddad's now, just to drop them off, before I have my first pantomime meeting.

I cannot, *cannot* believe I have somehow wound up agreeing to be in a pantomime. One thing that I have always stressed to my agent is, no matter what, I would happily throw myself off everyone's radar before I would resort to that. Pantomimes have this reputation for being for has-beens. It's the last-ditch career move for people who are well and truly out of any other plays – and I mean that in both respects. I know it's for a good cause but, an amateur pantomime, come on, it's going to be tragic. Let's just hope that it gets the local support it needs to be actually worthwhile, but that the buzz starts and stops there, I don't want anyone outside of Marram Bay hearing a word about this.

I don't have much to drop off at Granddad's. I don't even need to drop it off now, I'm just so curious to see the suggested plans for modernising, which Mum says are on the kitchen table.

When I arrive at the front door, strangely, it isn't locked. There are no cars on the drive, and no sign of anyone working here. Well, that's strike one for this builder. He can't even lock a door.

I dump my bags down in the hallway and head for the kitchen where, sure enough, the plans are laid out. It takes me a few seconds to realise that the mock-up 3D images of a house are of *this* house. Wow. Downstairs is still this large open-plan space, except the kitchen is ultra-modern, with a huge island, fancy lighting, enormous bi-folding doors that will open the room up into the stunning back garden. Most of the rooms will be modern and tastefully decorated, which makes sense, if the plan is to sell the place. Lots of whites and greys. White marble-look tiles in the bathrooms. I honestly can't believe this house is going to look like this plan in front of me. The builder might not know how to lock a door, but he sure as hell knows how to renovate an old house. My mum must have seen these, to say what she'd said about me falling in love, because this place is definitely going to be gorgeous when it's finished.

I snap a few photos on my phone, so that I can look at it all later, without having to trail the plans around with me. No doubt when I'm at my pantomime meeting I'll want my thoughts to drift off somewhere more pleasant, less boring, and not completely tragic.

My eyes snap up towards the ceiling when I hear the toilet flushing upstairs. Someone is in the house. They must be. Toilets don't just flush on their own, do they? Not unless the house is haunted which, even for someone with a wild imagination like mine, seems like a stretch. No, it has to be someone inside the house with me, someone creeping around upstairs. And *this* is why we should always lock our doors.

OK, OK, let's not be ridiculous. What kind of burglar (or ghost, if you're still floating that idea) stops to use the loo, never mind flushes afterwards? Exactly. None. I just need to go up there and see for myself that I'm just imagining things or that it's some kind of one-off or glitch with the loo. Still, no sense in being completely unprepared, just in case something awful is waiting for me up there, so I grab Granddad's old walking stick from the bottom of the stairs, brandishing it with all the enthusiasm and expertise you would a rounders bat in Year 8 (I was usually just so relieved it was something fun, instead of something I couldn't do to save my life, like athletics) and slowly make my way up the stairs.

The house remains silent. So silent that, by the time I've reached the door to the master bedroom, I feel silly, and decide to drop the stick and head back downstairs, but then I hear another noise, like a man clearing his throat, coming from the other side of the bedroom door. Right, there's no mistaking that, there's a man in the bedroom.

Emboldened by the fact playing Adelina has meant I've had training to pretend that I'm fighting, I figure what's good for the small screen will serve me well in real life. I don't even get a chance to think about how stupid it is before I charge in there – now with the walking stick extended out like a sword, which actually seems less useful – screaming like a maniac. Thankfully it's a big room, so I don't get to strike the man before I realise who he is. I've seen him before.

'*You*,' I blurt. 'What the hell are you doing here?'

He actually just laughs.

It's the man from yesterday, from the fundraiser, the one who asked me to take his photo. It can't be a coincidence that he spoke to me yesterday and now he's here in my house. He must be following me, the freak. I'll bet he knew exactly who I was yesterday, it was probably just a creepy excuse to speak to me. It's amazing what die-hard *Bragadon Forrest* fans will do sometimes.

'What's your problem?' I ask him angrily. 'Are you some kind of creepy stalker or something?'

'How do I know *you're* not stalking *me*?' he asks in that cheeky sort-of-cockney accent of his.

The fact he's smiling rubs me up the wrong way even more.

'You're in *my* house, you psycho,' I reply angrily.

'Funny, you say I'm the psycho, when you're the one threatening me with a weapon,' he replies, thoughtfully, although still clearly highly amused by this situation.

'The thing with the photo yesterday, pretending you didn't know who I was, now you're in my house, using my loo – are you an obsessive fan?' I ask, wondering if perhaps yesterday was just a stunt, to throw me off the scent, just to get close to me, to... oh, God, what is he going to do to me?

'Are you an egomaniac?' he claps back. 'I'm not using your lav, I'm fixing it. I've been doing a few jobs here – I didn't realise it was your house.'

'*You're* Vee's "lovely young man"?' I reply in disbelief.

'Aww, is that what she calls me?' he says with a smile. 'That's sweet. I take it you're her niece who is buying the house?'

'Emmy,' I reply, still sounding completely ticked off. 'And I'm not an egomaniac.'

I am starting to feel a little embarrassed

though, which only makes me more hostile towards him.

'You think it's normal to assume someone is
stalking you in a small town?' he says, in a tone that
implies it's supposed to make me think.

'I saw you in *two* places,' I say, emphasis on
the two.

'Oh, bloody hell, *two* places. *Two places*,' he
rants. 'Call the coppers.'

'I actually will, if you don't get out of my house,'
I tell him.

I think I'm just more annoyed than anything
right now, he's rubbed me up the wrong way.

'Gladly,' he says as he throws the last of his tools
into his bag and heads downstairs. 'I fixed your
flush, by the way. I'll send you my bill.'

'You do that,' I say, following him down the
stairs, ranting after him. 'And then I don't want to
see you within a mile of me.'

He laughs as he walks out the front door. I
follow him out, to make sure he leaves, my anger
increasing each time he laughs. He seems to think
this is hilarious.

'That's going to be difficult,' he tells me. He tosses his bag over the partition fence between my garden and next door, before vaulting over it himself. 'See you around, neighbour.'

He winks at me before heading for his front door.

Oh, fantastic. Bloody fantastic. This clown is actually my neighbour.

I head back inside and into the bedroom to make sure everything is OK up there and, sure enough, it is.

Well, at least I can get through this next month safe in the knowledge that I'm not going to actually be living here, and he did fix the flush in the en suite. There's always a silver lining.

19

I rock up to the theatre a little late to find Kay and Billy waiting outside for me.

'Oh, there you are,' Kay says, a combination of annoyed and excited. 'I was worried you'd had a change of heart.'

'Of course not,' I reply.

To say I'd had a change of heart, and didn't want to do it now, would imply I was down for it in the first place.

'Come inside, meet the owner,' Kay says. 'And the rest of the planning committee are in the meeting room, we can introduce you to them too.'

'Can't wait,' I lie.

It is actually interesting to step inside the theatre after all these years. I think it's been closed down for the best part of twenty years, and time and weather have well and truly ravaged it – I feel similarly about myself sometimes.

You can absolutely see where work has been done to fix the place up. Likewise, you can see where things like water damage have taken their toll. It's such a gorgeous old building though, with ornate details and original features intact. It does deserve to be saved, to be restored.

'Amazing, right?' Kay says, obviously noticing the wonder in my eyes. 'They were going to demolish it, before the owner put every penny he had into it… And here he is now. Emmy, this is…'

'Oh my God,' I blurt. 'You're Felix Valentine.'

Felix must be in his mid-seventies. He has grey hair, long on top, with a slight wave. His outfit – a pair of blue trousers with a purple corduroy jacket and a green scarf – is as outrageous as I would have expected. He has a pair of thick-rimmed, black-framed glasses on a chain that hangs around his neck. He is so bloody cool.

'For my sins,' he replies in what I can only describe as the ultimate thespian voice.

'You own this place? That's incredible. I had no idea. My name is—'

'Emmy Palmer,' he replies simply. Oh my gosh, he knows who I am. 'You play a fairy princess in *Bragadon Forrest*.'

'You... you watch it?' I blurt.

Felix Valentine knows who I am *and* watches my show. I can't believe it!

'Good heavens, no,' he replies, a little too quickly for my liking. 'I know the bigwigs on the show. Did you know they offered me 200k per episode to play your granddad?'

'You should've taken it,' Billy jokes, with a snort, as he glances up at the tired old lobby ceiling.

Felix shoots him a look that lets him know he does not find that funny. Billy retreats.

'Wow, I had no idea,' I tell him. 'That would have been amazing.'

Felix Valentine is an acting legend. He might not be the most famous on the big or small screen but if you know anything about theatre in this country he's the first name that springs to mind. He isn't just good, he's the best, and since he retired from acting there hasn't been anyone else like him. He would have been incredible as 'my' granddad in *Bragadon Forrest* but he's too good for a show like that, in my opinion, but it does sound like he knows it too.

He scrunches his face up at the suggestion.

'I'm retired,' he insists. 'I bought this money pit and now I'm trying not to die with it. Although I was born here, so it would be poetic, at least.'

Ugh, he's so dramatic, it's amazing.

'I take it you're in on this big idea of theirs then?' he asks me.

'I… I am, yes,' I reply. 'How do you feel about it?'

'Would you believe they haven't told me what it is yet?' he replies. 'Let us gather with the others and find out, shall we?'

He sounds almost sarcastic – intentionally so, I think…

Kay leads us into the meeting room. I don't know what kind of room it was before but it's a bit like a rec room now. There's a small kitchen set up on one wall of it. Then there are a few sofas and random other bits of furniture, but in the centre of the room is a big square table, and everyone else is already sitting at it.

'Let's all sit down,' Kay insists. She's obviously the driving force here, the one who manages everyone, the one who makes things happen.

'Why don't you sit next to Scott?' Kay prompts me.

Oh, God. I'm so nervous and kind of starstruck to be around Felix, I didn't even notice who was sitting at the table. Sure enough, there Scott is, and I'm sitting next to him. Great.

'So, Scott you know,' Kay says. 'Then we've got Alison and Pippa.'

Alison is a forty-something woman. She's curvy with bottle-blonde hair. Her clothing is loud and her make-up is louder – she looks fantastic. Next to her is Pippa, who I'd guess is my age. Pippa is perfectly petite. She has shoulder-length brown hair and, frankly, the most perfect eyebrows I've ever seen. If I could figure out how, I would steal them from her. They're so good they look like a filter.

'Emmy Palmer,' I say. 'Lovely to meet you both.'

'Palmer,' Billy says, mocking my accent (or lack thereof) just a little.

I get that a lot. Back in London, I, and everyone else, says 'Pah-mer'. Up here it's 'Par-muh' all the way. My entire family teases me about it. It really makes me wish I'd chosen a different name (or that *the* Emma Watson's parents had called her something else).

'So, we're all here to discuss the plan to save the theatre,' Kay says excitedly. 'We're going to put on a pre-Christmas show, for one night only, starring members of our theatre group, and the one and only... Emmy Palmer.'

'An interesting concept,' Felix muses. 'And Emmy will bring in a certain crowd, there's no doubt about that. What did you have in mind, something by the Bard?'

'Erm, not quite,' Kay says, stalling, buying herself a little time before she has to say what the actual idea is.

Now that I know it's Felix who owns the theatre it occurs to me that I'm not going to be the only person who doesn't want to be involved in a pantomime. Felix is going to *hate* it.

'We thought, with it being Christmas, something, er, seasonal might be the best way to go,' she says.

'*A Christmas Carol*?' he replies.

'A pantomime,' Kay says excitedly, breaking the news.

'Absolutely not,' Felix replies firmly. 'A pantomime? In *my* theatre?'

'We need to raise money and we need to do it fast,' Billy chimes in bravely. 'People love pantomimes.'

'Dare I ask which one?' Felix replies.

'We thought *Cinderella*,' Alison says. 'It's a classic.'

'It's unoriginal,' Felix snaps back. 'Honestly, a pantomime. And what do *you* think of this? Do *you* want to be in a pantomime?'

Oh, God, he's talking to me. Obviously, the answer is no, but...

'I want to save your theatre,' I tell him. 'And, whether we like it or not, a panto is the best way to get people in the seats.'

'And Emmy will pull in a huge crowd,' Scott adds. 'Her show is massive right now and everyone loves her character.'

'We're all valuable though,' Pippa adds, sounding a little put out. 'We can all make this amazing.'

'Every fibre of my being is telling me this is a terrible idea,' Felix replies. 'You're going to need to convince me otherwise.'

'We can do that,' Kay says, confidently, but her eyes tell a different story. 'In fact, if we can all set aside some time each day, we could have regular meetings to get things set up, and then schedule time for rehearsals. Those of us with jobs are willing to work around them, those of us without should be flexible.'

Those of us who had committed to house renovations are suddenly bricking it because they might have overstretched...

'Prove to me that this is a good idea,' Felix says. 'I fear I may loathe it regardless, but I appreciate the time and energy behind it.'

He might be the most gratefully ungrateful person in the world. I do understand why he would hate the idea of a pantomime, but it's like when you're an up-and-coming actor, you have to do the shit to get to the good stuff, that's why there's a video of me on YouTube advertising some weird cheese aerosol, wearing rollerblades and shouting 'Cheeeeeseaiiiir', because you have to do the things you don't want to do, before you can do the stuff you do. If Felix can just tough it out through this one pantomime then he'll be putting on Shakespeare before he knows it.

'OK, so the committee will meet back here to-morrow, same time as today?' Kay says.

Everyone agrees, so I do too.

'Great, see you all then,' she says.

'I didn't realise you were still acting,' I say to Scott.

'Oh, I'm not really,' he replies. 'Just bits for the drama group. Felix has been mentoring us so we wanted to do this for him. Hopefully, if we get the theatre back up and running, I can do a few plays, see if I can take things further.'

'Sounds like a good plan,' I tell him.

'Thanks for doing this,' he says softly. 'You'll make a big difference. No one would come to see us doing this without you.'

'I'm sure they would,' Pippa interrupts.

'Ah, it's nothing,' I insist.

There's an unmistakable whiff of awkward between us, but the fact Scott is being at least civil with me makes me feel a little less uncomfortable. I'm secretly excited that I'm going to have the opportunity to spend a bit more time with him.

'Gaffer, I'm going up the roof girders, checking that leak hasn't come back, then I'll have a look at what's next on the to-do list,' an annoyingly familiar voice says. I imagine Felix is the gaffer.

I turn around in my chair and see my new next-door neighbour standing in the doorway.

'*You* again,' I blurt. '*Again!*'

'Hello, darling,' he replies. 'Well, I think you're right, one of us is definitely stalking the other.'

'You two know each other?' Kay asks curiously. 'Terry is the builder doing a lot of the repair works at cost.'

'God bless you,' Felix says gratefully. 'This man is a godsend from the south.'

'My friends call me Tel,' he replies. 'And we already know each other because I've designed Emmy's new house.'

'*You* did that?' I reply. 'The plans I saw on the table?'

'All me,' he says with a smile. 'Anyway, I'm off up the roof. See you at home.'

Tel winks at me and, while he drives me absolutely mad, I can't deny that he's impossibly charming. Of course, the fact he charms me only makes me feel even more annoyed at him.

'So, any plans for this evening?' I ask Scott.

'I have a date,' he replies as he puts on his coat.

'Oh, nice,' I say. 'That's great.'

'You?' he asks, although I'm not sure how interested he actually is.

'Dinner with Dad,' I reply.

Scott shoots me a look.

'*My* dad,' I quickly add.

'Well, have fun, I'll see you tomorrow,' he says.

'Yeah, see you tomorrow,' I reply.

Billy wraps an arm around both of us, before either of us can leave.

'Isn't it great?' he says. 'The old club, back together.'

'Sure is,' I reply with faux enthusiasm.

Now, more than ever, I do really want to save this theatre for Felix, but, when it comes to pantomimes, I feel the exact same way as he does. But it's our best shot, right?

Oh no, it isn't.

Oh yes, it is.

Unfortunately, yes, it is.

20

My dad and his new family live in a beautiful detached house over on Hope Island. I'm standing on the garden path and I'm annoyed already.

When Dad left us we didn't have much money, and he didn't always give my mum money for Gracie and me, so it really pisses me off to see him doing well. I suppose that's one of the easiest ways to get rich, right? By not giving anything to anyone.

I think I'm hanging around in the garden, in the cold, because I don't actually want to go inside. I really don't want to be here, and I certainly don't want to sit down for dinner. It might be the one thing I want to do less than star in a pantomime.

I notice a face appear in a downstairs window. It's Patsie, Dad's wife. She smiles widely and waves wildly. Eventually, she appears in the doorway.

'Oh, Emmy, hello,' she says, calling me closer with her hands. 'Quick, come inside, out of the cold.'

The very first thing I see when I step through the door is an enormous family portrait on the wall, of my dad, Patsie and their daughter, Katie.

The funniest, most infuriating about Patsie is the way she looks – she looks like my mum. Honestly, the resemblance is uncanny. My dad cheated on his wife with someone who looked just like his wife. Even more annoyingly, Katie looks a lot like me, only she's five years younger than I am and five times bubblier. She worships our dad. So much so I find it hard to spectate. Then again, he didn't ruin her family for mine.

'Is that Emmy?' Dad calls out from the kitchen.

'It certainly is,' Patsie replies brightly. 'Let me take your coat, love.'

'Thanks,' I reply.

'Ooh, that's a good coat,' she says. 'So heavy.'

I just smile.

'Come on, have a seat at the table,' she insists. 'Katie has so much to tell you.'

I follow Patsie into the dining room. It's changed since the last time I was here. They've had one of those massive rear extensions that opens the house up, giving them this grand room with a huge round table at its heart.

Katie peeps around from behind the large floral centrepiece.

'Oh my gosh, Emmy,' she squeaks.

She stands up and hurries over to me.

'Sis, it's been forever,' she says as she hugs me.

I remind myself that it isn't Katie's fault that she was born.

'It's nice to see you with clothes on,' she adds.

It's probably her fault she's kind of a bitch though.

'Oh, I can't watch your show, unfortunately,' Patsie says, not sounding all that bothered. 'All the blood and nudity and swearing. Your poor mum must think it's a nightmare.'

She's had worse to deal with over the years.

'So, how are you both?' I ask politely.

'Doing well, thank you,' Patsie says. 'Yourself? Your dad tells me you bought a big house! We were sorry to her about your granddad. I met him a couple of times, he always seemed like a lovely man.'

'Thanks,' I reply. 'Yes, I bought his house. It's gorgeous but it needs some modernising, so I'm working on that at the moment.'

The room falls silent. Other than bitchy little remarks here and there, I don't have a bad relationship with Patsie and Katie, I just don't actually have a relationship with them at all. We're not close, we don't chat. I don't feel like I know all that much about them. I couldn't tell you what kind of things they like. My interactions with them both have always been minimal, formal affairs. I don't think I've been here for dinner since I was a teenager.

'I'm getting married soon,' Katie blurts eventually, filling the silence.

'Wow, congratulations,' I tell her. 'I didn't even know you had a boyfriend.'

'Yep, we've been together for three years now,' she replies. 'Look at my ring!'

Katie offers me her hand to admire her rose gold ring with a large diamond-looking stone in the centre.

'Beautiful,' I tell her.

'There she is,' my dad says as he walks into the room. He's wearing a black apron that says 'Licence to grill' on it. 'Come here.'

My dad hugs me like he loves me. I mean, I'm sure he does love me, even if he's not very good at it, but we're not exactly on hugging terms. It's like, when his new family is around, he puts on this perfect-family-man act, that I know couldn't be further from the truth.

'Hi,' I say as he squeezes me. I can't muster up much polite enthusiasm for him.

This – just like everything else – annoys me. He didn't hug me when he saw me at Granddad's funeral. Hugging me now just feels like taking advantage.

'Dinner is almost ready,' he announces. 'Emmy, let me borrow you in the kitchen, I want to make sure I cook your steak right.'

'OK,' I reply, dutifully following him, unable to hide the hint of caution in my voice. Sounds odd.

'Just, medium rare, I guess,' I tell him. 'Or however it comes.'

I just want to get out of here.

'Yeah, no worries,' he says. 'Stay here while I cook them, I need to talk to you.'

'Oh?'

'Yeah, you see, Katie is getting married before Christmas,' he starts.

'So I've heard,' I reply.

'Problem is, her venue had to move around a few dates this year, and they've somehow lost her booking,' he says, kind of casually for something that is such a big deal.

'That's awful,' I say genuinely. 'She just told me she was getting married, she seemed so excited, so calm, so... Oh, God, she doesn't know, does she?'

Dad just shakes his head.

'Thing is, I really want to make this day special

for her,' he explains. 'The church is still booked, so the ceremony can go ahead, I can give her away and all that. There just isn't going to be a reception.'

'I'd probably tell her,' I say, in absolute disbelief. 'I'd tell her *very* soon.'

'I'm hoping when I do tell her I'll have good news for her,' he replies.

He drops a steak in the pan, which sizzles loudly. It does smell really good, but there's something fishy in the air overpowering it...

'I was talking to your mum, she said you've bought Tony's house,' he starts. 'I remember when we would all get together there for Christmas, and the New Year's Eve parties, the number of people we could fit in that living-dining room... What do you reckon, that place could easily seat twenty-five for a sit-down dinner? And even more for the party. It's always been the ultimate house for house parties.'

And there it is. The reason I'm here. The reason he's talking to me. The reason he hugged me. I only agreed to come here because my mum made it sound like he was making some big effort, some grand gesture to get our relationship back on track, and as much as I hate him, he's still my dad. I feel so stupid for coming here.

'Yeah, it's a big house,' I reply.

'And your mum said you're tackling the downstairs first,' he continues. 'And that you're going to get it done ASAP, while you're in town...'

'Yep...'

'Love, listen, what would you say to letting Katie have her wedding reception at your place?' he asks, very optimistically for someone who walked out on me when I was a kid. 'I can help with the work there, money is no object, Patsie and I can make all the arrangements, we just need the space.'

'You're asking me if you can throw a wedding at my house that I'm not even invited to?' I say, unable to believe my ears.

'Not invited?' he replies. '*Of course* you're invited. Katie is going to invite you tonight.'

'She just mentioned her wedding to me and absolutely did not mention inviting me,' I point out. 'I don't even know the groom's name.'

'Lewis? He's a great kid,' Dad insists. 'And Katie

is so excited, she'll be devastated if this wedding is called off, Emmy, please, find it in your heart.'

I puff air from my cheeks. Pushing from my mind the fact that my no-good dad is asking for a favour – a favour for his new family, no less – I do really feel for Katie. I can't even imagine finding out my wedding wasn't going ahead a few weeks before, of course she'll be devastated.

'Do it for your sister,' Dad persists.

'Right, OK, fine,' I say. 'Once you've broken the news to Katie just let me know what you need.'

'You're a good girl, Emmy,' he tells me. 'Heart of gold. Now, how did you say you want your steak cooked?'

Whichever way is the quickest, ideally. I don't have much of an appetite this evening anyway, but watching Dad play happy families makes me feel sick. This good-guy family-man act is exactly that, an act, and I'm not falling for it for a second.

21

Is there anything worse than being woken up by a phone call and then having to try and talk to someone while you're half-asleep? Especially when you decide that, for some stupid reason, it's embarrassing to be caught sleeping, so rather than admit you've just woken up (explaining why you sound so weird and have no idea what's going on) you try and style it out. That's what I'm doing right now because Jane, my agent, has just called, and I'm hoping she has good news for me.

She could be calling me to tell me that Disney called, and they want me to play Spider-Woman in the next phase of Marvel movies, which would solve all my problems. She could be calling to tell me that *Bragadon Forrest* can't survive without me so they're going to scrap my exit scene or cut it short before I get my head cut off, or something, which would solve some of my problems. Finally, as a small consolation prize, I guess she could be calling to tell me that she's had a rethink about the panto and it's a terrible idea, which would solve my immediate problem of feeling like I'm resolved to filling out the rest of my career with Z-list gigs like pantos and reality TV, which is absolutely fine for some people, but I don't want to abandon my acting career.

'So, what's up?' I ask, semi-sleepily, after practically snoozing my way through the pleasantries.

'You should have received a delivery,' she tells me.

I did update Jane with my current address, just in case she needed to send any contracts (wishful thinking on my part), but I wasn't expecting her to send me anything.

'Oh?' I reply. 'I haven't checked my post yet.'

'Just a little something I think you'll like,' she replies. 'It's – Emmy, hun, I'm sorry, I'll have to go. I have Tom on the other line. Enjoy the present, speak soon. Good luck with the play.'

I love how she simply says 'Tom' when she's clearly referring to one of her biggest movie-star clients. He's just Tom to her. I also love how I'm clearly not as important as Tom. My stock is way down.

As much as I want to go back to sleep for a bit, before it's time to get up and head to the theatre, I'm excited to see what she's sent me, so I pull myself out of bed and shrug on my dressing gown. I'm not quite a-kid-on-Christmas-morning excited, but we always used to sleep here on Christmas Eve, the whole family, before celebrating the next day, so it does remind me of all the happy Christmases we spent together.

I rub the sleep from my eyes and head downstairs. Sure enough, outside the front door, there's a box with my name on it. It's quite big. I can't resist tearing it open and looking inside.

It's a heavily padded box, which makes me

think there's something fragile in it. There's a note on the top from Jane which simply states 'a souvenir'.

I carefully lift out the big ball of white paper that's wrapped around whatever this souvenir is. I slowly unwrap it and peep inside.

Oh my God.

Oh. My. God. This is horrendous. This is absolutely horrifying, in so many ways. Why on earth would Jane send me this without forewarning me?

Not only is it so final, to receive a parting gift from the set of *Bragadon Forrest,* reminding me that I really am well and truly off the show, but the last thing a person expects to find when they open a package, is their own severed head. Well, the replica severed head they had made for my final scene, but believe me, it is disturbingly lifelike. Oh, and obviously it's not *just* my head, it's my *severed* head, so I look all dead and bloody. Honestly, it's the stuff of nightmares. Why would I want this? Whether it's reminding me of my own death or the death or my career, I can safely say, I don't want it. I want it out of my sight.

I hurry down the driveway to the wheelie bins – three of them, each a different colour. I wonder, for a few seconds, which is the right one: green, black or blue. Back in London we have trash chutes, clearly marked with signs for: general waste, recyclables and glass. My best guess is that the black one must be for general waste, which I think is what prop severed heads come under, so I chuck it in there.

'Erm, what do you think you're doing?' I hear Terry's voice call out.

Damn, I almost made it back to the front door without seeing him.

'What?' I ask, reluctantly turning around, spotting him over the fence.

'They're my bins,' he informs me. 'Yours are in that wooden store, at the side of your house.'

'Noted for next time,' I reply as I make a move to head inside again.

I reach my front door when I spot him opening up his black bin, so I hurry outside again, marching up to him.

'You're not seriously taking it out?' I ask him angrily.

'No, I'm just checking it's recyclable,' he says. 'The fellas who empty them are sticklers for the rules. They won't empty them if everything isn't in the right bin.'

I stare at him, chewing my lip lightly as I wonder what to say.

'Is it recyclable?' he asks.

'The paper around it is,' I offer. 'Come on, don't go all bin police on me.'

'Green is for general waste,' he tells me, reaching into the black bin, lifting out what I had just put in there.

'I'll take that,' I insist, a little too heavy-handedly, because it piques his curiosity.

'What is it?' he asks with a slight smile.

'None of your business,' I reply.

'It's in my bin,' he points out. 'So, it's mine now.'

'Can I just have it back, please?' I say. 'I'll put it in my bin.'

I don't know if it's his intention or not, but as

Terry shifts my mystery rubbish in his hands, the paper opens up and he sees what's inside.

'Oh wow,' he blurts. 'What... what is this?'

He's an almost attractive combination of confused and amused. It's sort of charming. Well, it would be, if he weren't annoying me.

'It's my severed head,' I tell him, as though it were the most normal thing in the world.

'Can I have it?' he asks, equally as casually.

I feel my eyebrows shoot up, but they quickly fall again when I realise the implications of the existence of my character's severed head.

'Erm... yeah,' I reply. 'It's from a dream sequence, from a deleted scene, so it was never used. It doesn't mean much to me, so I don't want it. Wait, you're not going to do anything weird with it, are you?'

He laughs.

'Depends how you define weird,' he says. 'I thought we could have a laugh with it on Halloween, freaking out the kids who come to our doors. It will be so much fun to play around with.'

'Right,' I say, looking him up and down. 'Well, I

absolutely won't be here on Halloween, so you'll be playing with yourself.'

'Yeah, sorry, I forget you're not sticking around,' he replies. 'Well, thanks for the head.'

A man who is hovering at the end of the driveways, cleaning up after his dog, clears his throat loudly to alert us to his presence. Then it occurs to me how bad our last few sentences must have sounded.

Terry just laughs and heads back into his house, with my head in his hands. God, he infuriates me and charms me in equal measure but, just like with my old family memories, it's the negative emotion that dominates.

Well, I'm up now, I suppose I should get ready. I've got a pantomime to get on with. Oh joy.

22

Emmy Palmer, reporting for pantomime duty.

I'm here at the theatre, I'm on time, I'm ready to get on with it. I can't say I'm enthusiastic about this whole thing, but I am gently motivated by wanting to help Felix save his theatre. I know I considered trying to get out of it, somehow, and that Jane didn't come through for me, but I do genuinely have a lot of respect for Felix, and it's hard not to care about what happens to the theatre, especially now I've seen inside the old place again.

I still can't believe *the* Felix Valentine owns the theatre! No one seems to be as impressed by his presence as I am but, then again, if you're not a theatre nerd you're probably not going to be all that star-struck by him. I absolutely am though. I'm not sure I could be in a pantomime for anyone else... even if he did look down at his nose at the idea of playing my granddad in *Bragadon Forrest.*

Felix is the only one who isn't here yet. Kay and Billy are chatty as ever. Scott is being slightly awkward with me but that's understandable – I'm trying to pretend he isn't in the room too, mostly because now when I look at him I'm reminded of his dad. Pippa isn't saying much either – not with her mouth, at least, her eyes are a different (lowkey, hostile) story. I really like Alison though, she's lovely. She's so bubbly, so friendly, so interested and so interesting herself. She has grilled me about *Bragadon Forrest* but she's also talked a lot about herself. I know that she's divorced, she loves to crochet and she has three dogs. I've only been here twenty minutes and I already feel like I've known her for years. Some people just have that extra something about them that makes you feel at ease.

Felix walks in, his face like thunder as he slaps a piece of paper down on the table in front of us.

'*Cinderella*, cast and crew list, compiled last night,' he says. 'It's much of the usual although you will notice I've left the director blank. That's because I don't even want to put my name next to this hypothetically. Not until we've figured a few things out.'

Billy and Pippa are the two people who reach across the table to see the list but it's Pippa who snatches it up first. She sees something on there she doesn't like and quickly discards it, sending it floating back across the table to Billy.

'I'm Buttons and Scott is Prince Charming,' he says thoughtfully, processing the implications of this casting choice. 'I suppose, Buttons is the bigger part.'

'Yeah, but Prince Charming is the better part,' Scott adds competitively.

'Buttons gets more lines, more laughs,' Billy reasons optimistically, although he does seem slightly offended. I think he's reassuring himself.

'But Prince Charming gets the girl,' Scott continues to wind him up.

'You just strike me as more of a Buttons type,' Felix says. I honestly can't tell if he's sugar-coating his thoughts or not pulling any punches.

'Prince Charming is a smaller part,' Billy persists.

'There are no small parts, only small actors,' Felix says insincerely.

'There are some no-parts though, apparently,' Pippa says, rather confusingly.

Felix looks at her, mentally dismisses her comments, then looks away.

'What I mean is,' Pippa persists, pausing for a few seconds to gather her words. 'My part is a non-part.'

That doesn't make much more sense from where I'm sitting.

'You're our choreographer,' Felix tells her. 'You're *always* our choreographer.'

'But I usually star in our productions too,' she insists. 'And now you're relegating me to... to an understudy!'

Wow, and I thought Billy was offended at playing the friend-zoned buddy instead of the prince.

Felix pushes his glasses up his nose as he stares her down. Somehow this makes him seem like he means business.

'Pippa, this isn't the second-biggest room in the town hall, this is a prestigious theatre, with real seats – and lots of them – not pop-up chairs largely occupied by your own friends and family.'

Wow, Felix is brutal.

'It's a big room but it's not big enough for your ego,' he continues. 'We have a genuine star sitting at this table. Emmy is a big name who will draw a crowd. Granted, I find her show to be derivative drivel, lazily titillating the masses with torture porn – and often actual porn – but make no mistake, this pantomime is beneath her. Emmy can act, and people will actually want to see her playing Cinderella.'

OUCH! Absolutely savage.

'It makes sense that Emmy is playing Cinderella,' Alison says. 'We should have a star playing the star. Oh, and look at that, I'm the Fairy Godmother!'

Alison looks like she was born to play the Fairy Godmother. She looks friendly, sweet, helpful – all the qualities you would want. She's got that beaming smile too. I feel like she could make all my problems go away. Then again, maybe I'm just biased because she's saying nice things about me.

'Oh, and you've got the boys down for the Ugly Sisters,' Alison says with a giddy clap of her hands.

'The boys?' I ask.

'The *ladies*,' Kay corrects her. 'We have not one, but two incredible drag queens in our group. Naturally, they'll play the Ugly Sisters. Steve and Marc, also known as Rhonda Drinks and Lina Coke.'

'We can't put Lina Coke on a poster though,' Alison says with a shake of her head. 'That's not very family-friendly.'

'Pantos do have that element of innuendo though, right?' I say. 'Where the jokes for the adults are written to go over the heads of the kids?'

'So they're playing the sisters,' Kay asks as she

finally gets her hands on the cast list. 'And... oh my God. What? *I'm* playing the Wicked Stepmother?'

'Who else is there for you to play?' Felix replies. 'And Emmy raises an excellent point. Writing a pantomime is a subtle art form. I've only ever met one person I believed had truly mastered the art.'

'They're not dead, are they?' Billy asks with a snort. Then he clocks the look on Felix's face. 'Oh, God, sorry, they're not, are they?'

'I'm dead to her,' Felix replies. 'Anita Van der Boom. She lives on the island. If you don't get me one of her scripts, then this panto isn't happening.'

I notice a subtle little wobble in Felix's usually flawless delivery of every word he says. It sounds like there's some history there.

'But you just said you're dead to her,' Kay points out, her face scrunched with confusion. 'So surely she'll tell us to get lost?'

'Surely,' Felix replies plainly.

'Wait, so, I'm the only one here not in this thing?' Pippa says. 'How does that seem fair?'

'I am nothing if not fair,' Felix asks. 'Now go

and get me my script from the woman who loathes me.'

Felix leaves the room.

'I guess we could go see her tomorrow?' I suggest.

'Oh, do you think?' Pippa says sarcastically.

She doesn't look at me, instead staring at the pen she's aggressively twirling.

'Is everything OK with you?' Kay asks her carefully. 'You seem a bit...'

'A bit what?' Pippa snaps back. 'A bit like the part that should have been mine has gone to this rando? No offence, Emmy,' she says as she turns to me – a sentence opener that almost always precedes something really bloody offensive. 'But you don't even look like a Cinderella type.'

'It's a shame you didn't keep the long blonde hair you have in your show,' Alison says. 'Which I love, by the way. You'll need to wear a wig now.'

'It's not just that,' Pippa continues. 'You look dark and dreary. Cinderella is bright and beautiful. She isn't... emo or whatever.'

Loving the idea I'm a thirty-four-year-old emo kid.

'Perhaps I could redefine what it means to be Cinderella,' I say dismissively.

'See, this is what I mean, it's not that kind of show,' Pippa claps back.

'You do get to be her understudy,' Scott reminds her, as though that's going to make a blind bit of difference.

'So, I'm just supposed to sit here and hope something bad happens to her then?' Pippa replies. She sounds annoyed at first but then she raises a thoughtful eyebrow, as though that might be an option.

'Assuming I make it through the night,' I interrupt, getting the conversation back on track. 'Anyone up for going to see Anita with me tomorrow?'

I notice Billy open his mouth to speak but another voice gets in there first.

'I'll go with you,' Scott says. 'I'll find out where she lives tonight, pick you up tomorrow, take it from there?'

'Erm, yeah, great,' I reply.

I wasn't expecting Scott to step forward.

'Pippa, chuck us that pen,' Scott says as he tears a strip of paper off the bottom of the cast sheet. 'Emmy, write your number on there, I'll give you a bell later.'

I smile slightly as I write my number down for him. It's strange, just like that, I feel like a teenager again. My God, what I would have done to have a cool boy like Scott ask me for my number like that back when we were at school. By the time we did swap numbers, when we were in sixth form, talking about visiting unis together, it was such a bland transaction. This move, just now, feels like my teenage fantasy. He's still so cool.

'Class dismissed then, I guess,' Kay says. 'Oh, first, Scott, let me have eyes on Emmy's number, and I'll add you to the group WhatsApp.'

Oh, God, I hate group chats. I hate them almost as much as Zoom calls. They're just a whole thing, with bizarre, specific etiquette. Let's just hope no one in the group likes to drop memes in the chat, but I feel like I can already tell from Billy's eyes that he's picking out a welcome GIF because his eyes light up at the idea.

'Great,' I reply.

Scott is the first one to stand up. He pauses behind my chair and places his hands on my shoulders for a split second. Him touching me makes the butterflies in my stomach go crazy.

'See you tomorrow,' he says.

'Yeah, see you tomorrow,' I call after him, trying to play it cool.

Pippa is the next to leave, in a huff of course, and I do feel bad, having muscled in on her gig, but I'm only trying to help. I still absolutely don't want to do this. I don't know who wants it to happen the least, me or Felix, but I think we're both starting to see it as a necessary evil.

'Look at you,' Kay practically sings.

'Ooh, what are we looking at?' Alison asks excitedly. She was in the middle of putting on her coat but the thought of gossip has almost suspended her in time.

'You still fancy him,' Kay says.

'Emmy fancies Scott?' Alison replies, still frozen on the spot.

'For sure,' Kay starts. 'Come on, look at her face, she's practically blushing. And she did fancy him all the way through school.'

'We're adults now,' I point out.

'Then why are you so excited?' Alison says with a knowing grin.

'I'm not,' I insist with a snorty laugh but, now that I think about it, I suppose I am. I'm looking forward to spending time with Scott, one on one, with no theatre friends or awkward parents around. And now I've realised that I can't help but wonder, is Scott excited about spending the day with me too?

23

After a long day of whatever the hell this has been, I can't wait to get (not quite) home to (not technically yet) my house.

It's 5.30 p.m. and already completely dark out but I arrive home to a warm, welcoming glow. Mum's car is parked outside and there's that telling, flickering light coming from the living room that means she's lit the fire. Perfect on a chilly night like tonight.

Oh, and as if my evening couldn't get any more perfect, not only does the warm heat from the fire hit me when I open the door but so does the smell of whatever my mum must have brought me for dinner.

'You angel,' I call out as I make my way to the kitchen. 'I'm going to take this bra off and then...'

Sitting at the kitchen table, alone, isn't my mum, it's Terry the builder from next door. He's tucking into what looks like cottage pie and grinning like an idiot.

'Your mum said you liked my plans for the house but I didn't realise you liked it that much,' he jokes.

As if things couldn't get any more bizarre, my mum's head pops up – literally pops up – from the floor, behind the table, seemingly out of nowhere. She stays kneeled on the floor. They both stare at me, as though I'm the weird one.

'This is like that scene from *The Shining* only somehow much weirder,' I say, not that I expect my mum to have seen it – in fact, I'm counting on it.

'Spilled the peas,' Mum says. 'Otherwise, you're right on time. Sorry, I should have let you know we had company. I didn't realise you'd come in and say—'

'Do women always take their bras off to eat?' Terry asks playfully, in an attempt to defuse the awkwardness.

'Women take their bras off any chance they get,' I reply. He shoots me a look, even though he knows what I mean, so I clarify. 'Because they're uncomfortable.'

'Come on, sit down,' Mum insists. 'Have something to eat. I thought it might be nice to surprise you with dinner and Tel was just finishing up, so I invited him to stay.'

I suddenly regret allowing my mum and aunties to sort local tradesmen to handle the house renovations. I just assumed they would have more of an idea of who was good and trustworthy, and I didn't think to specify they hire someone who didn't annoy me.

I pull up a seat at the table. My mum cleans up the last of the spilled peas and plates me up a dish of cottage pie. She places it in front of me before heading back to her bag. She pulls out a bottle of ketchup and places it on the table in front of me.

'You put *ketchup* on cottage pie?' Terry asks in disbelief.

'I used to when I was a kid,' I reply, but his disapproving look doesn't shift. 'I put ketchup on *everything* when I was a kid.'

I meaningfully tuck into my dinner, without so much as looking at the ketchup, although truthfully, I would love some. I've always loved the stuff and it's something that I've brought with me into adult life. I'm the person in the restaurant who, when the waiter asks if anyone wants anything, always asks for ketchup for her chips. Well, why not? If you like something, like it unashamedly. Not tonight though, obviously, tonight I'm not giving Terry the satisfaction.

'Listen, Terry,' I start, but he stops me there.

'Everyone calls me Tel,' he interrupts through a mouthful of food. 'Except your Aunt Vee, she calls me M25, for some reason. I suppose because I'm from London.'

Oh, God, I've heard Vee name men she fancies after motorways before, and it's usually just so she can make reference to their hard shoulders.

'Tel,' I say, correcting myself. 'I've had a good look at your plans.'

'You love them, don't you?' my mum says. I regret telling her that because, as much as I do really love his vision for the place, no one is leaving this table until Tel has been relieved of his duties. He just rubs me up the wrong way, I don't think I could stand to be around him as much as I would need to be, especially if he's working at the theatre too.

'Your mum was telling me you're hosting your sister's wedding,' he says. 'That's really nice of you.'

I actually think my mum was weirdly proud of me for agreeing to this. Well, she's always been the bigger person. I think she saw this as some kind of character growth, a sign of me letting go of a little of my baggage, even if it's only my hand luggage.

'Thanks,' I reply.

'We were already planning things to a pretty tight schedule, but it's doable,' he continues. 'Luckily, I know everyone who can do everything in this town. So, if quick is what you want, it's all sorted.'

Quick is what I want – and what I need now, thanks to the wedding – and I do really love Tel's plans, and it does sound like he can do things well, and fast, if he's just done it all at his place.

'What's that?' I ask curiously, noticing some photos on the table.

'Oh, you're not going to believe this,' Mum says giddily. 'I was telling Tel about the dining table your granddad made and that we were going to have to throw it away, given how damaged it is.'

It's true and I'm gutted. I have so many amazing memories of sitting at that wooden dining table, that Granddad made with his bare hands, but it's old and damaged and has this big split down the centre.

'I've got a mate on the island, Ben, local carpenter,' Tel explains. 'We make these tables with resin in the centre.'

Tel puts down his cutlery and wipes his hands on his trousers before handing me the photos.

'Oh, wow,' I blurt.

I flick through photos of wooden tables with strips of resin down the middle. They're absolutely gorgeous. They do all sorts with them too. Layers of green resin to match the northern lights. Sandy yellow and blue with white foam that looks like the tide coming in. Real works of art.

'You can save Granddad's table?' I say eventually.

'Oh yeah. It's a good way to save old tables,' he says modestly. I'm not sure he knows how to react to my genuine awe.

'That would be amazing,' I say softly. 'Thank you. You're, erm, a real jack of all trades, aren't you?'

He smiles and shrugs.

'Master of *some*,' he says with a laugh.

OK, so, maybe it isn't the best idea to fire Tel. He obviously knows what he's doing, and he can clearly make things happen quickly. Plus, it sounds like he's managing the project, getting lots of different people to do jobs here. Oh, and if he's doing work at the theatre too, then it sounds like he'll be there a lot of the time.

My phone springs to life inside my bag so I

reach down and take it out. I notice I've been added to a group chat called 'Break a Leg' and the first message I see is a GIF from Billy featuring Sharpay and Ryan from *High School Musical* waving. Great.

A few seconds later I get another message, this time from a number.

Hey, it's Scott. Let's make a plan for tomorrow. X

I try not to get too excited or read too much into that kiss on the end of his message. Wow, I really am like a teen again. I am looking forward to it though.

'Your mum explained how special this place is to you all,' Tel says, snapping my attention from my phone back to him. 'Don't worry, I'm going to take really good care of the place, you're going to love living here – I love my place.'

'I'm not actually living here,' I insist, perhaps a little too forcefully. 'I'm heading back to London after Christmas.'

'Well, who knows, maybe when you see the

place you'll change your mind,' he says with a cheeky smile.

'You know, that's exactly what I said,' Mum replies.

Oh boy. Why do I get the feeling this is going to be a long month?

24

I remember when I was maybe seventeen or eighteen, standing outside my granddad's house on a Saturday morning, waiting for Scott to pick me up. Our media studies essays needed to be bound before they were submitted so we were taking them to a printing place in another town.

It was actually Scott's dad who was supposed to be driving us there. Imagine if he had, then I probably would have recognised him at the pub and all the awkwardness could have been so easily avoided. But his dad had plans so he entrusted his newly licensed son to drive his car instead.

I remember feeling so nervous. How had a dork like me managed to make plans to go somewhere (OK, to the printers, not exactly a date, or anywhere even slightly fun) with the coolest boy in school? Up to that point our interactions as teenagers had been strictly limited to drama club so, when he asked if I wanted to go together to have our projects bound, I basically went into shock. The only thing more shocking was when we went for lunch together after, and then made another plan to go on another drive, to visit the universities we were looking at. We all know how that ended.

Today, being a mature woman (ha!) I don't feel quite so nervous, but I do have those butterflies in my stomach. I tell myself I'm being stupid. That I'm in a TV show watched all over the world, sometimes wearing next to nothing, constantly being interviewed and approached by strangers. I'm not *not* confident. But there's just something about being around Scott. It's like the schoolyard hierarchy is still in place, like I'm supposed to feel intimidated by him, but it could just be because I still fancy him.

I glance over at Scott. Sitting in the driver's seat, in some ways he looks just like the skinny teen I remember from all those years ago but now that he's a confident, grown man I potentially fancy him more now than I did then. Back then he seemed so lanky, in his Green Day hoodie and his baggy jeans, constantly, carefully looking over his shoulder as he nervously drove. He does it so effortlessly now. So much so he takes his eyes off the road and catches me staring at him. He just laughs.

'Do you think we're wasting our time?' I ask him. 'Chasing a woman around town who Felix is sure is going to tell us to get lost?'

'I don't have anything better to do today,' he says with a smile. 'Do you?'

Things were awkward between me and Scott a few days ago, to say the least, but it's as though somewhere around the time we realised we'd be sharing the stage again we decided to just let go of it, probably only for the sake of the pantomime, but still, it's nice.

'I have a small army of men in my house banging and screwing and...' It's like my brain starts actually listening to the words I'm saying and pulls rank on my mouth, stopping me from saying another word. I laugh. 'I have lots of workmen in my house. It's nice to be out of there. I'm hoping, in a few weeks, the downstairs and the master bedroom will be finished.'

'And then you're heading back to London?' he replies.

'And then I'm heading back to London,' I confirm. 'Back to work.'

Hopefully, I guess.

'I'd love to move to London,' he says. 'I just need something to give me that push to do it. I'd still love to pursue acting professionally, not just for fun like I do with the theatre group, as fun as it is.'

'You should just go for it,' I tell him. 'If I hadn't, I'd still be here, doing something else.'

'I was sad when you moved away,' he says, suddenly quite serious. 'But you were right to, it was absolutely the right thing for you to do. I would love to be on a show like *Bragadon Forrest*.'

God, so would I, it turns out.

'The theatre group are a fascinating bunch,' I

reply, changing the subject, because talk about my soon-to-be-non-existent career really freaks me out. 'I've been trying to get the measure of everyone.'

'Well, me you know,' he starts. 'Brilliant actor, devilishly handsome, adored by everyone. Felix is great but he's an absolute savage. I think he thinks he's acting royalty.'

'He *is* acting royalty,' I insist.

'Whatever he is, he's a miserable git,' Scott continues. 'I didn't want to do this pantomime for him. Sure, it will be fun, and it's great to save the theatre, don't get me wrong. But putting myself out there for him, doing him a favour, to probably just get obliterated... I'm excited about starring alongside you again though. Kay is the best at organising us all, Billy is still a bit of a nerd, but he makes me laugh. Alison is a sweetheart but a total meddler so don't ever tell her anything. Pippa is... well, Pippa is not happy you're in town.'

'I feel awful,' I reply honestly. 'I think she feels like I'm taking her place. It was never my intention. Truthfully, I didn't really want to do this either.'

'That makes me, you and Felix,' Scott chuckles. 'Remind me why we're chasing this woman all over town?'

'Because we offered,' I reply through a smile.

To say we're chasing Anita Van der Boom across town is a slight exaggeration. We went to her cottage on Hope Island where one of her neighbours told us she'd already be propping up the bar at The Hopeful Ghost, a pub over on the mainland.

We're just pulling up outside now (funnily enough, only a matter of metres away from where we started, across the road at the theatre).

I think I must have only been to The Ghost, as the locals call it, two or three times when I was in my teens and once when I visited home in my early twenties. These days it's nothing like I remember it being. Before it was just a pub-pub, all pints and pork scratchings. Sure, it was in a beautiful spot on the seafront, with views over to the island. From the beer garden you get a perfect view of the old abbey ruins over on Hope Island. Hope Abbey has been in ruins for hundreds of years. We all heard the stories growing up; supposedly, there's a secret tunnel network that runs underneath it, that the monks who lived there used to escape from... I want to say Vikings, but you know how these types of stories change over the years. One of the times I did sit in the beer garden with my friends, a drunk old man, who looked exactly how I would imagine Santa Claus to look, tried to convince us he'd seen the ghost the pub was named after – a dead, scorned bride who got trapped in the tunnels on her wedding day. It kind of turned me off coming here, but seeing it how it is now, it doesn't have so much of a dark vibe.

These days The Hopeful Ghost is a popular local bar and restaurant. It's so bright and airy and everything is modern and chic, but still with that double dose of local charm everywhere around here seems to have. Between the roaring fire and the gentle music, I could actually see myself settling down here to hang out today, if only that were an option. We're here for business.

'Excuse me,' Scott says ever so politely as he approaches the bar. 'We're looking for someone who drinks in here. Anita Van der Boom?'

The barman doesn't say anything, as though he might be breaking some sort of barman code if he did tell us where Anita was, but he does nod in her direction.

Sitting on a sofa, over by the fire, nursing a glass of what looks like whisky is a woman in her early seventies maybe. There's a glamorous vibe about her. If you told me she used to be a Bond girl I'd believe you.

'Hello, are you Anita Van der Boom?' I ask as we approach her.

'That depends,' she starts, looking us both up and down. 'Are you after money or an autograph?'

'Oh, neither,' I quickly insist. 'We're here on behalf of Felix Valentine.'

Anita practically chokes on her drink.

'That old bastard. What does he want?' she replies.

'Well, er...' I find myself getting a little tongue-tied. I know he said he wasn't her favourite person, but that reaction has really taken me aback.

'Come on, kids, sit down,' she insists. 'Oi, Glenn, bring us another three of these.'

Anita, who has the same accent all the theatre luvvies have, suddenly sounds quite Yorkshire as she shouts at the barman.

'You two drink?' she says.

'I'm driving,' Scott tells her.

'So, you can have *one*,' she replies. 'And what about you? I know you.'

'You know me?' I reply.

'Yeah, from the critically acclaimed *Bragadon Forrest*, I'm a big fan,' she replies. 'Only reason I'm buying you a drink so, come on, take a seat.'

Scott and I look at each other for a second, wondering if we have any other options, before sitting down as instructed.

'You're the best thing about that show,' she tells me.

'Thanks so much,' I reply, hoping the fact she seems to like me means she might just help me out.

'I tell you what I liked the most. That episode where you're in the bar, in The Unclaimed Lands, and you play Five Finger Fillet – what do you call it in your show?' she asks.

'We just call it the old knife game,' I reply.

'Yeah, we call it Five Finger Fillet,' she says. 'Was that actually you doing it, in that scene?'

She eyeballs me curiously.

'It was,' I reply proudly.

I am actually quite proud of that fact. You know the old game where you spread your hand out on the table in front of you and stab the gaps between your fingers with a knife, one at time, as fast as you can? Well, my character had to do that in a scene, so I spent weeks learning how to do it, getting faster and faster each time I practised, until it was good enough for the show.

'I was very impressed,' she tells me, and she does sound it. 'I'm not as fast as I used to be, but I was the Five Finger champ in here, back in the day, before it went all posh.'

I can see Scott stifling a smile.

'Come on then, what does he want?' Anita asks as our drinks are placed down in front of us. More whisky. Not exactly my thing.

'Felix owns the old theatre,' Scott tells her. He sips his drink and then scrunches up his face. Whisky must not be his drink of choice either.

'So, the old bastard bought the place,' she says. Her eyes wild and her smile beaming.

'He did,' I say. 'But it does need a lot of work done.'

'Oh, I'll bet he's absolutely bankrupt himself,' she says gleefully.

'I don't know about that,' I reply uncomfortably. 'But we're putting on a pantomime the week before Christmas to raise funds.'

'Ha!' Anita blurts loudly. So loudly it attracts the attention of the other day-drinkers. 'Felix? A pantomime?'

'Well, only on the condition that it's one of yours,' I reply. 'He said you were the only person he knew who had mastered the art. It's you or no one.'

'Then it's no one,' she replies. 'Did he tell you what he did to me?'

'Oh, erm, no,' I reply. There's clearly a lot going on here that we don't know about. I think it's time for us to leave. 'That's OK though, we'll leave you to it.'

'Sit back down,' she insists before we've even finished standing up. 'I just want you to know why, so you don't think I'm some bitter old hag, or perhaps I am a bitter old hag, but let me tell you. Felix and I were an item. We used to dance in the theatre dance hall – did you ever see it? I'm sure that room closed before either of your time but, my God, it was spectacular. Legend has it, during the Blitz, people kept dancing in that hall, even as the bombs were falling. Before mine and Felix's time but they continued having these bygone-era dances right into the sixties. I slowly but surely fell in love with him but then he frigged off to London *to be famous*.'

Anita says these last three words in such a mocking tone. I can't help but look over at Scott who is already looking at me. I hope he doesn't think that's what I did to him.

'I always wondered if he'd come back for me, surprise me with some bold gesture, or even just an apology, but it never came,' she says with a sigh.

'Well, we're not going to try and convince you,' Scott says. 'You clearly have your issues. To be fair, he knew you wouldn't say yes.'

'Sorry to bother you, Anita,' I say. I feel sorry for her, for Scott, I feel guilty and selfish. I don't know the details and I'm sure our situations aren't as comparable as they seem, but things seem to get to me far more easily these last few weeks, what with everything going on with work, and then everything here. 'Thanks for the drinks.'

'Ah, it's not your fault,' she reasons. 'And it is nice to have some company. You don't fancy a game of Five Finger Fillet before you go, do you? There's never much competition in here, now it's a fancy *wine bar.*'

I love the tone of voice Anita uses when she talks about the things she thinks are dumb. I wish I had the confidence to pull that off.

'Oh, I don't know about that,' I say with a laugh, assuming she's joking. 'I'm painting a feature wall in my bedroom tomorrow. I can't do that if my hands are bleeding.'

'Not unless you want your wall red,' Scott jokes.

'We'd play with a pen, obviously,' Anita says with a roll of her eyes. 'I'm not as fast as I used to be, so I play with marker pens.'

Oh, wow, she's serious. I consider playing a round with her, just because she seems like she'd really enjoying the company, but then inspiration strikes.

'How about I play you for a panto script?' I suggest. 'The best version of *Cinderella* you've got.'

Anita looks at me thoughtfully. Then her eyes light up at the thought of a challenge.

'You're on,' she says. 'If you're faster than me you can have your script but, if I'm faster than you, then you two have to spend the day drinking with me. It's nice to have some company. You have to pay though. And you can't ever ask me for a script again, obviously.'

'Sounds good to me,' I say confidently.

'Emmy, can I borrow you for a second?' Scott says, standing up, edging away from Anita.

'Yeah, sure,' I reply.

'I'll find the pens in my bag,' Anita says giddily. 'Oh, it's been so long since I had a challenger.'

'I've absolutely got this in the bag,' I tell him in hushed tones once we're alone.

'Do you really think so?' he replies.

'I mean, never mind the fact we have nothing to lose, Anita said it herself, she's not as fast as she used to be, and she said I was great at it. I did practise forever for the show. I really think I can win us our script.'

Scott laughs.

'Well, I'm right behind you,' he says. 'Go kick this old lady's arse and get our script, I guess, and if not, let's at least drink her under the table.'

'Sounds like a plan to me,' I reply. 'But don't worry, I've got this. By tomorrow morning we'll have a script to show everyone and we can start rehearsals.'

'Good,' Scott replies. 'Because if we don't, we're screwed.'

25

Has the meeting room at the theatre always twirled around like this, slowly spinning around the table we sit at, or is it the table that's moving?

I do actually know the answer to this question and it's a simple one. I've had too much to drink. So has Scott. And, not content with how much we drank, we left the pub and staggered across the road to the theatre (Scott was definitely in no fit state to drive us anywhere else), and now here we are in the meeting room, slumped on the table, sharing one of the bottles of Prosecco left over from the fundraiser. I thought it might be too warm, given the fact it hasn't been chilled, but it's actually so cold in the theatre that it's chilled enough to be enjoyable. Or it would be if all the drinks we had with Anita hadn't removed my taste buds already.

'Do you want to talk about it yet?' Scott slurs.

'I just can't believe she beat me,' I reply. '*She* beat *me*. But she didn't just beat me. She *thrashed* me.'

'You said you were good and she said she was slow,' he says, baffled. 'But then *she* won.'

'*She* did.' I sulk. 'How though? I was *sooo* fast on TV.'

Scott thinks for a moment. He swigs from the bottle of Prosecco before the answer hits him like a sledgehammer.

'Now that I think about it, I'm sure I read something online once, some trivia about the show, that said it was a hand-double doing that for you,' Scott says.

'What?' I reply, my drunken shriek getting on my own nerves. 'No way. They had me learn it, and I did it, and I remember thinking it wasn't fast enough but I watched the episode and it looked so fast and... oh my God, it must have been a double. Shit.'

'You tried your best,' Scott chuckles. 'You were faster than I would have been, just no match for Anita.'

'Good on her though,' I say, taking the bottle from Scott, raising it to toast Anita. 'She deserved to win. I kind of feel like she sharked me, giving it all that about being old and slow. It made it all the more amazing when she killed it.'

'And at least we had an excuse to drunk in the day,' Scott reasons. 'Drink in the day, I mean.'

'And the evening,' I remind him. 'Because here we are.'

'And I can't even drive home because I've had too many, and because the tide is in right now, and I live on a stupid island, and because my dad will kill me.'

'And... actually that's all I've got,' I say with a snort.

'And we don't have a script,' Scott says.

'I'll drop a message in the group,' I reply as I fumbled around next to me for my phone.

Scott stands up, takes the almost-empty bottle of Prosecco from me, walks over to the sofa, plonks the bottle down on the shelf behind it, and then flops face down into the cushions.

I follow him and perch on the edge of the sofa next to him.

'We'll just have to convince Felix to let us use a different one. Anita is just one writer,' I reason.

Scott sits up.

'Thing is, Felix is stubborn, and if he thinks pantomimes are hacky, that's it, no pantomime. He would rather see his theatre crumble to the ground than watch two men in a horse costume, lifting one of the legs and firing a water gun at the audience.'

He has a point.

'Shit,' I say under my breath.

This isn't even my fight, or my problem, and I'll be gone in a few weeks but... God, I feel so frustrated. Everything really is getting to me at the moment.

'Come on, it's going to be OK,' Scott says as he wraps an arm around me. He pulls me close and rubs my shoulder.

'I just feel so involved now,' I reply, turning to face him, not realising just how close our faces suddenly are.

For a moment we stare into each other's eyes, neither of us moving a muscle, not even blinking, until – I swear – it seems like Scott is moving in to kiss me. Does he want to kiss me? I know I want to kiss him, so I move ever so slightly closer to him, so slowly that he probably can't tell for sure if I'm moving.

Scott quickly pulls away so perhaps I wasn't moving as subtly as I thought, and he wasn't moving at all.

'Shit, sorry,' he blurts. 'I wasn't trying to kiss you, I swear, I'm seeing someone, that girl you saw me with the other day.'

'You're seeing someone?' I reply. 'I had no idea. That's great though, really great for you.'

'And obviously I know you're seeing my dad, so...'

Scott's voice trails off awkwardly and I realise Mike has obviously never set him straight.

'Oh, there's nothing going on between me and

your dad,' I insist. 'I'd say we were just friends but we're not even really that. My auntie Vee and his friend Ken are kind of a weird thing. She actually roped me in as her wing-woman, so bizarre, but your dad and I were just hanging out because we didn't want to sit and watch them kissing all night. Nothing romantic, at any point, we said that up-front, and the thing you walked in on, I spilled wine all over my dress, I was just getting cleaned up, I couldn't get my dress off...'

Oh God, I just straight babbled at him, so much, for so long, I don't think either of us knows what I'm on about.

'Oh,' is all Scott says. 'OK. Where's the Prosecco?'

'*He's behind you*,' I joke, panto style – I love a crap joke to fill an awkward moment – spotting the bottle behind him.

Scott erupts with laughter, somehow making him look even more handsome, which is even more annoying now I know he's seeing someone.

'See, this is what's so annoying, pantomimes write themselves,' he says with a big sigh. 'We could knock out a *Cinderella* tonight, if we wanted to.'

'We could,' I reply.

We both sit in silence for, I don't know, a few seconds, a minute, it could be an hour and a half for all my drunk arse knows. But inspiration strikes us at the exact moment.

'Are you thinking what I'm thinking?' he asks.

'*We* write the panto,' I reply.

'Come on, there's a computer in Felix's office, let's do this,' he insists, taking me by the hand, dragging me along with him.

'This theatre is pretty creepy at night,' I say anxiously, taking in our dimly lit, decaying surroundings in one of the corridors that hasn't been given a makeover yet.

'It is,' Scott replies. 'Apparently, bits of it are haunted too.'

I stop dead in my tracks. I felt far less creeped out in the newly refurbished, brightly lit meeting room.

'Come on,' Scott insists, dragging me again. '*Everything* around here is supposedly haunted. Rumour has it that any cast who used to perform here back in the day would all go crazy and turn on each other. Some of them still walk the corridors, just waiting to whisper malicious ideas into the ears of actors who dare to take the stage.'

I shift uncomfortably.

'Let's just hurry up,' I insist.

Inside Felix's office, it's hard to tell if his room has had a makeover or not. It looks clean and, you know, not like it's about to cave in because the walls are damp (truthfully, I have no idea what would make walls cave in) or whatever. But, still, it looks so plain and unfinished, like perhaps he spent the absolute minimum time, effort and money on a room that was just for him, in favour of putting everything to better use elsewhere in the theatre. You've got to hand it to him, he does seem to really love this place.

Scott fires up the computer and opens a blank document. I stand behind him and we both stare at the screen, that little cursor flickering expectantly, almost menacingly, daring us to write a pantomime.

I glance around the room as I ponder how to kick things off. We've both had eyes on a lot of scripts over the years so we know how to write them, we just need to work out what exactly we want to write in this one.

'What's his deal?' I ask curiously, noticing a framed photocollage on the wall next to us.

It's one of those with spaces for multiple photos and seems to be showing a montage of the very first photos taken here, before any work was done. The picture I'm referring to is one of Felix and Tel, standing together in the doorway, both brandishing sledgehammers. It seems like perhaps it might have been a staged photo for the local news or something, metaphorical sledgehammers, because if you so much as brushed this building with the tails of your coat it feels like it might just fall down around you.

'What, Felix?' Scott replies.

'No, Tel,' I say, trying not to sound too interested, but I am. I just can't quite work him out.

'Pssh,' Scott replies. I didn't realise people actually said pssh. 'That *Love Island* looking chump?

With his overinflated muscles and his cheeky cockney charm that *everyone* loves? Doing all his free work, being so nice to everyone? With his big house and his easy-going attitude and all the guys love him and all the girls fancy him and he just can't seem to do any bloody wrong and Felix thinks the sun shines out of his arse?'

'Yeah, that one,' I reply. I wasn't expecting that little outburst. 'What's his deal?'

I repeat my question, but I suppose Scott just answered it in a way. Tel is Mr Perfect. Mr Too Perfect. But no one is that perfect really, are they?

'I don't like him,' Scott says simply. 'And I definitely don't trust him.'

'He's doing some work at my house,' I say. 'Lots of it, actually. Well, he's managing it. I've been trying to avoid him, to be honest.'

'Yeah, do,' Scott slurs keenly. 'Something isn't right there.'

I glance at the blank screen again.

'Can I sit there for a minute?' I ask.

'Knock yourself out,' he replies, moving for me.

I hover my fingers over the keys for a second or

two before I start typing. Scott watches.

'That's pretty good, you know,' he says excitedly. I type a bit more. 'Brilliant, in fact. Hang on, let me add something.'

I watch him shoehorn in a panto-sized dose of innuendo in the first few lines and snort with laughter.

'I love that,' I say excitedly. 'That's so funny!'

'We're going to absolutely knock this out of the bag,' Scott says giddily, mixing up his metaphors. 'Felix is going to love this.'

'Do you think we can get it done by morning though?' I ask.

'If we stay here all night,' he replies. 'I will, if you will?'

'OK,' I say with a few giddy claps. 'Let's do it!'

We take it in turns writing, bouncing off each other, absolutely creasing each other up with our brilliant jokes and edgy but family-friendly dialogue. I feel so happy that we're solving this problem so easily but, whenever I've thought about spending the night with Scott, I have to admit, this is the *last* thing I imagined us doing.

26

'You two look like you've had a good night.' I immediately jolt upright on the sofa because I know where I am before I've even opened my eyes. Waking up on the sofa in the meeting room is not a shock. Waking up with Kay and Billy standing over me is.

'Shit,' I say under my breath. I cough to clear my throat before attempting to explain myself. 'This isn't what it looks like.'

'What *does* it look like?' Pippa asks.

Alison is with her. Now all four of them are

staring at us and, somehow, Scott is still fast asleep on the floor.

I tap him lightly with my foot but he doesn't wake up. I kick him a little harder.

'I'm up, I'm up,' he says, reluctantly pulling himself upright.

It only takes him a few seconds to realise he's not in his bed. He's puzzled until he looks around and sees the rest of the gang.

'Oh, morning,' he says with a smile. He only has one eye open as he adjusts to the light. 'I'm glad you're here. We need to tell you all about last night.'

'Oh, we don't want to hear it,' Pippa insists angrily. 'After that message Emmy sent to the group. Actually vile.'

'*I* sent a vile message to the group?' I say in disbelief.

Pippa can hardly look at me. She's standing there in her tightly belted coat, her nose turned to the ceiling, and I'm pretty sure whatever this is, it's still about me getting a part she believed should be hers. I do wonder if she might have a crush on Scott too...

'I thought it was funny,' Kay says. 'You said "With Scott. No panties."'

'I wondered what you meant,' Billy says, for some reason looking like a kid who's just found out there's no Santa. 'I think I understand now.'

'Oh my gosh, no,' I say, unable to hold back the laughter. 'Sorry, we'd had a few drinks, but that's not what I meant, it must have been a dodgy auto-correct. It was meant to say no *panto*, meaning we didn't get the script.'

'Oh,' Pippa says simply. 'So, no panto at all then?'

I swear, she looks delighted, I can see it hiding in her eyes.

'Not to worry, we've saved the day,' Scott announces as he pulls himself to his feet. 'Emmy and I wrote a script ourselves last night and, honestly, it's brilliant.'

Scott wipes his eyes with the backs of his hands as he heads over to the table to pick up our freshly printed *Cinderella* script.

'I present you all with the best pantomime

script I've ever seen… if I do say so myself,' he announces rather grandly.

Honestly though, I think the script deserves it. Not only did we write it in one night, but I don't think I've ever laughed so much.

'Ooh, let's see,' Kay says excitedly. 'So… Act One, prologue, blah, blah. OK, here we go: "Dramatic music. Dark stage. Smoke creeps along the floor before (pyro?) a flash reveals the Fairy Godmother. She narrates DSP…" Alison, these are your lines, why don't you read them?'

I can't help but smile. How professional do we sound?

'Honestly, you're going to laugh your arse off,' Scott insists.

'Yay, OK,' Alison says excitedly as she takes the script. She does a few clichéd theatre-actor mouth stretches before she starts. '"Once upon a time, in a land far away, lived a prince in a very big castle. He had even bigger balls" – oh my!'

'It's innuendo,' Scott insists, but he looks over at me, as if to confirm that we actually wrote that. We must have, but that's not the fantastic script I re-member from last night...

'Oh, OK,' Alison says, shifting uncomfortably as she takes a seat at the table. '"At the other side of the village lived a kind, old baron, with his lovely wife. They loved each other so dearly that one day they... they went up to the..." – OK, I'm not reading this, this isn't innuendo, this is filth.'

I quickly snatch the script from her and skim-read it.

'Oh... my... God! This is awful,' I can't help but announce. 'Take a look.'

I hand the script to Scott, who only needs to look at a few pages to come to a similar conclusion. He winces as he reads it.

'It's possible that, when we were drunk, we thought we were much funnier than we are,' Scott says. 'Which I guess is pretty funny.'

'Except Felix is going to be here in about ten minutes and we're not going to have a script for him,' Kay reminds everyone, as though we'd forgotten.

'We're screwed then, aren't we?' Billy says as he

sinks into the sofa. 'No pantomime, no theatre. We'll have to go back to the town hall, to trying to perform Shakespeare while tempers are flaring in the room next door because the Nation of Shop-keepers are meeting and someone wants to open up a shitting KFC.'

His rant takes me aback a little.

'All might not be lost,' Alison says timidly.

She picks up her handbag and clutches it in front of her, as though one of us might be about to try and steal it. Eventually, she loosens her grip, places her bag down on the table and takes out a wad of papers.

'I've written a script,' she says.

Pippa snorts.

'Is it a guide on how to crochet your own hats?' Pippa asks rather cruelly.

Alison shoots her the dirtiest look.

'It's a *Cinderella* script,' she says clearly, even though we all know. 'It was actually something Emmy said, about redefining what it means to be Cinderella, that gave me the idea for it.'

'Can I have a peep?' Kay asks gently.

Alison nods and hands it over but you can tell she's terrified of showing it to anyone. Let's hope this lot are nicer than they were about my and Scott's script. I can't believe how bad it is. In fact, I grab it and take another quick look. Christ, it's worse than the first time I looked at it. I don't just want it out of my own sight, I stuff it in my handbag. No one else can *ever* see this.

I look up at Kay who is smiling widely as she reads Alison's work. She reads a few pages, the smile on her face growing with each line.

'This is brilliant,' Kay says. I can tell from her bright eyes and her big grin that she means it. 'Billy, look at this.'

He eagerly takes it from her and starts reading.

'I love what you've done with it,' Kay says. 'You really are shaking things up. Emmy, you'll love it, you're not playing the Cinderella you thought. It's got a modern twist.'

'Ooh, does this mean I don't need to wear a wig after all?' I say excitedly.

'Oh, no, you still need to wear a wig,' Alison informs me. 'It's a classic set with classic costumes.

It's just the dialogue that's modern. Oh, and re-member Jean, who did the music for our spring fling collection?'

I have no idea who Jean is, or what that is, but everyone else seems to know what she's talking about.

'Well, he said he'd do the songs, so we can have a few original musical numbers, isn't that great?'

'Are there usually musical numbers in pantos?' Scott asks curiously.

'Yeah, definitely,' Kay replies. 'Not many, but some. Oh my God, Alison, it's amazing. You've saved the day, you really have.'

'Let's see it,' Pippa reluctantly says. 'I can't imagine Felix coming around, he was very clear, he only wanted a script from that one woman. I wouldn't even show it to him.'

'Emmy, what do you think?' Kay asks.

I think it can't be worse than my effort. I take the script and have a look for myself. I can tell from the first few pages that it's not only better than mine and Scott's mess, it's actually really good. It's fun and fresh and I'd really love to do it.

'I think we can convince him it's a good idea,' I say confidently. 'Once Felix sees that it's something a bit different, honestly—'

'I thought my ears were burning,' Felix announces as he walks into the room. 'Is that my script?'

'It is,' I say, owning it. 'It's not the one you were expecting, but it's the only one you're going to want.'

'A bold claim from the fairy princess,' Felix says. 'And where is this script from?'

Alison raises her hand. She seems a little more sure of herself now that we've all praised her work but Felix is Felix. He could turn at any moment.

'From our very own Fairy Godmother,' he says. 'Interesting, very interesting. Well, let's see.'

I hand the script to Felix who reads a few pages before folding the script closed again. He never gives much away with his body language but he always instils fear.

'Is this your only copy?' he asks Alison.

'No,' she says cautiously, grimacing, like she's

preparing for Felix to throw it in the bin or, worse, throw it at her.

'Print some more,' he says plainly. 'I'm taking this one to read. Give copies to everyone and begin learning your parts. We'll have a table read next week and then we're on with rehearsals.'

I think, as Felix goes, that's a compliment.

'Yes, sir, right away,' Alison babbles like a schoolgirl.

Her smile is so wide and she looks so pleased with herself. She deserves it.

'You're all dismissed,' Felix announces with his back to us as he leaves the room.

'Great job, Alison,' I tell her. I'd hug her but I probably stink of booze and I'm in the clothes I slept in. 'You've smashed it. He clearly loved it!'

'I think I'm going to be sick,' she says through a smile.

'Me too,' Scott says. 'But I think it's from mixing my drinks. I'm heading home for a nap and a shower – in that order.'

'I think I'll join you,' I say, cringing immediately

at my choice of words. 'To my own home, bed, shower.'

'This is really exciting,' Billy says. 'I can't wait to tackle this, Alison. I'll schedule the table read and put it in the group chat so keep your eyes peeled.'

I don't need to keep my eyes peeled because so far the group chat has been pretty non-stop, even if it is mostly just Billy posting crap memes and Kay being the only one who laughs at them.

I usher Scott to one side.

'Let's never write again,' I say under my breath.

'I'm with you there,' he replies. 'Right now I could happily agree to never drink again either. I'm going to get going for that shower. I'm sure I'll be far more relaxed, now I know I'm not going to find you and my dad in it.'

'Ha! No,' I say with a snort. 'Anyway, see you at the table read, Prince Charming.'

'Yeah, see you then, Cinderella,' he replies.

I honestly can't believe I'm saying this but, from what I read of Alison's script, it's such a cool, fun, much-needed twist on the classic panto format. Sure, the set will be the same, and the naff costumes, but the contemporary dialogue and references gives it an edge. We've got our USP. Now I can't wait to get stuck in, let's just hope everyone else is as excited about it as I am. This may not be quite so embarrassing after all.

27

I find my mum sitting at the kitchen table, nursing a cup of tea.

'Oh, stick the kettle on,' she says, before even saying hello, when I walk into the room.

'*Hello*,' I hint.

'Sorry love, hello,' she says with a laugh. 'I was miles away and I've let my tea go cold. I wasn't expecting to see you until later. I thought you had your club all day, I've not even got the tea on.'

When you're northern you just develop this sixth sense for knowing when tea means a cup of tea and when it means dinner. My mum just hit me with one of each.

'We finished early today,' I tell her. 'I was hanging out at Granddad's – at home – but all the noise from the workmen was doing my head in.'

'Workmen is such a sexist term,' Megan chimes in as she grabs a bottle of water from the fridge. 'I thought you were supposed to be a feminist icon.'

'My character is,' I reply. 'And it's not sexist because they're all men. You have a problem with that then I guess all you can do is be a plumber when you grow up.'

'Gross,' she replies before leaving us alone again.

'Don't tell her to be a plumber,' my mum insists.

'No?'

'No, because they're both going to university, and Roy and I can't wait to have the house to ourselves,' she says quietly.

It's funny, I was worried she was going to say the job was beneath Megan, or something else equally untrue, but she just wants a house without kids in it.

'Fair play,' I reply. 'They're not exactly a bag of laughs to be around.'

'You say that, but – I was actually going to talk to you about this today – you know it's the twins' birthday on the seventeenth? They always feel like it's a little overshadowed, being so close to Christmas, and this is their eighteenth, so we're having two parties. A nice dinner party for the family and then we've hired that arcade by the seafront, the one with the speakeasy upstairs, for a friends-only proper party-party.'

'Nice,' I reply. 'Well, just let me know when the dinner is. Unless I'm trying on a glass slipper in front of God knows how many people, or throwing a wedding I wasn't originally invited to, I'll be there.'

I'm kidding, of course. The panto and the wedding are much nearer Christmas. I'll make more of an effort to remember the dates of them nearer the time.

'Well, actually, the twins would love you to attend their party-party too,' Mum says with a smile, like I'm going to be touched they want me at two parties.

'Didn't you say it was a no-family party?' I say.

'Yes, but they want you there! Isn't that nice?' she replies.

'Not exactly,' I say with a laugh. 'Megan was just in a room with me, didn't invite me, and was actually quite rude to me. Also, if no family are going, why am I invited?'

The look on my mum's face says it all.

'Mum, you're kidding me?' I say.

'Listen, I know you might think they're using you...'

'I thought they were embarrassed of me?' I reply. 'And that's why they're so off with me?'

'Well, turns out, given that a lot of their friends are fans of yours, and the fact they know you're related to Megan and Louis, they've all assumed you'll be there, and the twins would never say as much, but I believe there's an unspoken worry that no one will come if they find out you're not going to be there, so...'

I can tell my mum is embarrassed to ask me

this, but I get why she's doing it. They're her kids. She would have done the same for me.

'I really don't feel comfortable being wheeled out at parties,' I say. 'Especially when they're having you ask me, and they're not usually nice to me.'

'This might make them nice to you?' she says. 'Or at least pretend to be.'

She laughs.

'Don't tell the others I said this, Gracie included, but you were the best teenager,' she tells me.

'And you were the best parent,' I reply.

She frowns playfully.

'Well, that's no competition, is it? Unless you count Roy...'

'I meant out of biological parents,' I reply with a cheeky smile. 'Otherwise, Roy wins all categories.'

'Oh, Emmy Watson, you devil,' she laughs. 'Make me a nice warm cup of tea and I'll forgive you.'

I have to admit, it's really nice being able to just pop over and have a cup of tea with my mum. It's little things like this that you take for granted when you live locally, and then you move away, and on those days when all you need is a cup of tea and a cuddle with your mum, you can't just get one.

I feel a heavy tug in my heart. I suddenly feel so guilty about living so far from home. Not because I feel like people are upset with me for it, or because I can't stand being away from my family (as much as I do miss them) but because you can't control what you miss, when you are miles away. You tell yourself there will always be other dinners, other barbecues, other impromptu get-togethers just because the sun is shining that day and everyone fancies hanging out. You even tell yourself there will be other birthdays, if you have to miss those, but I've suddenly realised that's just not the case. Sometimes there isn't another time. When I think about all the time I spent away from my granddad, no matter how many presents I sent him or how many long phone calls we had, there's no escaping the fact that I hadn't seen him in months, and I'll never see him again. As I watch what is left of him slowly disappearing from his house, sometimes it's much easier, with less things around to remind me of him, but other times it's so much harder. I feel like I'm erasing him. I'll glance at the old clock in the hallway, the one he always used to lift me up in front of so I could watch it gong (I have no idea why I wanted to watch it make sounds, I was a kid), and it won't be there and feeling the absence of these seemingly unimportant things makes me feel the absence of one of the most important things in my world.

I make my mum her cup of tea with a real lump in my throat, and as we gossip about why Gracie is being so quiet lately, and what's giving Vee such a spring in her step (I *had* to tell her, she's my mum), I just can't shake the feeling that there's a gap in my life. While I might be worried about my lack of a job, and it might seem impossible to find one right now, it's not actually impossible, I'll get a 'regular' job if I need one, but with Granddad, it really is impossible to see him again. And that's a missing piece of the puzzle I just don't know how I'm going to replace.

28

It's 8 p.m. when I finally arrive home and I'm absolutely shattered, so I'm annoyed to see that the lights are still on, and the front door is wide open. I approach it just as Tel is walking out.

'Oh, there you are,' he says cheerily.

'Hi,' I reply. 'I thought you'd be gone by now.'

'Yeah, well, I figured I may as well keep working until you came home, get as much done as possible, seeing as though we need to be ready for a wedding now,' he says with a smile. 'I suppose time just got away from me. This isn't me stalking you.'

I roll my eyes. He's not letting that one go, is he?

'Right,' I say as I walk past him. 'God, it's freezing in here.'

'We fit the bi-folding doors today,' he tells me. 'It's been a chilly one though, sorry. Get that fire on.'

'Cheers,' I reply simply, stalling the conversation.

Am I being a bit rude? I'm not trying to be but there's just something about Tel. Somewhere between when he annoyed me and Scott telling me not to trust him, I decided I needed to keep him at arm's length.

'Right, well, I'll get off then,' he says, picking up on my tone. 'Oh, before I go...'

Tel picks up a cardboard box from the floor and hands it to me.

'One of the lads says this was delivered at some point and they put it to one side, forgot to give it to you,' he says.

He hands me the cardboard box. I glance down at it and see my granddad's name on it. It's only as I'm opening it, lifting out what's inside, that I remember what it is. I hand it to Tel as I burst into tears, running into the living room where thank-fully there is still a sofa to sit on, for now at least.

I think it's the shock, perhaps, coupled with a feeling like I've seen a ghost. Whatever it is I just can't keep my emotions locked up inside me any longer.

Tel hurries in after me.

'Are you OK?' he asks me. I don't answer him, I just sob.

'Of course, you're not,' he says, sounding like he's kicking himself for asking.

I place my head in my hands, suddenly seri-ously embarrassed to be ugly-crying in front of a stranger.

I hear Tel fussing around for maybe a minute before I hear the front door close. I suppose some-where between my unsubtle hostility toward him and my outpouring of wild emotion, he decided to scarper. I can't really blame him.

After a few minutes it's the warm of the fire I feel first. Then I open my eyes and see Tel standing in front of me.

'You were shaking,' he tells me. 'So, I thought

I'd grab some logs from outside and light the fire. Can I...?'

He gestures at the sofa.

'Yeah, sure,' I reply.

I rub my teary eyes with the backs of my hands so forcefully I see into another dimension.

'Sorry about this,' I tell him. 'That bottle of whisky... I sent it for my granddad, they tried to deliver it on the day he died, he never got it.'

'That's rough,' Tel replies. 'Emmy, I'm so sorry. I know what it's like to lose a granddad. I don't have any grandparents left now. You mum told me you live in London?'

I nod.

'Yeah, well, I'm like a reverse you. But instead, I moved from the south to the north, and I wasn't very successful,' he says with a cheeky smile. 'I got a job working for a property developer who travelled around sticking up new builds, didn't make it home much, and I swear, every time I did head back, someone else was missing.'

'How did you end up staying here?' I ask curiously.

'Just fell in love with the place,' he says with a shrug. 'I started doing odd jobs, bit of building here and there, and I scraped together what little money I had to buy the smallest, shittest, but most importantly cheapest, house in Marram Bay. Business increased, and I did that house up, flipped it for a profit, and used the money to buy next door. Anyway, I just wanted to say that I get what you're going through.'

'I don't have any grandparents left either now,' I reply. 'Granddad was the last one. He was more of a dad to me than my actual dad ever was, so I feel like I've lost such a big part of my life.'

I don't know why I just told him that. I don't ever tell anyone anything about my dad.

'He will have known how much you loved him. It certainly seems like you spoiled him,' Tel says, holding up the bottle of whisky. 'This isn't the cheap stuff.'

'It was his favourite,' I reply. 'I don't really know what to do with it. Do you want it?'

'It might be nice if we poured a couple of glasses now, raised a glass to your granddad?' Tel suggests. 'I know you had the funeral and stuff, but those things never really feel like they achieve what they're supposed to.'

'I always say funerals are pointless,' I say, amazed we seem to be of a similar opinion. 'But, yeah, I think that's a great idea.'

'I'll grab some glasses from the kitchen,' he tells me. 'You stay here, keep warm.'

I sniff loudly.

'I'll bring you some tissues too,' he adds.

'Thank you,' I call after him.

I pull my legs up onto the sofa and hug my knees. I feel a little calmer for letting it all out, and I really like Tel's idea of raising a glass to Granddad, even if the last thing I want to do right now is have a drink – especially not whisky.

'Loo roll,' he tells me, placing it down in front of me.

'Thanks,' I say with a smile. 'Sorry again for the outburst.'

'No apology necessary,' he replies. 'You've recently lost someone who meant a lot to you. I think you can get away with anything right now.'

Tel pours us a couple of drinks before sitting back down next to me and raising a glass.

'To Anthony,' he says. 'We only chatted a few times over the garden fence, but he seemed like a great geezer.'

'To Anthony,' I say. 'Probably the best man this shitty world will ever know.'

'Not even going to fight you on that one,' Tel says, clinking his glass with mine. 'Cheers.'

Tel swishes the whisky around in his glass. Granddad always used to do something similar and it sets me off again.

'Do you want me to get your mum or someone?' Tel asks.

'No, no,' I say quickly. 'Thanks, but everyone else is dealing with just as much as I am. I don't want to set anyone else off, as much as I need a hug right now.'

'Well, I could hang out for a bit?' he suggests. 'I could update you on house progress, grill you about your job, or just sit in silence. It's been a long day.'

'Thanks,' I say with a smile.

Tel places an arm around me and rubs my shoulder, but he doesn't get too close or make me feel uncomfortable. Now I really do feel like a cow because I was so rude to him and now I'm just so happy that he's here.

'I got everything ready to paint the wall in my bedroom this evening,' I say with a sigh. 'I'd been looking forward to it. Now it just seems silly.'

Tel clicks his tongue.

'Swooping in to do the fun and easy jobs,' he teases. 'And then everyone will compliment the gorgeous wallpaper, but no one will say a word about the toilet that flushes now.'

I laugh.

'I really appreciate the toilet that flushes,' I tell him sincerely.

'Why don't I help you paint your wall?' he suggests. 'If you're hell-bent on doing it yourself, I won't paint a lick of paint, I'll just hand you brushes and mansplain how to use them.'

He really is so funny and so charming. It's hard not to smile.

'Thanks,' I say with a big sniff. 'I'd really like that.'

This is the reality of grief for most people, isn't it? You don't sit around actually mourning loved ones after they pass – in this day and age who even has time? Instead, you do your best to get on with things, go through the motions, keep a careful lid on it so you can function, but at some point that lid comes off, and I'm so glad I wasn't alone when it did.

29

Things are really coming along in the house now.

It's amazing what some money and a small army of men can achieve. And, no, I'm not being sexist, it's like I told Megan, there *are* only men working here, unless you count me but I'm not really doing much. Tel was right last week, when he said I only liked to do the fun and easy jobs that got the most glory.

It's odd, having only been here a couple of weeks, but feeling like so much has changed, it almost makes it feel as though years have gone by.

Tel is being great. He splits his time between

here and the theatre and I don't know how he does it. He just has so much passion for these things. I remember when I used to feel that way about my job. I remember when I *had* a job.

Things aren't just looking good at home, they're looking amazing at the theatre too. Sure, we have big chunks of the huge place that are completely unusable, but the bits we need are really coming along.

To 'get a feel for the stage' we'll be performing on, Kay has set us up a table in the small auditorium, so we can read in here. It's my first time seeing the room properly, especially since the work has been done, and it's amazing. Not too big, but grand enough, and with decent capacity. I'll bet you can fit three or four hundred people in here.

'So, what's everyone doing tonight?' Scott asks us as we kill time, waiting for Felix and Kay to turn up. 'Any hot dates?'

I get this horrible feeling that this might be Scott trying to remind me that he's seeing someone. If he weren't such a nice guy, I'd think he were doing this to teach me a lesson, but I think that's just me feeling sensitive after what Anita told us about Felix. I can't stop thinking that perhaps that's what Scott thinks I did to him. That we were finally getting together when I took off.

'I have a date,' I blurt, incredibly unconvincingly for someone who is – y'know – an actor, before I've really thought about whether or not it's a good idea.

'You do?' Scott replies, taken aback, like that's the last thing he was expecting me to say.

'I do,' I reply. 'Really looking forward to it.'

'And who is this mystery date?' he asks, a little too curiously.

I make eye contact with Alison across the table who gives me a knowing look. She knows I've only said this because I fancy Scott.

'You're looking at him,' the only other male voice at the table chimes in.

The three of us all turn to look at Billy. He smiles back at us.

'I'm her date,' he says again, just in case we didn't get it.

'I didn't realise you two had a thing,' Scott says, unable to hide his confusion.

I can't help but laugh to myself, inside my head, because no one did. I guess I just need to go with it now.

'Oh, totally,' I insist. 'Well, we do go way back, and everyone used to think we were a couple, of sorts, when we were younger so... we just thought... why not?'

'It's actually feeling pretty serious pretty fast,' Billy adds, laying it on way too thick.

'Yeah, I guess when you have history with someone, you always think you'll be able to get together eventually,' Scott replies.

I wonder, is that a dig at our decade-spanning 'will they, won't they?' But he's the one who said he was seeing someone first. He can't expect me to stay single, just waiting for him to be available too, so we can finally get together.

'So, what about you?' I reply, trying to act like I'm not bothered by it, even though I am. 'I take it you have a hot date with the girl you're seeing?'

'Actually, I'm not seeing her any more,' he says.

'That never really got started so... probably just a night in with my dad, if I don't get a better offer.'

Shit. Shit, shit, shit. Was this all a set-up, so that he could ask me out? I wonder if, now that he knows there's nothing going on between me and his dad, he thinks the road is finally clear enough for us to move forwards, and I've gone and totally shagged it by pretending to have a date. The worst thing of all is that I can't just undo it, I can't just say Billy and I are off, not after only just saying we're on, and Billy laying it on so thick about us. I'll just seem like I'm bouncing from one person to the next, just anyone who crosses my path, like I'm trying to fill my boots while I'm home. I'll just have to give it a little time, say that things didn't work out between us, naturally kill off the idea there's a me and Billy so that Scott can see we really might be able to actually, finally, go on a date.

'I'll give you a better offer,' someone says.

'Oh, boys,' Alison says excitedly. 'Emmy, these lovely young men are Steve and Marc, aka Rhonda Drinks and Lina Coke. They're playing the Ugly Sisters.'

'Lovely to meet you,' I say.

The boys, as Alison calls them, are actually grown men. They're not in drag right now, obviously, but I can't wait to see them in costume. I'm always so fascinated by drag queens, or anyone who can achieve that level of make-up, to be honest, because anyone who has tried to replicate those looks at home knows how it never ends up looking all that great.

'God, the pleasure is all ours,' the man who propositioned Scott says as he hurries over to shake my hand. 'It's not often we get a genuine star like you gracing our little performances. How brilliant, to have Emmy Palmer, fairy princess, on board. We usually have to make do with this queen.'

He nods towards his friend who rolls his eyes.

'It's lovely to meet you both,' I reply with a giggle.

'I'm Steve,' he continues. 'Also known as Rhonda. Marc here is Lina.'

'It's a genuine honour to meet you,' Marc adds.

Steve is larger than life, a laugh-a-minute, full-on personality, whereas Marc seems much quieter.

He might be one of the most beautiful men I've ever laid eyes on, with his perfectly chiselled facial features, and his swimming-pool-blue eyes.

'Are you boys excited for the table read?' Alison asks them.

'I'm raring to go,' Steve insists. 'This one is nervous though.'

'I'm a fashion queen, not a comedy queen,' Marc reminds him. 'Making outrageous jokes and trying to pull off laughable eye make-up is your gimmick. My job is simply to look beautiful.'

'I've seen people laugh at you,' Steve quips.

'Don't worry,' Alison starts with a reassuring smile. 'I had both of your personalities in mind when I wrote the parts and I've carefully constructed the dialogue so that all the humour comes from Steve. Marc, you mostly just set jokes up, so don't worry about comedic timing or anything like that.'

I smile. Alison has really surprised me. I think perhaps when I met her I just saw her as this lovely, friendly woman who loved her craft, but she's so much more than that. Her script really is brilliant, I read it a few times over the weekend, to prep for today, and I honestly think she has a future doing this sort of thing.

'We're here,' Kay sings, announcing her and Felix's arrival.

She appears to be her bright and bubbly self and Felix is as intense and moody as always.

'Just before we get started, we have some updates,' she announces. 'So, the show is locked in for the twenty-third of December, with a full dress rehearsal on the twenty-first, which we will perform for friends and family.'

Wow, I can't believe we're going to put this whole thing together in little more than three weeks. But, just like with the house, if you have a big enough, talented enough team, you can achieve anything.

'And, we have some more news,' she continues, her excitement growing with each word. 'We started spreading the word, over the last few days, and looking at the interest we've gathered, we could fill this room four times over.'

'But I thought this was a one-time-only kind of thing,' Scott says.

'Follow me,' Felix announces.

Eager to find out where Felix could possibly be taking us, we all scramble to our feet, like kids eager to get to lunch, and follow him dutifully.

We're through the door by the time we realise where we are.

'Oh my God,' I blurt.

Watching this derelict theatre being restored to something beautiful is really something to behold but, here in the main auditorium, despite some major clean-up work needing to be done, it almost doesn't matter. This enormous room is nothing short of breathtaking. The size and ornate finishes in everything from the stage surround to the painted ceiling give you a glimpse of the grandeur that made this place so special back in its day, and it's still so special now for still being here. It could have been taken out during the Blitz, it could have been left to become truly dilapidated, if Felix hadn't bought it to try and save it, but it has survived it all.

I used to come here when I was a kid, and I did wonder if the place might seem smaller, now that I'm an adult, but it doesn't seem any less magnificent. Just tired. It looks how I feel.

'We'll be performing the pantomime in here,' Felix announces.

'What?' Marc says, his perfectly chiselled jaw hitting the floor.

'You must be able to fit a thousand people in here,' Steve adds. 'I don't think we've ever performed in front of more than fifty.'

'Actually, it's closer to two thousand,' Kay says through her grin. 'Can you believe we're actually going to perform in here?'

'I feel sick,' Billy says quietly.

'I feel excited,' I admit. 'Don't worry, we're going to smash it.'

I take Billy's hand in mine and give it a reassuring squeeze which he seems to appreciate it.

'He doesn't need babying,' Kay insists, a little ticked off. 'He needs to realise how brilliant he is.'

'I think we all do,' Scott adds. Even he sounds nervous.

Sure, I feel butterflies in my stomach, but only in an excited way. I am *so* excited. More than I thought I would be.

OK, so it needs some more work doing in here, but what an incredible space. All the little complexities of every inch of it feels like it's absorbed decades of performances on the stage and emotions from the audience. I think that's why I'm buzzing about getting up on this stage, and actually feeling excited about acting, which I haven't felt for the longest time.

'We'll have to do so around Tel and his team, to a degree, but we'll start with rehearsals right away,' Felix announces. 'As they say in the business, the show must go on. Let's make this one hell of a good one.'

'That's the spirit,' Kay says as she punches the air.

'And if it turns out to be the abomination I fear, let no one say we didn't burn out in a blaze of fire,' Felix adds, potentially dampening the pep talk, just a little.

'I guess all that matters is that we have fun,'

Billy says before puffing air from his cheeks as he slowly comes around to the idea.

'Boy, if you ever say anything like that again in my theatre I will murder you, chop you up, cook you into a pie and then feed it to your mother, do you understand me?' Felix says seriously.

A quick glance around the room confirms who is familiar with the plot of *Titus Andronicus* and who thinks Felix is a homicidal monster. Billy is clearly one of the latter because he appears to be briefly paralysed with fear.

'So, those who are able, if we can grab the tables and chairs from the other stage and bring them into here,' Kay says, snapping back into organisation mode. 'Let's get this table read on the way.'

'Well, this is cool,' I say with a smile as I walk with Scott.

'Seriously cool,' he replies. 'I'm excited to get stuck into this script.'

'Me too,' I say, and it's so nice to mean it, not like when I used to have to repeat in every interview that I loved played Adelina, even though I really grew to resent the part towards the end.

'Liar,' he teases. 'You're just raring to go so that your date comes around quicker.'

I laugh awkwardly.

I can't be annoyed at Billy for stepping up for me like that. It was so very clear to almost all involved that I was making up the fact I had a date. He was just doing his best to cover for me. More than anything I am mad at myself for lying in the first place, but at least now I can focus on rehearsals, while slowly phasing out the idea of a me and Billy, and then who knows what's going to happen?

No, seriously, who knows? Because I have absolutely no idea how all of this is going to go.

30

After rehearsing pretty much non-stop for two weeks now, the thought of having afternoon tea with the ladies in the family is a more than welcome distraction. What's even more exiting is that Tel and his crew have completed so much of the renovation work, including the kitchen in its entirety – it's amazing how much you can get done with a big enough team of brilliant workers. So that's where we're having afternoon tea today.

In other, equally exciting news, Granddad's house is now officially my house, so tea today is about celebrating that too. My mum instructed me that I didn't have to lift a finger, that she was going to prepare everything, and that Megan was very keen to help her.

So, sitting around at my swanky, new grey kitchen island, with sleek white worktops, and the comfiest padded grey bar stools, there's me, Gracie, Bev and Vee. Buzzing around us my mum and Megan are setting down platters of sandwiches, cake stands loaded with sweet treats and pots of tea.

'Don't forget this,' Vee says, removing a magnum of Prosecco from her handbag, in a move Mary Poppins herself would be proud of.

'Ooh, get that cork popped,' Bev says with an enthusiasm not usually reserved for 11.30 in the a.m.

'Mum, can I have a bit?' Megan asks.

She's on her best behaviour today and it's suspicious.

'You can have a splash in your orange juice,' Mum says as she wrestles with the cork. 'But don't tell your dad.'

Megan eagerly takes a swig of her orange juice

to make room for a little Prosecco. She is turning eighteen in a week, so there's no harm in it, but the space she optimistically makes in her glass is not filled when Mum eventually pops the cork and starts pouring.

'I do love what you've done with the place,' Bev says. 'That Tel is brilliant.'

'Didn't I tell you?' Vee says smugly.

'I'm wondering if he might have built your house,' I tell Gracie, dragging her into the conversation. Once again, she's oddly quiet. 'He told me he was here putting up new builds when he decided to stay so he must be talking about yours. He's bringing me some wood for the bedroom.'

'That's my girl,' Vee says with a wink before she practically chugs Prosecco from her glass.

'He's helping me put it up in my bedroom,' I clarify, but that doesn't satisfy her innuendo radar, it only makes her worse.

'Ha!' she splutters.

I roll my eyes.

'For the panelling we're building behind my bed,' I add.

'You say "we"—' my mum starts.

'Yeah, genuinely, I've done loads of jobs here and there, it's a lot of fun,' I insist. 'Tel has been teaching me a few bits. I'm really enjoying it.'

'Sounds like you and Tel are spending a lot of time together,' my mum says. 'Could love be in the air?'

'Now, now, ladies, calm down,' I insist. 'We're not spending time together, we've done a few jobs – *don't.*'

The 'don't' is for Vee, who will almost certainly be triggered by my use of the word 'jobs'.

I pick up one of the delicate, triangular prawn sandwiches from the table in front of me. God, it's good. I'm really enjoying this eating whatever I want lark and, thanks to all my work at the theatre and here at the house, it's more than replacing my need for a gym. It makes me wonder if I even needed to starve myself for my part all these years.

'It sounds like Vee has finally met her match,' Bev says through a mouthful of sandwich. 'This mysterious Ken character we're yet to meet.'

'Emmy has met him,' Vee says with a shrug.

'She knows he's real. And I know he's real, and that's all that really matters.'

'Come on, Emmy, tell us what he's like,' Bev insists.

'Young,' I reply, not meaning to sound judgey, but it does come across that way a little.

Vee wears it like a badge of honour.

'Turns out I like them young,' she says with a shrug. 'I know you like them older, Emmy, love, but—'

'I don't "like them older",' I insist. 'Vee, you know I was only on that date because you asked me to go, there was nothing between me and Mike.'

'I wasn't on about Mike,' she says. 'Your married TV fella, in the papers, the one we're not allowed to mention.'

This is the first time *he* has come up for a while. To be honest, I've been living in a bubble, but that's not to say it hasn't been on my mind. Not having my work phone or checking my social media accounts helps, and everyone is too polite to mention it, of course. You know what it's like in these small communities, everyone does everything they are supposed to – to your face – but behind your back you know they're talking about you, you can see the looks they give you. I am so, so tempted to go on-line and see what's being said about me but it would be like picking at a scab. I used to feel this way about reviews and even tweets but I eventually realised you can't worry too much about what people think of you or you'll just stop doing things altogether. I'm just hoping that I'm not big time enough for them to keep on at me. I don't imagine it's still being talked about, but that doesn't mean people have forgotten.

I imagine that's in retaliation to my judgey remark.

'Cheese and pickle, Emmy,' my mum says, pointing out a particular sandwich to me, as though that's going to distract me. It does a bit.

'None of us believe that nonsense in the news,' Bev reassures me. 'And it sounds like this Tel is your age, so that will dispel any rumours.'

'Oh my God,' I say through an annoyed laugh. 'There is nothing going on between me and bloody Tel.'

Everyone is silent.

'He's standing behind me, isn't he?' I say pointlessly.

'Oh yeah,' Megan informs me.

I turn around to see Tel standing in the doorway. He's wearing a scruffy pair of jeans and a vest under an open shirt. He must have just popped in from next door because you'd be freezing, out and about like that today, although I don't think there's a woman in this room who would tell him to cover up right now.

'Any chance you didn't hear that?' I ask him.

'Erm, not really, no,' he replies through a smile.

'Great,' I say sarcastically. 'How did I guess, of course you would have caught the end of something so mortifying.'

'In the interest of full disclosure, gaffer, I was about to walk in the room sometime around when your mum first mentioned me. I politely gave you some time to move on while I carried things in but that didn't happen,' he admits. 'So, I figured hiding in the hallway was weird, best I come through and nip the awkward in the bud.'

That is just beyond embarrassing. I need to say something, anything, to move things along and make this less weird.

'I told Gracie you built her house,' I blurt.

Yep, that bizarre statement with absolutely zero context definitely makes this seem less weird.

'I mean, erm.' I laugh uncomfortably. 'I told her you might have built her house. She lives in The Willows.'

'Oh, really?' he says, turning to Gracie. 'Which one did you buy?'

'One of the ones with trees at the back,' she says, not seeming all that interested. 'The corner one.'

'Huh,' he says thoughtfully. 'That's a great spot. Definitely one of the ones I worked on. There's a little bit of me in that house.'

'That's a lovely sentiment,' she says politely.

'No, I'm talking literally, there's an actual part of me in that house,' he tells her. 'I was cutting the wall cavity insulation to size, I sliced off the end of my finger and the little bit that came off fell into the wall cavity. See?'

Tel holds up his left hand and, sure enough, one of the fingertips on his left hand looks much flatter than the rest. Lucky for him it's healed nicely and is almost unnoticeable, unless you're looking, but Gracie is completely grossed out.

'Lovely,' she says.

'Do you want a sandwich or a cupcake, Tel?' my mum offers.

'Go on then, I'll pinch a cake,' he says with a smile. 'Cheers, Deana.'

'Just, don't take that big one at the top,' Megan tells him. 'That's literally just for Emmy, I actually got that one for her.'

'You got it for me?' I say in disbelief.

'Yeah, of course,' she says with a scoff, as if to say, like, how on earth could I be surprised be that?'

'So, what time do you want me over for the bedroom?' Tel asks me innocently.

I expect something from Vee in three... two... one...

'Wow, you really do give good service,' she says, right on cue.

'Any time this evening,' I tell him. 'No plans here.'

'OK, well, I'll take this and let you get back to your lunch,' he says. 'Have fun.'

'He is lovely,' Mum says when he's gone. 'I could go for someone like that.'

I shoot her a look.

'If Roy wasn't the love of my life, obviously,' she says with a giggle.

'Ah, but remember, Mum, Emmy only has eyes for one boy in Marram Bay, and that's Scott Allen,' Gracie chimes in.

Mum laughs.

'I remember that boy,' she says. 'Always the lead in all the plays – wasn't he the Romeo you were upset with because you didn't get to kiss him?'

'That's the one,' Gracie answers for me.

'Bloody hell, it took all I had to talk you out of writing a letter of complaint to your drama teacher,' Mum says.

Ha! I'd forgotten about that.

'He's Prince Charming in the panto,' Gracie informs the room.

'Ooh,' Mum coos. 'Well, poor Tel won't get a look-in, will he?'

'Get you, Emmy,' Megan joins in.

'We're starring in a pantomime together, we're not getting married,' I remind everyone.

I can hear my phone ringing where I left it in the lounge, which gives me the perfect excuse to bail on this conversation for a few minutes.

'Back in a sec,' I say, leaving the ladies to chat amongst themselves. Bev goes back to grilling Vee about Ken, Megan talks to Mum about party clothes and Gracie just sort of sulks in silence. I've tried asking her what's wrong lately, but she always says it's nothing. I'm going to have to get to the bottom of it one way or another though, I'm really starting to worry about her.

I feel a fluttering in my stomach when I realise it's Scott calling.

'Hello,' I say brightly.

'Hi,' he replies. 'I was just thinking, it's Emmy's day off, she's probably sick of the sight of me, and of working for free at the theatre so... how would you like to do me a favour this afternoon?'

I laugh.

'I would love to do you a favour this afternoon, if I can,' I reply.

'Will you be free at 3 p.m.?' he asks.

'I will indeed,' I reply. 'What's going on?'

'I'll pick you up at 2.50 then, if that's OK?'

'How mysterious,' I say excitedly. I'll bet he can hear me smiling down the phone. 'I'll see you then.'

'Ooh, was that him?' my mum asks the second I hang up.

'Bloody hell, Mum,' I say, jumping out of my skin. 'These old houses don't do much to alert you to lurkers, do they?'

'Was that him?' she asks again with a wiggle of her eyebrows.

'It was, he needs a favour this afternoon,' I tell her. 'He's picking me up later.'

'That's exciting,' she says. 'And speaking of favours... Megan and Louis' birthday party?'

'Oh, God, I thought we'd let that go,' I reply.

'You have to admit, she's being extra nice today,' Mum points out in a whisper.

'Erm, she's being extra nice because she wants something,' I say, keeping my voice down to match Mum's.

'They want you there because you're cool,' she tells me, as though that will work.

'I gave up worrying about looking cool a long time ago,' I tell her. 'I also gave up doing appearances in nightclubs so, even if she went to my agent and offered her my usual fee, it would still be a no.'

God, I hated doing those. I took it so seriously the first few times. I learned how to DJ, even though they told me I could just pretend if I wanted to, but I soon realised no one gave a shit if the music was down to me or not. People just want their photo of me pretending to strangle them and that's it, which I don't mind, but drunk people are the absolute worst.

'Think about it, will you?' Mum pleads. 'Come and try the cake she got you, that will change your mind.'

I head back into the kitchen and resume grazing on the spread all set out across the island.

This kitchen is the kitchen of my dreams. It really is. It's going to be amazing in the summer, when the bi-folding doors can be open for more than a few minutes just to test them. It's such a shame I'm not going to be here to enjoy it.

I'm not thinking about that now though, or the impending teenage party I'm supposed to be guest starring in, all I'm thinking about is Scott, and what he could possibly have in store for me this afternoon.

31

'I have to admit, as favours go, I have no idea what you want from me at the town hall,' I tell Scott as he leads me through the doorway.

I probably dressed a little nicer than whatever the hell he could possibly have brought me here for but, as I'm often reminded, my preferred colour palette always kind of makes me blend in, so I'm sure I won't look too out of place in my skinny jeans and nice top.

'Just follow me this way and all will be revealed,' he tells me.

Eventually, he leads me into a small function

room where there is a mixture of parents and children all of whom appear to be below the age of ten, but I've never been great at identifying kids' ages.

'This is my drama group,' he tells me. 'I teach these kids acting, help to boost their confidence and stuff.'

'Wow, you're a teacher?' I say. 'I had no idea.'

'I'm not a real teacher,' he insists modestly. 'Just drama and football. This group of kids though, they're great, honestly, and I know they would love to meet a real, famous actress.'

'Let's do it,' I say. 'Looking forward to it.'

'OK, kids, let's all sit down in the centre of the room, and parents, see you all at four,' he announces. He's never seemed more grown up and, in a very strange way, he's never seemed sexier.

One of the parents, a dad with a toddler in tow, sidles up to me and leans in to whisper.

'Hi, I'm Alfie, I'm a huge fan,' he says quietly.

'Cheers, Alfie,' I tell him.

I make a move to follow Scott but then Alfie says something else.

'I really want to ask for a photo of you strangling me, but I get that it might seem a bit weird in front of the kids.'

I laugh.

'I'll get you after,' I tell him. 'While no one is watching.'

Alfie leaves happily.

'Today we've got a real-life TV star here,' Scott tells the kids. 'Emmy Palmer from a show called *Bragadon Forrest*.'

'My dad watches that,' one kid says.

'My parents watch it too,' adds another. 'They say I'm not allowed.'

'It's a bit scary for kids,' I reply. Among other things. 'But maybe you can watch it when you're older.'

'Emmy grew up here – she even went to Acorn School, just like most of you,' Scott continues. 'And while she's home for Christmas she's going to be starring in the pantomime with me. Emmy is playing Cinderella and I'm playing Prince Charming, so we thought it might be fun to teach you some of our lines.'

'Does that mean you both have to kiss?' a little

boy calls out.

'Yes, Rowan, it means we have to kiss,' Scott replies.

There are a few totally expected childish moans of 'ew' and 'gross' from the kids.

'We don't have to kiss, do we?' a girl asks, clearly horrified at the thought.

Scott laughs.

'Sorry, no, Aria, of course you don't have to kiss,' he quickly adds. 'Emmy and I used to act together when we were at school, and they used to make us pretend by sucking our thumbs.'

'How does that work?' Aria asks.

Scott offers me his hand.

'For old times?' he says with a smile.

'Sure,' I reply.

Scott and I lock hands, as though we're about to arm-wrestle, but then we rotate our grip so that our own thumbs are facing ourselves. It's an odd one to explain but you just kind of move close together, as though you're going to kiss, but then you suck you own thumb instead. Your hands are hidden by your faces and then you just kind of move around a bit and make noises like you're kissing.

We do it and it makes the kids laugh.

'Just like that,' Scott says. 'But we have to kiss for real in the pantomime because Prince Charming dips Cinderella when he kisses her, and you need both hands for that.'

A little girl raises her hand.

'What does dip mean?' she asks curiously.

'It's when you sort of drop the person backwards as you kiss them,' Scott explains but the kids don't get it. 'Tell you what, we'll show you.'

It's worth mentioning that so far, during rehearsals, we've just been saying '...and then the kiss' rather than actually kissing.

'Ready?' he asks me.

I hope I'm not showing how absolutely terrified I feel right now, not that the kids would be able to pick up on it, but Scott would.

'Go for it,' I say with a confidence that gives me faith in my acting abilities.

Scott slips one arm around my waist and the other across the top of my back. He dips me in a kind of juddery motion before planting his lips on mine. He holds me for a few seconds and then, just before he brings me back up, he lightly sucks my lip before he pulls me back up to eye level and releases me. He gives me a slight smile and winks at me before turning back to his audience.

His sneaky, cheeky little kiss inside the stage kiss makes me blush a little but I can't say that I didn't like it. I'm surprised, given that he thinks I'm seeing Billy, but obviously I'm not seeing Billy really so that's not anything for me to worry about.

Wow. It happened. I can't believe we've finally kissed.

I've thought about my first kiss with Scott a lot, ever since I was a teenager, but I have to admit, I never imagined it taking place in front of a crowd of children.

32

I don't know how I thought panelling was built but the reality isn't what I thought it would be. I suppose I expected it to be one big piece of something that covered the whole wall, perhaps, but Tel is teaching me that it's lots of skinny pieces of wood, stuck to the wall equal distances apart, and then the whole thing is painted.

See, this is why I'm glad I've got Tel on my team. I thought I was happy with my painted feature wall but then I was scrolling Instagram and saw someone with panelling behind their bed and that was it, I wanted it, but I had no idea how to do it. Tel not only knew, but he said he'd help me do it.

I'm currently holding up pieces of wood against the wall while Tel marks up where they need to be stuck.

'You seem like you're in a really good mood,' he says. 'It's nice. It really suits you.'

'Thanks,' I reply. 'I taught at a kids' acting class today and... I just found it so rewarding.'

'I bet,' he replies. 'Something different to get your teeth stuck into.'

God, he doesn't know the half of it.

'How are you finding rehearsals?' he asks. 'I'm not really one for theatre but even I'm enjoying watching you all. I feel like I've seen the show twenty times, just from working in the background. I probably know all of your lines better than some of you.'

I laugh.

'I am actually really enjoying it,' I confess.

We move back over towards Tel's temporary workstation to cut some more wood – I say 'we' but obviously it's all Tel.

'I keep meaning to ask you, actually, when it comes to Felix, how do you work him?' I ask curiously. 'He's an absolute pussycat with you but a total hard-arse with the rest of us.'

'That's just Felix, innit?' he says with a smile and a shrug. 'He'll be trying to get the best out of you all. With me, it's different, with the work on the theatre and stuff, that's stuff he doesn't understand so he doesn't feel like he needs to push me.'

'Trying to get the best out of us by being a bit of a dick?' I say, lowering my voice on that last part, although it's not as though he can hear me, I guess.

'That's the way he helps people though,' Tel insists. 'He's thinks if he's hard with them, he'll get the best out of them, or do right by them – like with Anita.'

'You know about Anita?' I say. 'Scott and I met her. We got drunk with her, actually.'

'Nice,' Tel says with a laugh. 'Yeah, Felix said he'd sent you on a fool's errand and told me all about what went on between them. Did she tell you what happened?'

'She said she and Felix were an item but that he "frigged off" to London to be famous,' I reply.

'Just between us, just so you better understand the man,' Tel says, pausing work for a moment to sit on the dustsheet-covered bed. 'He might sound all la-di-da now, but Felix didn't come from money, the opposite actually. So, when he got the chance to go to London, he knew he had to take it. He also knew that Anita's mum wasn't well and that she'd never be able to leave her. Rather than make Anita choose between her boyfriend and her mum, he chose for her. That's what Felix is like though, he's like the tide. He pushes you away, only to pull you back in. I think he always intended to come back as soon as he could, but life doesn't always work out like that, does it? I swear, that's why he's ploughed every penny he has into this theatre, he feels like it's theirs.'

'Don't get me wrong, I'm not saying builders can't be smart,' I say carefully. 'But I had no idea you had all this going on.'

I wave my hand around although I have no idea

what I'm pointing out either. He just has these hidden depths that don't ever stop surprising me.

'We're both living here alone, no family around,' Tel explains. 'I've got a cousin who visits me every now and then, but that's it. Felix doesn't even have that any more. And I've been working on the theatre since he bought it, so we chat. He's a sound old geezer.'

'I feel a bit sorry for him now,' I admit. 'Anita too. They're both lonely, both so clearly pining for the other.'

'You're right, you know,' he replies. 'He keeps that dance hall like a shrine to her. I keep offering to work on it and Felix always says it's not a priority, but it's like he can't bear the thought of plastering and painting over their room.'

'Hmm,' I say thoughtfully. 'I'm seeing a whole new side to him now. And you, you dark horse.'

Tel laughs it off.

'I know what I keep meaning to ask you,' he starts, gearing up for a subject change. 'Seeing as though so many of the jobs are wrapped up now, are you thinking of putting up some Christmas decorations?'

'Shit, I'd not even thought about it,' I say. 'Don't get me wrong, I knew Christmas was coming, I've already done all my shopping online, but putting up decorations here just totally slipped my mind.'

'You've been renovating,' Tel reminds me. 'There hasn't been room, and you don't have to put any up, but there's still two weeks until Christmas.'

'My granddad loved Christmas,' I tell him. 'He'd be horrified, knowing I didn't have decorations up. He's got loads of them in the loft.'

'Well, when we're finished up here, how about I nip up and get them and we stick a few up where we can?' he suggests.

'Are you sure you don't mind?' I reply. 'And can you please make sure I'm paying you properly for all of this?'

'Tonight is a freebie,' he says with a wink. 'It's just nice to have someone to decorate a tree with.'

By the end of the night not only will I have fancy panelling behind my bed, and Christmas decorations throughout the house, but I feel like I've gained so much more than that. I've not only seen a different side to Tel but I feel like I know so much more about Felix too. And I can't stop wondering how I can help him, but I think I might have a few ideas...

33

Just in case you thought things were going well with panto rehearsals, and that it might not actually be completely embarrassing, let me assure you that that is not the case at all.

There's an elephant in the room. Something that was initially addressed – rather tactfully for Felix – but that has now gone on a little too long with no improvement.

Almost everyone is at the theatre for rehearsals already. Alison is in the office, sorting out the posters, because she knows a guy who can do them for cheaper than usual. Pippa is in the smaller auditorium with the children she teaches dance to, going over their routines with them. Steve and Marc are getting into costume because they both feel like it helps them perform when they're in drag. Tel is knocking around somewhere, fixing something, I believe. Felix is in his place on the front row, where he usually directs us from, and me, Kay and Billy are sitting on the edge of the stage. I swing my legs anxiously as we discuss our biggest problem: Scott, the only one who isn't here yet.

You see, we have a handful of musical numbers in the panto, but while the rest of us can sing, Scott absolutely cannot. It wouldn't be so bad but one of the best numbers in the whole thing is a song performed by Cinderella and Prince Charming when they realise they're falling in love. It would be such a loss to the panto if we cut it, but Cinderella can't exactly sing it on her own, that would seem like only she was in love with him, rather than it being the beautiful, mutual thing it's supposed to be.

'I told him to practise,' Felix insists. 'You all told

me to give him a chance, I gave him a chance, but he isn't improving.'

'Perhaps if he just had a bit longer?' Kay suggests. 'It's such a beautiful song, I don't want us to cut it.'

'And Emmy sings it so beautifully,' Billy adds.

I give him a grateful smile. Billy is always so nice to me.

'To even give him the chance to practise was foolish,' Felix says. 'Some of us just cannot sing. I hold my hands up, I'm one of them, but that just means that I know one simply cannot learn to sing over a couple of weeks, especially if they never seem to show any progress.'

'It just seems such a shame to cut it,' Kay insists. 'It really does.'

Felix massages his temples.

'We've been talking about this song so much it haunts me,' he says dramatically. 'I can *hear* it in my head.'

'Actually, I can hear it too,' I say. 'Listen.'

'It's clear as day to everyone who walks by...'

'But... it sounds good?' I say in disbelief.

'...*That me and you, you and me, us and I...*'

'Really good,' Felix adds.

'And you said Scott practising wouldn't pay off,' Kay says smugly. 'He's nailing it.'

'...*Look from the stars to the sea, but it's just you and me...*'

'Erm, that's not me,' Scott says as he joins us.

We all stare at each other for a second.

'Quick, it's coming from behind the curtain,' I say.

I don't think I've ever seen Felix move so fast. The five of us hurry towards the curtain, like a poorly cast *Mystery Inc.,* to see where this incredible voice is coming from.

'...*The one from my dreams, is it you? Could it be?...*'

Our mystery vocalist holds on the last word, rather impressively, around the time we unmask him. Behind the curtain, up a ladder, singing away while he works, is Tel.

'*Terry,*' Felix shouts up at him. He sounds almost angry. 'Your singing—'

'Sorry, gaffer,' he calls down. 'I just love to sing while I work and, let me tell you, I've heard this song so many times now, and it's a definite earworm.'

'Come down here,' Felix insists.

Tel actually looks a little worried as he hurries down the ladder.

'Wow, Tel, you've got pipes,' Kay says, practically swooning.

I give him a nudge with my elbow.

'What did I say last night?' I say to him, giving him another nudge with my elbow. 'You're a real dark horse.'

Scott looks completely put out by this revelation. So does Billy actually, just a little.

'I was just messing around,' Tel says, clearly ever-so-slightly embarrassed all of a sudden.

'Can you act too?' Felix asks him.

'Oh, definitely not,' Tel insists as he wipes his hands on his jeans. 'I can't even lie.'

I smile.

'You're in the show,' Felix tells him. 'Congratulations.'

'What?' both Scott and Tel say in unison.

'You're giving him my part?' Scott says in disbelief.

'I'm giving him your *songs*,' Felix corrects him. 'You'll play the part, as planned, but Tel will be standing behind the curtain with a microphone, and he's going to sing your songs. Now, seeing as though Tel is warmed up, let's start things off with Act Two. I'm going to fetch myself a drink. Positions in fifteen minutes.'

'Did he... did he just *Singing in the Rain* me?' Scott asks in disbelief.

'I'm really sorry, mate,' Tel says sincerely. 'No hard feelings?'

Tel offers a hand for Scott to shake but he turns his back on him.

I do feel bad for Scott, he must feel like Tel has muscled in on his part, but it's obvious Tel didn't intend to. Tel will just see this as an extension of him helping Felix and I think that's clear to everyone but Scott. I would defend him, convince Felix to reconsider, but Scott really, really can't sing, so this really does feel like the best solution. Scott did say he would practise, but he did confess to me that he was hoping they would just cut his song, because he was never going to be able to learn to sing in time. I'm sure Scott will come around to the idea, once he realises it means he doesn't need to worry about his singing voice.

'Do you guys want a laugh?' I say, breaking the awkward silence.

'Oh, always,' Kay says, following my lead.

'What's going on in here?' Pippa asks.

'Emmy is about to make us laugh,' Kay tells her.

'Have you guys heard of Nauti Nauti?' I ask.

'That's the floating nightclub,' Tel says. 'It's parked up just offshore.'

'Is that the one only in town for a couple of nights?' Kay asks.

'Yes, tonight is the last night,' I reply. 'My sister, Katie, the one who is having her wedding at my house, is having her hen party there tonight. I said I would go, thinking me and my other sister Gracie could have a laugh. Turns out Gracie can't go because she's got kids.'

I am sure that people with kids can't do a few things that people without kids can do – or at least can't do them as easily – but I actually sometimes think Gracie uses it as an excuse to get out of doing things she doesn't want to do.

'And that's funny, why?' Pippa asks.

'Because now I have to go to this boat nightclub with a bunch of strangers,' I tell her.

'That is kind of tragic,' Pippa says.

Anything to take a swipe at me. Over these last couple of weeks it's like she's tried to undermine me at every opportunity. If she can trip me, or make me look silly – or even if she can't, she still gives it her all.

'Well, why don't we come too?' Tel suggests. 'We could just be there at the same time, that way, while your sister is hanging out with her friends, you can hang out with us.'

'You'd really do that?' I reply.

'Of course we would,' Billy chimes. 'You know, I especially should be there for you, given that...'

'Oh, even though we said we'd just be friends?' I quickly interject. 'You'd still do this for me?'

Billy actually looks deflated. The thing is, ever since that day he said he was my date, I've been trying to slowly but subtly undo what he did. Distance seemed like the best way to go and now I feel like enough time has gone by that I can really drive home to everyone that we are not an item. Consider the Emmy-Billy relationship arc officially retconned.

'Count me in,' Scott says.

'Me too,' Kay adds. 'Sounds like fun.'

We all look at Pippa. I'm actually hoping she says no.

'Go on then,' she says. 'If everyone else is going.'

Ah well, you can't win them all.

'See, now I'm looking forward to it,' I say.

'Let's crack on with this rehearsal then,' Kay says. 'Tel, come with me, let's get you set up behind the curtain to sing.'

'Wait, Tel is singing now?' Pippa says.

'For Scott,' Kay tells her.

'Oh, but Scott was so good,' she insists.

I can't help but roll my eyes.

As we all prep to practise Act Two, now with Tel's incredible vocals in the mix, I suddenly feel much lighter. Well, I was so worried about tonight, and thinking about how I could get out of going, but now I'm actually quite looking forward to it. A nice, fun night out with my theatre group – the most dramatic people I know – what could possibly go wrong?

34

Set over three floors, Nauti Nauti is exactly what it says on the tin: a floating nightclub.

It's a cool idea, I suppose, especially in somewhere like Marram Bay where, if you want to go to a nightclub you have to travel to York or Leeds, but then you're looking at one hell of an expensive taxi home or a night in a hotel.

The top floor is a chic bar with the best views. From there, you can see Marram Bay from one angle and Hope Island from another. My little home town is really something to behold. Being back here is reminding me just how much I miss it.

It's not just scenery. I miss the lazy pace of things here. I miss my family. I miss having friends who aren't potentially only friends with me because I can get them into clubs or want me on their TV shows. Here, apart from a handful of people recognising me (and nothing more than a brief, completely positive interaction resulting from it), no one really knows or cares who I am. No one shouts offensive stuff at me in the street and, best of all, I don't have to constantly worry about what I look like because there's no paparazzi, no one to catch me on a bad day, and therefore no magazines printing pictures of me with a big red ring around a spot on my chin or cellulite on my thighs.

The two floors below the bar are nightclubs. One playing dance music and one playing more poppy stuff. We haven't been here long, but I decide that the first thing I should do is find Katie and show her that I turned up, so I leave the gang over by the bar and look around for her and the rest of her hens. It doesn't take me long to spot them. They're a blur of hot pink and penis-shaped things. Honestly, we're talking the absolute hen party works. Everyone is wearing the same shade of pink topped with a sash that says things like 'Bride,' 'Maid of Honour' and 'Bridesmaid'. Katie's penis-based tiara totally distracts from how cheap it all looks.

'Hey,' I call out over the music.

Katie's eyes widen before she hugs me.

'Emmy, what? You came?' she says in disbelief. 'Hello!'

'You invited me,' I remind her.

'But I didn't think you'd come,' she says. 'Seriously, thanks again, so, *so* much, for letting me have my wedding reception at your place. Dad keeps going on about how you've saved the day.'

When Katie says 'thanks again' she is referring to the first time she thanked me, which was in the text message inviting me on this hen do, tagged on at the end as a Ps.

'You're welcome,' I say. 'I was doing the place up anyway.'

'Oh really?' she replies. 'Hmm, I should have told you what colours I wanted. Never mind, eh?'

Yes, never mind. As though I would paint my

house to match her wedding colour palette. If it's anything like I'm sure the Pinterest board for this hen party was it'll be all fuchsia and phalluses.

'Ahh, you're Emmy Palmer,' the girl next to Katie squeals as she clocks me. 'What the *fuck*, oh my God!'

She screeches every single word at near point-blank range, overpowering the music, making my ears feel like they're going to pop.

'Let me get my phone,' she says, still squealing. 'Will you strangle me?'

'Happily,' I reply.

'Emmy, this is Kylie, she's my maid of honour,' Katie tells me.

Katie and Kylie, in their matching dresses, the exact same face of make-up plastered on them both – so exact it could have been done by a stamp – the same hair, the same nails, the works.

'I love your dress,' Kylie says.

'Ah, thanks,' I reply.

When I was shopping for Christmas presents, I decided I probably needed a new dress for tonight, so I ordered a few online. They were all pretty much the same, and all my usual style, aside from one that was definitely out of my comfort zone and not only did a voice tell me to buy it, but that same voice told me to wear it tonight. It's a short *white* off-the-shoulder dress that is ruched all the way down the front, edging it into daring-low and daring-short territory. Teamed with a bright red pair of heels and a matched clutch, I actually felt kind of good in it when I left the house, then I felt wildly uncomfortable in it, walking around the street, but now that I'm in this dark club I feel at ease again.

'You guys look great too,' I tell them.

'We wanted to match,' Katie says. 'She's my best friend, my maid of honour, she's like the si... erm... she's just like the second part of me, you know?'

I swear she was about to say 'like the sister I never had' but I'll never know for sure.

'Anyway, a few of my friends are here, so I might go see them,' I tell them.

'Ooh, where?' Katie asks.

I scan the room for my friends, eventually spotting them hanging around by some standing tables on the edge of the busy dance floor.

'Oh my God, who is that?' Kylie says through a jaw that is certified: dropped.

Tearing up the edge of the dance floor, it's Tel. He scrubs up really well in a pair of black jeans, a white T-shirt and trendy bomber jacket. As Dua Lipa's 'Don't Start Now' plays and Tel grooves effortlessly, I can't help but wonder: is there anything he can't do? It's not even like he's a professional dancer, he's just got that perfect combination of being able to move to the music but also not taking himself too seriously. He's almost funny, but in a way that makes you smile, like he's letting you in on the joke.

'That's my neighbour Tel,' I reply. 'And he's doing work on the theatre, to get it ready for the panto.'

'There's a panto?' Katie says.

At the same time as Kylie says: 'There's a theatre?'

'Yes,' I reply to both.

'Well, let me give you a drink,' Katie says. 'To thank you for coming.'

She thrusts a mini bottle of Prosecco into my hand.

'Thanks,' I reply.

'Go over there and put a good word in for me,' Kylie commands me. 'Talk me up to him.'

'Sure,' I lie.

I turn to walk away but Katie stops me.

'Hang on,' she says. I wonder if she's going to ask me to hang out a bit longer, but instead she just shoves one of her penis-straws into my drink. 'Right, now you can go.'

I'm only a few steps away before the combination of the straw and the glass bottle causes the Prosecco inside to fizz out of the neck of the bottle.

I plonk the bottle down on the table, flick the liquid off my hand, before picking up my elderflower gin fizz.

'Nice straw,' Tel says as he approaches me.

'I brought it for you,' I tell him. 'By the way, don't look now, but you've got an admirer over there – I said *don't* look!'

He looks immediately, of course.

'Wow, she is staring at me,' he says.

'Oh yeah,' I reply. 'She asked me to put in a good word for her.'

'I'm asking you not to,' he jokes.

'Not your type?' I ask curiously.

'It might be all the dicks on her person throwing me off but, no, I wouldn't say so,' he says with a laugh. 'And speaking of dicks.'

Tel gestures behind me with his eyebrows. I turn around and see Scott, sat cradling a beer while Pippa, who is sitting close next to him, strokes his arm. He's shooting daggers in this direction. Now that I'm looking, so is Billy. I'm surprised he cares about Tel providing the vocals for Scott's musical numbers, especially because, you know, Scott is a terrible singer. And then Kay – what the hell? – she's got a face like thunder too.

'Erm, hi there,' Kylie says, springing up between me and Tel, from out of nowhere.

'Hello,' he says politely.

'I was just wondering if you wanted to dance with me,' she says, kind of intensely.

'Oh, I'm so sorry, I just asked Emmy to dance,' he says. 'Maybe later on?'

'Oh, OK,' she says.

Kylie joins the filthy-look club, mutters something about 'girl code' under her breath and then walks away.

'Wow, way to throw me under the bus,' I say through a laugh.

'You think that was savage?' he says. 'Now you have to dance with me.'

'I don't actually have to, do I?'

'Of course you do,' he says. 'Or she'll be back over here in a flash to make me dance with her. Just remind yourself who climbed a tree in your garden at 11.30 last night to wrap Christmas lights around it.'

'Wow, it was all for this?' I joke. 'OK, fine, just one dance.'

'I'd better hope they put a long song on then,' he replies.

'Watermelon Sugar' by Harry Styles is playing, which gives us this weird middle ground between regular club dancing and slow-dancing. Still, we both naturally gravitate into a slow-dance position. I wrap my arms around Tel's neck and he places his around my waist, holding me close. I feel so comfortable in his arms.

I was going to take this opportunity to talk to Tel about what I'm planning for Felix – that I will absolutely need his help for – but there's something so relaxing about being in his arms, moving to the music with him. I forget everyone else in the room and place my head on his chest, snuggling in, so close that all I can smell is his aftershave. I feel almost drunk on him.

As the song comes to an end, I come to my senses.

'Erm, I was wanting to talk to you actually,' I say, completely ignoring what just happened. 'I've had an idea for something we can do for Felix.'

'What's th... erm... where have the others gone?'

Tel dances me around, so that I'm facing where the others were sitting, and sure enough they've gone. I look over at the bar, glance around the dance floor, but there's no sign of them. That's odd. Eventually, I look towards the door and spot someone I recognise, but it isn't our friends that I see, it's Carl, my brother-in-law. For a second, I'm excited, thinking perhaps Gracie has bagged a babysitter and the two of them have come to join us, but then I notice the woman leading him by the hand is *not* my sister. She pauses in the doorway, pulls him close, kisses him, then drags him up the stairs.

'Shit, that was my brother-in-law,' I tell Tel. 'With another woman. They just kissed.'

'What?' he replies. 'Is that Gracie's bloke?'

'Yeah, I just saw him, plain as day, one hundred per cent him kissing another woman,' I say. 'It looks like he just left with her.'

'What a bastard,' Tel says. 'Are you going to tell Gracie?'

'Definitely. It's too late tonight, she and the kids will be asleep, but I'm telling her in the morning. That's not on at all.'

'Do you want to just get out of here?' he says. 'We could go somewhere quieter, and you can tell me what you're planning for Felix?'

'Yeah, definitely,' I reply. 'Let's just go home. I'm starving and I've got a brand-new kitchen just waiting to be messed up.'

'I could make you my famous spaghetti bolognese?' he says.

'That's sounds great,' I reply. 'I'll just need to show you my famous shopping skills on the way home because the chances I have the ingredients are slim.'

He laughs.

'Well, that's the beauty of me living next door,' he says. 'I can just pop over and get whatever you need.'

'Oh, best neighbour ever,' I reply, but I can't quite get my mind off poor Gracie. She's going to be devastated.

'I'm sorry about your brother-in-law,' Tel says as we eventually step off the boat. 'Generally, and on behalf of all men.'

'Thanks,' I reply. 'Come on, let's go get this spaghetti on, I'm really looking forward to it.'

I'll tell you what I'm not looking forward to though, telling my sister about her shit of a husband. No one wants to be the person who breaks up a marriage (I might already have one on my conscience, according to the papers) but surely, she'll want to know, right? She would want to know the truth, rather than just turn a blind eye? I'm sure she would.

I guess we'll find out in the morning. I just hope she doesn't shoot the messenger.

Scott hasn't turned up for rehearsals today and, oh boy, is there an atmosphere. It's as though we're suspended in a state of chaos, with so many things going on at once.

Tel is spinning several plates today. He's been alternating repainting the deep-red areas that surround the stage with doing odd jobs, fixing things like whatever it is that makes the curtains open and close, the backdrop change, and the trapdoors open. We need all of them to be in full working order for opening night.

In the interest of making sure it will all be all

right on the night, Alison and I are wearing our big dresses, to make sure they're practical, otherwise we'll need whole new ones making and that will take some time. Time we don't really have.

So, I'm knocking around in my ball gown, terrified of grazing it on the dusty areas or, worse, the wet red paint. Actually, the worst thing I could do in it would be to fall down the currently open trapdoor, into the mucky pit below. Felix says you usually have a crash mat down there, so that if you want an actor to disappear you open the trapdoor, they fall safely onto the mat, and seemingly vanish into thin air. Very effective – well, it would be, if it weren't currently jammed open, while Tel attempts to fix it. That's the next thing on Tel's ever-increasing to-do list, but Felix says it's not the priority right now. Right now, he's having to fill in for Scott. Not just his vocals, his part too, otherwise the rehearsals wouldn't be able to go on, and then we'd be seriously behind.

Of course, Pippa is being her usually catty self, if not more so. She's really, clearly not happy about my presence here, but I'm not going to back out, just so she can be the centre of attention, am I? Kay and Billy don't seem their usually friendly selves either. I guess the pressure is getting to them – it's getting to us all.

I am somewhat relieved to report that there is something Tel can't do. He was absolutely right when he said he couldn't act, so maybe he isn't quite as perfect as he seems, but I like that. He isn't too good to be true, he's just good.

The fact Tel isn't the best actor actually makes him a lot more fun to share the stage with, at least the rehearsal stage, because we seem to be laughing every few minutes.

We're currently acting out the big final scene. Tel is reading from pieces of paper because he doesn't quite remember the dialogue as well as he does the catchy songs, but that's fine, he's only a placeholder so that I can practise my lines.

'I finally have my Prince Charming,' I say, projecting my lines towards Felix, who is sitting in his usual spot on the front row. 'My happy-ever-after starts today – and I finally get to uninstall Matcher too.'

A few of the spectators laugh. There's something so fresh and funny about the modern-day script Alison has written – especially when we'll all be wearing old-fashioned clothing and standing in the middle of olden-day sets.

'Felix, I don't think anyone is going to be able to dip me in the dress,' I say, breaking character for a moment. 'It's the corset, it's too stiff.'

'Tel, can you practise the dip with her?' Felix asks.

'Yeah, no problem, gaffer,' he replies.

Tel takes me in his arms and slowly leans me back to see how far we can go. It feels stiff and clunky and when I'm as far back as I need to be I don't think he could reach my lips with his, it's like I'm attached to a metal rod.

'Can you feel how stiff it is?' I ask Tel.

He sniggers.

'Something like that,' he says with a cheeky smile.

I can't help but laugh.

'I don't think he'll be able to reach me,' I tell Felix.

He massages his temples for a moment.

'OK, sorry to put this on you, Tel, but do you mind?' Felix asks in a tone I'm not entirely happy with. He makes it sound like kissing me is some kind of horrible chore that he can't believe he's asking him to do.

'You want me to kiss her?' Tel confirms.

'If you don't mind,' Felix says.

'Man, I'm in the wrong job,' Tel jokes. 'Do you not mind?'

'It's fine, I'm a professional,' I say with a smile and a casual bat of my hand.

'If you can do it, hold for a few seconds, and then return to your positions,' Felix says.

'Ready?' Tel asks.

'Ready,' I reply.

Tel scoops me up in his big, strong arms and tips me back with ease. He leans forward and plants his lips on mine, holding them there for a few seconds, as instructed, before he returns me safely to my feet.

'Are you fucking joking me?' Scott's voice bellows through the auditorium.

I look out into the mostly empty audience and see him angrily marching down the aisles. Why do I feel like I've just been caught cheating on him?

'Scott, I thought you were under the weather?' Felix replies – I'm not sure if he's being polite or passive-aggressive. 'How nice of you to join us.'

'Is it nice?' he replies. 'Or are you giving my part to this meathead?'

'You stand your ground, Scott, tell them,' I hear Pippa call out supportively.

'Actors,' Felix muses to himself under his breath. 'Scott, come with me to my office, let's iron this out, you've got the wrong end of the proverbial. Everyone else, take fifteen minutes.'

'Well, that was weird,' Tel says to me quietly.

'The kiss? You get used to it,' I reply as casually as I can.

The strange thing is that, while you do totally get used to the kissing, it's mostly because you see it as just another part of the job. When Scott kissed me at his drama class he overstepped a line, making it about more than the scene, essentially stealing a kiss from me. I've spent years thinking about kissing him and I guess I thought it was different, but it was only different because he made it different. I'm not sure how I feel about it now. But with Tel he did exactly as Felix told him to do. He played it by the book, a total professional. And yet I felt something in that kiss I've never felt before. Usually with scenes like these I'm just willing them to be over. Everything from the staged lingering kisses to having giant elf characters thrashing away on top of me for take after take. They're an uncomfortable part of the gig that I professionally endure. This kiss with Tel, just now, has made *me* feel unprofessional, because *I* didn't want it to end.

'Not the kiss,' Tel laughs. 'I've kissed girls before. I'm talking about Scott's outburst.'

The door flings open again. This time it's Gracie! And the kids too.

I hurry down off the stage and over to her. Something must be really wrong for her to turn up here.

'Hey, are you OK?' I ask her, cutting to the chase.

'You messaged me, said you needed to talk in

person, and then I tried to call you a few times but you're not answering, I've been worried sick,' she tells me.

I glance back at the stage. It's just Tel and Billy up there now.

'Hey guys, can you show Darcy and Oscar the stage while I talk to their mum?' I ask them.

'Of course,' Tel says. 'Come on up.'

'Don't let them near a microphone unless you like *Frozen*,' I joke. 'They're a big hit at wakes.'

I look at Gracie, who that joke was intended for, but she doesn't laugh.

'Come on, what's going on?' she asks me once we're alone.

'Sit down for a second,' I say.

'No, just tell me,' she insists.

'OK, fine,' I reply. I take a deep breath as I search for the right way to say it. 'I was at Katie's hen party last night and I saw Carl there.'

'I see,' she replies, not showing me a flicker of anything.

'He was with another woman,' I continue. 'I saw

them kissing and then they left together. I'm so sorry.'

I watch Gracie's face change. Her muscles tighten, her cheeks flush and her eyes narrow.

She doesn't say anything, she just turns around and marches out of the door.

'Gracie?'

'Watch the kids,' she calls back through gritted teeth.

Shit.

I hurry up on to the stage to find Tel.

He's standing by the curtain where Billy and the kids are literally running rings around him.

'Wow, you can't take your eyes off kids for a minute, can you?' he says. 'They've already got in the red paint.'

'Caught red-handed,' Billy jokes, catching both Darcy and Oscar by an arm each, one and then the other.

'Unbelievable,' I laugh.

'I'll take them to wash their hands,' he says.

'OK, but, seriously.' I lower my voice. 'Watch

them like a hawk because they're fast and they're dangerous.'

Billy's smile drops.

'Be good for Billy, kids,' I say brightly.

Safe in the knowledge it's just me and Tel now, I tell him that I've told Gracie about last night.

'That's awful,' he says. 'But there was never going to be an easy way to tell her. Do you think she's OK?'

'If I know my sister, she's probably gone to scream at him,' I reply. 'God knows what happens after that.'

'Alison is cleaning the kids up, I figured she's better with kids than me,' Billy says as he joins us again.

'That's great, thank you,' I reply.

'Oh no, Emmy, you've got a red handprint on the back of your dress,' Billy informs me.

'Oh, what?'

I twirl around, like a dog chasing my tail, trying to get a look at it.

'One of the kids must have touched it,' Billy says.

Tel grabs hold of the skirt of my dress and holds it still for me, so I can see it.

'That's a pretty big handprint for a—'

I don't get to finish my sentence.

You know all the stories about the theatre being haunted? Well, you're going to think I sound crazy, but it's as though the big, heavy old curtain just lashes out at us. It moves so suddenly, and clearly so forcefully, because it sends Billy flying. It's almost as though it happens in super-slow motion *and* in the blink of an eye. As Billy loses his footing, I can't help but let out the most blood-curdling scream as I watch him stumble towards the open trapdoor. He falls through it face first.

As Tel and I hurry towards it I quickly strip off my ball gown, leaving me in nothing but my underwear. Well, I can hardly move with that thing on, never mind help.

'Oh my gosh, what happened?' Pippa asks, seemingly coming from nowhere. The look on her face changes when she realises it's Billy who is hurt. 'Billy! Billy, are you OK? Oh, God.'

As her faux sincerity vanishes and is replaced

by pure panic, I wonder whether Pippa might have just tried to *Hamlet* me through the curtain.

Tel drops down into the hole in the floor. I follow close behind him.

'Mate, are you OK?' Tel asks him.

'It's my leg,' he says. 'I can't move my leg.'

As we both fuss around him, trying to work out how we're going to get him out of here, I notice a pile of human bones on the floor. I scream again, scurrying away from it.

'Emmy, Emmy, it's OK, it's a prop,' Tel reassures me. 'It's fake. Steve threw it down here earlier, he thought it would be funny for whoever came down here to find it.'

Another scream comes from the trapdoor above us. This time a scream of delight.

We all look up and see that it isn't just Pippa staring at us now, Steve and Marc are there too. Well, technically it's not Steve and Marc, it's Rhonda Drinks and Lina Coke, and Rhonda is laughing her ass off.

'Oh my God, the bones paid off already,' Steve cackles until he starts coughing.

'See, this is what I'm talking about, you're juvenile,' Marc ticks him off. 'Those gigantic fake tits are stopping you breathing. And Billy is clearly hurt and you're laughing.'

Steve leans a little closer and narrows his eyes.

'Shit, sorry, Billy,' he says. 'I didn't see you were hurt.'

'Also because of the fake tits,' Marc says under his breath.

'You're the fake tit,' Steve replies, but then I catch his attention. 'Emmy, love, are you naked?'

'I took my dress off,' I reply.

'That's all well and good,' Steve calls back. 'And I'm sure it will make him feel better, but he'd probably do better with some medical attention.'

I roll my eyes.

'How bad is it, mate?' Tel asks Billy, who is lying on the floor, clearly in a lot of pain. 'Can you move it?'

Billy tries to move again, and you can see the instant regret on his face.

'Nope,' he replies. 'Nope, nope, nope.'

'It's OK, it's OK,' I reassure him. 'Do you want

us to try and lift you out or do you want an ambulance?'

Billy scrunches his eyes tightly closed and grits his teeth.

'I'm just trying to work out which will be the least embarrassing,' he says.

'I'm sure I could lift you, no probs, mate,' Tel reassures him, but it has the opposite effect.

'The ambulance,' Billy says quickly. 'Definitely the ambulance.'

I look up just as Steve disappears.

'Already on it,' I hear him call out. Marc goes with him.

As Tel tries to get Billy comfortable, I stare up at the trapdoor opening. Pippa stares back down at me. I know how crazy it sounds but I really am wondering if that shove was meant for me, but she wouldn't do that for a part, would she? Surely not...

36

When I arrived at rehearsals this morning, I knew things were going to be difficult, but I never would have guessed we'd all end up where we are now.

An emergency crisis meeting has been called by Felix. There's me, Scott, Alison, Tel, Pippa, Steve, Marc, Kay *and* Billy. Billy is in a wheelchair though.

'I can't believe you broke your leg,' Kay says as she strokes Billy's hand on top of the table.

'I can't believe what a deathtrap this place is,' Billy says angrily. 'I thought Terry was supposed to be sorting it?'

'I was sorting it,' he says. 'But I had to fill in for Scott. I did warn you all about the trapdoor.'

'And then there's whatever fell behind the curtain to knock me over,' Billy continues.

'Well, someone was clearly hanging around behind the curtain, with adult-sized hands, trying to sabotage things, because they put that handprint on my dress too,' I point out, glaring at Pippa in a not-so-subtle way.

'If you're going to make an accusation, make it,' she insists.

'OK, children, enough,' Felix interrupts. 'This petty squabbling gets us nowhere. Thankfully we opted to have Emmy only on the poster, so that will be fine.'

Felix holds up a poster in front of us. God, I look so dorky in that crappy blonde wig.

'Hang on a minute,' Marc speaks up. 'You've got my name wrong. It says Lima Coke instead of Lina Coke.'

'We can't put Lina Coke on a poster,' Alison says. 'But I thought that was still pretty funny.'

'I don't get it?' Marc replies.

'It's funny,' Alison insists. 'And family-friendly. *And* not our biggest problem.'

She subtly nods towards Billy – as though he doesn't know he's our biggest problem.

'I knew we should've had understudies for people other than just Emmy,' Kay says. 'Even if she seemed like the one most likely to bail.'

I would resent that comment if I hadn't been so unenthusiastic at the start.

'I told the orthopaedic surgeon who examined me that I was supposed to be performing in a pantomime. He said that if I keep the weight off it until then I should be able to stand for a while, so long as I don't walk on it. I suppose I can stand in one spot, on the side, and use crutches when the scenes change,' Billy suggests, having clearly given this a lot of thought. I admire his show-must-go-on attitude. 'It's going to be fine, it's going to be fine. That's what we'll do. It will be fine.'

'That's partially what we'll do,' Felix says. 'Yes, to the standing on the side, moving when we fade to black, but you can't possibly play Buttons that way. For one, he moves around a lot, especially for the godawful audience participation segment you all insisted we include. Regardless, we'll see your cast. The audience *cannot* see your cast.'

'Well, what do you suggest?' Billy asks.

'You and Marc are swapping parts,' he tells him.

I don't know who is more horrified, Billy or Marc.

'Did you just say you want me to play an Ugly Sister?' Billy asks in disbelief. 'Or have I taken too much codeine?'

'The dress will hide the cast,' Felix reasons.

'I can't play Buttons,' Marc insists.

'Why not?' Felix replies.

'Even if I thought I could play it straight, come on,' Marc says. 'No one is going to buy into me having an unrequited crush on a woman. That's Billy's job.'

Marc smirks a little. Billy glares at him.

'You're an actor,' Felix starts.

'No, I'm a drag queen,' he replies. 'And I'm not funny. Steve is funny. Have Steve swap roles with him.'

'I can't play Buttons,' Steve says with a laugh and a shake of his head.

'Why not?' Marc replies.

'I'm fifty-fucking-five,' Steve replies. 'She must be half my age. I'm not Leonardo bloody DiCaprio.'

'I hate this,' Marc insists. 'I absolutely hate this.'

'Just try and read a few lines,' Felix insists.

He tosses a script to Marc who lets it fly off the table past him. Steve picks it up for him. He reluctantly takes it and opens it on random pages until he finds some dialogue for Buttons.

Marc clears his throat and rolls his eyes before he begins.

'Wow, Cinderella looks so beautiful tonight, doesn't she, boys and girls?' he says, in no way selling it, his droll Yorkshire accent that he makes no attempt to hide making it seem all the worse.

'You're not even trying,' Steve ticks him off.

'Wow, Cinderella looks so beautiful tonight, doesn't she, boys and girls?'

His second attempt is even worse.

'Why are you doing it like Phil Mitchell now?' Pippa asks.

'I'm trying to sound macho,' Marc insists. 'I'm trying to sound like him.'

He nods towards Tel, who is horrified.

'I don't talk like that, do I?' he asks.

'You don't,' I reassure him.

'You do a bit,' Scott chimes in.

'It's going to take a bit more work, but this is what we're doing,' Felix says. 'Adapt. This is theatre.'

'I can't believe I have to wear a dress,' Billy says to himself sadly.

Just when I had started to feel more confident about the pantomime not being totally embarrass-ing, this happens. With a theatre family in ruins, an understudy potentially trying to kill me, and two actors having to swap roles – and just three days until our friends and family performance and only five until the show itself, which has *sold out*, by the way... I don't have high hopes for this one, do you?

37

'Do you want to come inside for a cup of tea and a debrief?' I ask Tel as we're pulling into his drive.

'I'd love to,' he says. 'But it looks like you've got company.'

I glance over into my driveway and see Gracie sitting there in her car.

'Oh boy,' I say. 'I don't think this is going to be good.'

'I'll take that tea in the morning,' Tel says. 'We can talk about how screwed we are then.'

I laugh.

'OK, see you then, then,' I reply.

Gracie sees me walking up the driveway and jumps out of the car.

'I thought you'd be back ages ago,' she says, almost annoyed, as though I'd known she was waiting here for me in the cold.

'Yeah, we had a bit of a crisis at work,' I tell her. 'Remember, when you came back for your kids, and we were all fussing around that guy in the wheelchair? Spoiler alert: he wasn't in a wheelchair earlier.'

'Sorry, sorry,' she says. 'Is he going to be OK?'

'He's not happy about having to wear a dress to hide his cast,' I reply. 'Long story. Anyway, quick, come inside. Where are the kids?'

'I left them with Carl,' she says. 'They're all at home.'

As soon as we're inside, I light a fire and put the kettle on. I grab a couple of the new sofa throws that arrived today and we get comfortable on the sofa.

'Listen, there's something I need to tell you,' Gracie starts. She pauses to take a breath, clearly stalling telling me what she's about to say. 'I haven't actually told anyone this yet and I'm worried I won't be able to say it... Carl left me.'

'*He* left *you?*' I reply in disbelief. 'You should be the one leaving him. He cheated on you.'

'He left me a while ago,' she says. 'We're separated.'

'Oh my God, Gracie, I had no idea,' I reply.

'Well, you wouldn't,' she says. 'We haven't told anyone, he still lives at home, still turns up to family events. The kids have no idea. But he promised me – swore to me – when he told me that he didn't love me as a wife any more, and that he wanted to see other people, that he wouldn't start until he had moved out.'

'What a prick,' I say. 'So, you're stuck at home looking after the kids and he's out doing whatever he wants?'

She shrugs.

'That's why I saw red when you told me, I think,' she explains. 'He's the one who ended our marriage and I'm the one who has to suffer. But, really, I don't even know how to be that mad at him. Our marriage was boring – our whole life was boring. We live in that soulless new build, which I hate. I hate it even more now I know that part of Tel's finger is rotting in the wall. We never have fun. We hardly talk. Good on him, I guess, for trying to change his life.'

'You made this life together,' I remind her. 'He shouldn't just get to walk away scot-free, leaving you trapped in it.'

'So, what do you suggest I do?' she asks, clearly not expecting an answer.

Gracie breaks down in tears. It just erupts out of her, out of nowhere. She was talking things through so calmly before, so it jolts me into shock for a second.

'What am I going to do?' she asks. 'I'm pathetic – my life is pathetic. I've wasted all this time with him and now I'm going to be a single mum. Everyone is going to forget about me. No more sleeping in. No more going out. No parties – God, what I'd give for a proper party.'

I wrap an arm around her and squeeze her tightly.

'The kids will be in bed, right?' I ask.

'Yeah, I put them to bed before I left,' she replies.

'Call your lousy husband and tell him you're sleeping here tonight,' I demand. 'And tomorrow night. What you need is a break from being a wife, and from being a mum. Just a couple of days off. Sleep in in the morning, I'll even bring you breakfast in bed. Then tomorrow night we are having a girly sleepover and, the night after, after the shitty friends and family test performance of the pantomime that you are going to dutifully sit through, I'm going to throw you a house party. How about that?'

Gracie laughs and pats my leg.

'Gracie, I am totally serious,' I tell her. 'It's happening. Call Carl and tell him you're having a few nights away. Don't worry, you can pop home and see your kids in the daytime, put them to bed before you come back here, whatever you want, but you need this, so let me do this for you, OK?'

She starts crying again.

'Oh, Emmy, it's so good to have you back,' she says. 'I've been bottling all this up for months.'

I feel that guilty tug in my stomach again. I really should be here for my family when they need me. And they don't just need me, I need them too.

'I'm thinking about keeping the house,' I tell her.

'What?' she replies.

'I think I'll just keep it – it's still a good investment, but it gives me somewhere to stay when I visit, and somewhere for us all to hang out. When this place was Gran and Granddad's it was always our family hub. I think we need it.'

'Sounds good to me,' she says. 'You got me excited then. I thought you were going to say you were staying.'

'We'll see if you still feel that way after our party,' I tell her. 'It will be just like the one we never got to throw when we were teenagers, except we're old enough to buy booze now. I just hope you have some friends to invite, otherwise it will be just me, you and my theatre crew.'

'They're not so bad,' she says. 'I quite like Tel.'

'Yeah, I think I do too,' I reply.

38

'Felix, you're really taking things too far this time,' I hear Scott telling him from the stage.

'What's going on?' I ask.

'This is Art Moss,' Felix says. 'Seasoned theatre heckler.'

'*Heckler*?' I reply.

'He thew an egg at me during what was frankly the best *Richard III* performance of my life,' Felix says. 'I broke his jaw after the show. We've stayed close ever since. He's travelled up from Shoreditch, just to be here.'

'So, Art is going to do what?' Kay asks.

'Stress-test this performance,' Felix replies. 'If you can stay cool under that sort of pressure, we might just be OK.'

'I don't know how I feel about this,' I say cautiously.

'Big baby,' Art calls out.

Wow, he's started already.

Art is a sixty-something, balding man. I can tell he's on the short side, even though he's sitting down. I don't know why but he just looks like someone who would be an internet troll – but it's as though he hasn't quite mastered the technology involved so he just shouts at people on stage.

'I've instructed Art to do his worse,' Felix tells us. 'No hard feelings involved. This is all for your own good. For the good of the show.'

I watch as Felix settles into the seat next to Art, ready to watch the fireworks.

'Buttons, Sisters, Cinderella – in your places for the scene where the ball invitations arrive. Everyone else off the stage,' Felix demands. 'Let's start after the Sisters have torn up Cinderella's ticket.'

'Oh, Buttons,' I start. 'I feel like I'll never get to the ball.'

'Try relaxing your muscles,' Art calls out.

I feel my eyes widen in horror.

'Oh, boys and girls, I love Cinderella so much,' Marc, as Buttons, says to the audience, in one of those typical panto fourth-wall breaks that the other characters aren't supposed to notice.

'Oh no you don't,' Art heckles.

'No one wants you at the ball anyway, Cinderella,' Billy, as an Ugly Sister, says half-heartedly. 'The prince wants to meet *beautiful* women.'

'That's right,' Steve replies. He holds his arms out. 'He wants to meet a ten, like me. Or a nine, like my sister.'

'Oh, the cheek of it,' Billy adds without a hint of enthusiasm.

'Cheer up, love,' Art shouts at him. 'Your calendar might be wrong.'

'My sisters are right,' I say. 'Why would—'

'Can't hear you,' Art shouts.

'Why would—'

'You're too quiet,' he sings.

'*Why would the prince want to meet a girl like me?*' I practically shout, aggression creeping into my voice.

'OK, love, calm down,' Art replies. 'Christ, have you got your period or something?'

His sexist remark makes me so angry I feel sharp prickles all over my skin.

I look at Felix, irritated that he's put us in this position, and notice him looking at me expectantly, slowly nodding his head.

Screw it.

'I might do,' I reply. 'You're like period pain in human form.'

'Ooh, OK,' Art replies. 'Don't be so thin-skinned. I'm just trying to toughen you up.'

'Well, you know what they say, what doesn't kill you makes me disappointed,' I reply. I look at the watch I'm not actually wearing. 'There's a bus back to London in half an hour, why don't you go lie under it?'

For the first time, Art is speechless. I look over at Felix who smiles and gives me a thumbs up. If this was a test, I think I've passed it.

The other cast members on stage are all smiling. I think they feel emboldened by my outburst. Like there's nothing this heckler can say now.

Let's just hope the audience are gentler on the night. It took all my courage to call out Art and he's just one man. Imagine when there's a room full of them.

After my scene, I hurry to the dressing room, keen to get out of these clothes, and go home to see Gracie.

'A moment, Emmy?' I hear Felix from the doorway.

'Of course, come in,' I reply.

'You certainly know how to handle a heckler,' he says, clearly impressed.

'Yeah, well, when you've been on a TV show for so many years, and have people stopping you in the street to have a go at you for something your character did, as though you had any say in it, you develop a thick skin,' I reply.

'I suppose that's true,' he replies thoughtfully. 'Anyway, I just wanted to thank you, because I don't believe I have yet, for the role you are playing.'

I'm a little taken aback by his gratitude, so I make a joke.

'I'd always fancied playing Cinderella,' I say with a shrug of my shoulders.

'Not just your role in the production, your role in all of this,' he points out. 'Things were getting... difficult, to say the least, here. But with this sell-out show, and all your hard work. And of course, there's another happy side effect, you are bringing out the best in everyone, tapping into qualities they didn't know they had.'

I smile.

'Especially with the script,' he says. 'Alison really has a talent for writing. I did worry about the script, and with Anita... Well, I appreciate you trying.'

'Do you miss her?' I ask him, way overstepping the mark. He must think so too, because I finally see some genuine emotion in his face. He seems surprised, and yet somehow like he feels better for being asked.

'I do,' he replies. 'Very much so.'

'Do you think you made a mistake?' I ask him.

Felix sighs.

'Make the most of people while you can,' he tells me, patting me on the shoulder, before leaving the room.

I think perhaps that's as much as I'm going to get out of him, but it feels good to know that I'm really, truly doing some good, and helping people, which is far more than I thought I was going to achieve with this panto. It's almost made me even more determined to do something nice for Felix, and I've had the best idea...

39

I think I'm getting softer as I'm getting older. I know, I know, after what I said to Art yesterday, I don't seem like a softie, but I am with those whom I care about – to my own detriment.

Take last night, for example. I had it all planned out for my sleepover with Gracie. I wanted to do it just like we used to when we were younger. Have the special teas we used to have with Gran and Grand-dad, on their old foldaway table that they used to put in front of the TV for us. We would eat those little individually wrapped pieces of cheese and watch whatever was on one of the four channels available to us, or old VHS tapes of *Fawlty Towers*. Our favourite episode was always the one with Basil the rat, and I even found it on Netflix for us to watch.

But then Gracie got a call from Mum about the twins' party, which I had totally forgotten about (probably because Mum had stopped nagging me to do a personal appearance, or a PA as we call them in the biz), saying their DJ had cancelled because he was unwell. I figured I was doing all this for Gracie, and letting Katie have her wedding at my house, so I may as well step up for my other two siblings and not only turn up to their party, but DJ too, so it really was like a PA.

I did my best to blend into the background, almost like a prop, there for what they needed me for, but in no way stealing any of the attention.

At one point, when I nipped to the toilets, Megan chased after me. It's rare she goes out of her way to talk to me, unless she wants something, so I didn't have high hopes for this exchange.

'Emmy, can you play some Anne-Marie?' she asked me.

'Sure,' I replied.

I continued towards the toilets when she called my name again.

'Emmy,' she started. 'Thanks so much for doing this. It's seriously cool.'

Is there any higher honour than being called cool by a teenager?

Even Louis, who is moody at the best of times, never mind with me, came over to thank me. He also asked me to ignore his friends if any of them asked me on a date – presumably out of manners, not because he thought I might say yes. Teenage boys will always be teenage boys though – all talk. Other than a few requests for photos (mostly the usual strangulation requests) no one dared to talk to me.

I'm really happy I turned up for the twins, and I'm hoping they might start seeing me in a different light now, or at least stop worrying about their friends knowing who I am.

Gracie and I got our sleepover afterwards, but it was thinking about helping out all my siblings equally that reminded me of something: Katie's wedding.

No, I hadn't forgotten that she was getting married, or that she was doing it at my house, I suppose I'd just lost track of the dates. So, I told everyone about the party tonight, after the friends and family performance, to either celebrate or commiserate, but mostly just to show Gracie a good time. Then I remembered that Katie's wedding is tomorrow. I'm not too worried though, we're all adults, it's not going to be a wild house party. And the clean-up will be easy because I'll have Gracie with me, and she's amazing at cleaning and tidying. She's already doing it non-stop, above and beyond what I would usually do. I'm learning all sorts from her, about what you're supposed to clean and how often. It will be nice to socialise her a bit, I feel like she's watching too much YouTube.

I can't worry about any of that now though because I have lunch plans. On the subject of me going soft, Tel and I have arranged a little surprise for Felix. He's done so much for us, and thanks to Tel I feel like I understand Felix way better. He's just doing his best for people, albeit in an un-orthodox way.

Tel and I are standing in one of the corridors at the theatre, outside a door, waiting to show Felix what we've done on the other side of it.

'I hope he likes it,' I say, chewing one of my fin-gernails. 'What if he goes mad?'

'He'll love it,' Tel replies. 'And you're worrying too much. After this panto, you can run out of this theatre and never look back. Back to London, back to your fancy job.'

'Yeah,' I say with a snort. 'Won't that be great.'

'What's wrong?' he asks.

'Nothing,' I insist. 'Ignore me.'

'You don't like your job?' Tel says curiously. 'I would have thought a role like that was a dream for an actor. You must have more job stability than movie stars, and less hecklers than theatre actors.'

I laugh.

'You would think so,' I reply.

'Emmy, talk to me,' Tel says. 'I can tell you're bottling something up.'

I don't know what it is but suddenly the urge to

tell *someone* is overwhelming, and my gut instinct is that I can trust Tel.

'Can we keep this just between us?' I ask him.

'Of course,' he replies.

'I've been killed off,' I admit. 'Shit, sorry, you don't care about spoilers, do you?'

'I haven't seen the show, don't worry,' he assures me. 'Emmy, I'm so sorry. Did they give you plenty of warning?'

'Not exactly,' I reply. 'I don't suppose you read the tabloids?'

'I sometimes lay old ones on the floor to protect it while I'm working,' he says. 'But mostly, no.'

'There was a story recently, about me and the married showrunner, saying that we were having an affair,' I explain. I'm about to tell him it's not true when...

'I don't believe that for a second,' he says. 'And you got sacked for that?'

I smile. It's nice to have someone just *know* that it's not true.

'It's a bit messier than that,' I tell him. 'Danny, the showrunner, tried it on with me at a party and I knocked him back. Then, on a night when we were working late, he tried again. He was much keener that time. It didn't seem like he was going to take no for an answer but, well, bizarrely a lot of my show choreography helped me nip his advances in the bud. Next thing I know, I'm being killed off.'

That's the first time I've told anyone what happened. I never thought I'd tell anyone, never mind our friendly neighbourhood builder, but it does feel good to tell someone, especially someone I know I can trust.

'That bastard,' Tel says. 'Honestly, my blood is boiling, I'm so angry. So, you get sacked and he gets away with it?'

'Who would believe me?' I reply. 'Maybe some people would, maybe some people wouldn't. Nothing actually happened to me, so I guess I just counted myself lucky and left it at that. I don't know if you saw it, but there was a story in the tabloids, saying there were rumours we had a full-blown affair, which weren't true. An unknown source said that we'd been at it for years, and they published it with a photo of the two of us on set, where he had his hand on the small of my back. Sometimes, I wonder if he leaked it, to absolve himself of any guilt, but that's probably crazy, surely he'd never suggest he was having an affair to cover up the fact he's a creep? Anyway, after the shock of being killed off wore off, I was almost happy about it. I didn't ever want to work with Danny again.'

'What a scumbag,' Tel says. 'I feel like I want to do something, but I don't know what.'

'It's not a very nice environment and I'm just one girl on my own.'

'Please, don't be so hard on yourself. You were in an impossible situation.'

'The worst part of all is that now, not only am I looking for work, but the stories about my supposed affair were in the news cycle for less than a week. It's as though people accepted the information and moved on. So that's that. I'm down as a homewrecker, which isn't going to help me find a new job, and no one really mentions it to me, but I know so many people must have read about it and have this horrible opinion of me. I don't know what I'm supposed to do.'

'Right, I'm here,' Felix's voice interrupts. I'm relieved, to be honest, I was starting to get upset. 'Come on, what disaster do you have to show me now?'

I exhale before putting my own drama back in the box in my brain where I've been hiding it these past few weeks.

'We actually have a good surprise for you,' I tell him. 'So, a little birdie told us that this room used to be a dance hall, and that you used to spend a lot of time here when you were younger.'

'That may or may not be true,' he replies with a raised eyebrow.

'Come inside,' Tel insists as he opens the door. 'So, it's going to take some real work to get it looking nice, but for now, we thought we might recreate a little of that wartime magic and play some of the songs you used to dance to, when you would come to 1940s dances here.'

'For one night only – or lunchtime, at least –

we've brought the old ballroom back to life,' I say proudly. 'Come see.'

As we enter the room the band starts playing. We managed to get a group of vintage enthusiasts, all obsessed with the forties, everything from the fashion to dancing, to come and hang out. Marram Bay actually has an annual 1940s weekend and everyone takes it *so* seriously. People put tape on their windows, dress up – some of the more extreme participants even eat rations for the weekend, although it is just an excuse for a bit of a piss-up, so even though no one really breaks character while they're celebrating, they never feel the need to ration their alcohol intake. So, no one took much convincing to get involved today, in something so authentic, getting to dance to a live band in a theatre that hosted dances throughout World War II, no matter what was going on outside. It's hard to imagine Felix as one of these enthusiasts until I see him breathing in the music, and the atmosphere, and it doesn't matter that the walls are tired and that we've had to light it with Tel's work lights, pointed at the walls. In fact, it adds to the mood of the place.

A room that seemed so tired and past it has blood surging through its veins once more. The high ceilings and fancy wall decorations might not be what they once were, but I see a side of Felix that I haven't seen before. And then, at the heart of the dancing crowd, he notices one woman standing alone in between all the couples. Anita.

For a second, he just stares, like he's seen a ghost. A tear appears in one of his eyes.

'She swore she'd never look at me again,' he says.

'Well, maybe someone had a word with her,' Tel says with a wink.

Knowing that Felix missed Anita, and that Anita was spending her days propping up the bar, both of them as lonely as the other, I just knew I needed to find a way to get them talking again.

'Go on, go see her, don't leave her dancing alone,' I tell him through a huge smile. It feels so good to be able to help him – to help them both. They seem so lonely and like they've been missing each other all these years. Someone needed to bring them back together.

'Thank you,' he tells us. 'Thank you both.'

'Come on, let's join them for a dance,' Tel suggests.

'OK, but everyone seems like they know the steps,' I point out.

Tel just shrugs.

'I've never really cared about what people think of me,' he replies.

We only dance for a few seconds before I can't resist asking him a question that's on my mind.

'So, have you really never seen my show?' I ask him.

'I'm not a big TV watcher these days,' he replies.

'I mostly just meant because, if I met someone, and I knew they were in a TV show, the first thing I would do is look them up,' I say. 'Just out of curiosity.'

'If I'm being honest, I did think there was something familiar about you, so I looked you up briefly, to see where I knew you from, but I didn't think you'd want me to mention it.'

'Why not?' I reply.

'Because I realised you're the Cheeseair girl,' he says through a stifled smile. 'Cheeeeeseaiiiir!'

'Oh, God,' I blurt. 'Yes, let's go back to never mentioning that, please.'

'I loved it,' he confesses. 'What happened to it?'

'I think it was outlawed,' I say with a laugh. 'Kids were using it to get high. It was awful, really.'

'Wow, I wasn't expecting you to say that,' he replies. 'OK, I'll never mention it again.'

That would be great because my family *do not* let me forget it.

As we watch Felix go and get his girl – decades later than he should have – I can't help but wonder about my own love life. Perhaps patience is the key. If you meet someone when you're younger, and you think you're perfect for each other, maybe you will find a way back together. Maybe for me that person *is* Scott. But then there's Tel, my right-hand man. The one who made all this possible. It might have been my idea originally but that's all it was, an idea.

Tel and I worked together to develop it and bring it to life and it's worked out better than either of us could have expected.

Whatever is right for me, I just hope I figure it out. Felix and Anita might be together now but think of all those years they spent apart. I don't want to be lonely. I don't want life to be happening here while I'm in London alone, doing a job that is sucking the life out of me. It's all I know though. I suppose I need to think long and hard about that too.

40

In the most shocking plot twist of all time – even more shocking than Edrym beheading Adelina while they're in bed together – the pantomime is a roaring success.

Well, I don't want to get too excited, it is just the friends and family performance, so they're probably going to be more supportive than paying customers, and there's still a scene to go, but there is just such an incredible vibe in the theatre.

Throughout the whole thing everyone has been so clearly enjoying themselves – the cast, the audience, even the crew. And I actually think it's all coming across really well. The jokes are landing, the twist with the present-day dialogue is really working, and despite the last-minute hiccups, it's all working out brilliantly. Everyone has really pulled it out of the bag, even Billy and Marc, who have totally adapted to their new roles and completely knocked it out of the park. Marc is so proud of his performance as Buttons that he joked at intermission that even his mum would be asking him if he were going back in the closet, he 'played it so straight'. Scott even sucked it up to do what he needed to do, lip-syncing perfectly to Tel's vocals as he sang the songs behind the curtain, *Singing in the Rain* style. Thankfully, he wasn't exposed.

I have to admit, it's felt amazing to be back on-stage, or even just back to acting generally. But it's not just the performing, I think it's more than that. It's being a part of something that excites me. Something I want to work hard for – somewhere I can see my hard work paying off. I know that working on *Bragadon Forrest* wasn't leaving me feeling fulfilled any more. The reviews aren't as good as they used to be, some fans are getting upset at the way the plot is headed (just wait until they find out what happens to Adelina!), and it always just felt like the same old, same old, not wearing much clothing, fighting, getting doused in fake blood. I've been over it for a long time, I just haven't had anything better to do. This theatre group may be small-time, but it feels like a big deal to me.

All that's left to do is deliver the final few lines, take our bows, and then we can celebrate.

'I finally have my Prince Charming,' I say, with real enthusiasm, really giving it my all for the audience, even if it is only made up of people we know. 'My happy-ever-after starts today – and I finally get to uninstall Matcher too.'

Everyone laughs at my joke. I'm really enjoying making people laugh.

'And perhaps the guys at work can stop trying to set me up with their friends,' Scott replies, in his corny Prince Charming voice. 'Well, at least they would if I had a real job.'

More laughs.

'He's a William, not a Harry,' Steve ad-libs.

'So, what happens now?' I ask, once the laughter has died down.

'This is the part where you live happily ever after,' Alison, my fairy godmother, tells me. She gives me a wink that isn't in the script, and that she hasn't done in any of the rehearsals. I don't even think the audience can see it. 'Now kiss!'

'Gladly,' Scott says.

He takes me in his arms, dips me, and kisses me on the lips.

I don't know if it's more or less of a kiss than the first one. We've kissed in rehearsals a few times now and, if I'm being honest, they feel a bit flat. I mean, of course they do, they're stage kisses, but considering I thought we had some kind of spark, you'd think I would feel something, but I don't.

I get more of a rush from the audience clapping and cheering, wolf-whistling, shouting out for an encore.

We all take a bow and, as the curtains close, and Tel emerges from his hiding place, it's him who I can't wait to run over to and hug.

'We absolutely smashed it,' I tell him.

'We did,' he replies. 'We just have to make sure we do it again.'

'I have every bit of faith in this squad,' I tell him.

'Still back to yours for the party?' Steve asks, as he runs up behind me, and wraps his arms around me.

'Yes, definitely, we need to celebrate,' I reply.

We do need to celebrate. For once, finally, something has gone right, and it's made me wonder about what the future could hold for me. Something that, up to now, had felt so hopeless.

41

It feels like forever since I attended a decent house party.

I'm in the kitchen pouring glasses of champagne when Gracie comes rushing in.

'Erm, Emmy, Alex Forbes is at the door,' she says, like it's the most normal thing in the world, but her face tells a different story. She lowers her voice. 'I just met Alex Forbes.'

I was a little annoyed when my agent told me that, after hearing about my panto gig, my ex-*Bragadon Forrest* co-star (my on-screen lover/murderer), who is also a client of hers, wanted a ticket. At first,

I thought he only wanted to come and laugh at me, so I said he could come to the friends and family performance, thinking I could at least write off anything that went wrong as opening-night bugs.

'You can let him in,' I tell her with a chuckle.

'Right,' she says. 'Of course.'

Gracie eventually heads back into the kitchen with Alex, shortly followed by Vee and Ken, neither of whom I was expecting.

'Hey, Alex,' I say.

'Oh, Emmy, you were amazing,' he tells me. He gives me a showbiz kiss. 'Honestly, when I heard you were doing panto, I was shocked, I thought it was going to be awful but, genuinely, you were fantastic. The whole thing was great. I was really surprised.'

I can tell Alex means that because I'm not sure he's a good enough actor to lie so convincingly. At least he's honest, I suppose. Hopefully, anyone else coming to gawp, to see if the mighty have fallen, will also see that I'm doing the best job I can for a wonderful cause.

'Thanks, Alex. And thanks so much for coming,' I reply. 'There are stiffer drinks in the dining room.'

'You know me so well,' he replies.

'I can't believe you get to shag that for a living,' Vee says.

I wince. No one wants to hear their auntie say shag. But there's so much to unpack there. I can't ignore it.

'You know I don't actually sleep with him, right?' I say. 'You know I'm an actor?'

'He's bloody lovely,' she says. 'No one would blame you if you did do it for real, like they were rumoured to have done in that film.'

'*Don't Look Now*?'

'Why, is he coming back?' she asks, glancing over her shoulder.

I laugh.

'What are you doing here, Vee?'

'Scott told his dad he was coming to a party here and I thought, hmm, there's no way my favourite niece is throwing a party and not inviting me!'

'I'm literally standing maybe four feet away

from you,' Gracie, her *other* niece, points out with a wave.

'But Emmy has champagne,' Vee says. 'Anyway, we're only stopping for a quick one.'

God, I hope she means a drink.

Gracie's phone rings in her pocket. The party is in full swing now. It's nothing wild, but she still has to put her finger in her ear to hear properly.

'What?' she says, a concerned look on her face. 'I'll be right there.'

'Is everything OK?' I ask her when she's done.

She smiles at me.

'I have to go,' she says. 'Oscar needs me. He had a bad dream and wants me there. He's crying for me, Carl can't calm him down. My family needs me.'

'Go on, go,' I tell her.

Gracie runs around the kitchen island and hugs me so tightly.

'Thanks for this,' she says. 'For all of it.'

'Well,' Vee says once Gracie has left the room. 'This is why I never had kids.'

'I'm going to mingle with my guests,' I tell her. 'Behave.'

As I pass through the dining room, I spot Scott hovering by the buffet.

'Emmy, can I have a word?' he says.

'Of course,' I reply.

'Sorry if I've seemed a little off these last few days,' he says. 'Honestly, I felt like Tel kind of snaked my part, and then it seemed like he was trying to keep you all for himself.'

'Nothing to apologise for,' I tell him. 'I'm just glad it all worked out in the end.'

'Speaking of things working out, guess what?' Scott starts excitedly. 'We've finally aligned. I'm single, you're single. Is there anything getting in our way now?'

I must make a face that suggests I'm a little taken aback by his forwardness.

'I know what you're thinking, you live in London, but what if I came back with you?' he suggests. 'We can take things slowly. But I'm just thinking, life is short, we need to go for it. I could come right away, if I could crash with you? Maybe you can get me a spot in your TV show? You would unlock so much more potential if you had a famous boyfriend.'

'I, erm, I just need the loo,' I tell him. 'Back in a minute.'

Have you ever had a seemingly harmless conversation that has completely changed your life?

I think back to yesterday, with Felix and Anita, losing so much time that they could have spent together, and my decade spanning 'will they, won't they?' with Scott. I've realised that, now we're both available, and there is seemingly nothing getting in our way, there is actually something stopping us, and it's a pretty big hurdle. I don't want to be with him. I thought I did when I was a kid but, as I've grown up, those feelings have gone. Maybe I thought us being apart and then coming back together was romantic – it certainly seemed that way with Felix and Anita – but really it's nothing short of a tragedy that they spent so long apart, they've been pining for each other for years. But I've been living without Scott just fine. Just because someone is so deep-rooted in your past, it doesn't mean they have to be with you in the future, and there's something so peaceful about finally accepting that. At least I hope that's the right call...

I nip to the bathroom and, on my back through the hallway, I spot Felix through the window next to the door.

'Hello,' I say brightly as I open it. It's so lovely to see him here. I didn't think he'd want to celebrate with us.

'Hello, Emmy,' he replies. 'I was in two minds whether to come or not.'

'Well, I'm so happy you decided to,' I say. 'Come inside, it's freezing out.'

'Actually, this won't take long,' he says. 'I just wanted to share my thoughts on the performance with you.'

'Wasn't everyone amazing?' I reply.

'Not everyone,' he says. 'Everyone but you.'

I laugh, but then I notice the serious look on his face.

'Wait, what?' I blurt. 'Is this a joke? Are you heckling me?'

'I wish I were,' he says solemnly. 'I think the

harsh fact is that you're not cut out for theatre. You're a TV actress. Pippa is a theatre actress, I think she would be a much better fit for Cinderella. I have to go, but I shall leave this with you. I had a word with Pippa, she says she is ready and willing to step in, if needed.'

'I thought the whole point of all of this was for *me* to bring in the audience?' I reply in disbelief.

'But that means nothing if you don't have the talent to back it up,' he says harshly. 'Stick to TV.'

I don't know what to say. I don't think Felix does either, so he just walks off, leaving me standing on the doorstep with my mouth open. Wow, so that's what you get for helping someone? I can't believe it. You do develop a thick skin as an actor, and you have no choice but to get used to knock-backs, but I was doing *him* a favour – a favour I didn't even want to do. How can he just drop me like this?

I head to the living room – the last place I saw Tel, because he's the only person I want to talk to right now – but instead I find the gang. Pippa, Kay, Billy and Alison. Scott spots me and wanders over too.

I want to walk away, ignore them all, go and find Tel, but I just can't...

I march over to where Pippa is sitting. They're all gathered on the seats by the large, old window in the lounge. It's usually such a gorgeous, chilled-out place to sit but tonight the scene is going to be far from pretty.

'What the hell are you playing at?' I ask her. 'I just spoke to Felix, he says you told him you were prepared to take over my role in the panto.'

'He told me you probably weren't going to show up,' she says. At least Felix didn't tell her he was pushing me out because he found my performance so unwatchable. I never would have heard the end of that. 'Come on, Emmy, you've been out to replace me since you got here. I'm only taking back what's mine.'

'Taking back what's yours?' I say. 'I didn't seek this part out, you know, Kay and Billy talked me into it. They said they needed my help. My life was just fine as it was. I was doing fine on my own...'

'Well, not quite as fine on your own,' Alison

says proudly. 'Let's just say, you might have had a fairy godmother giving you a push.'

'Woah, OK, what does that mean?' I ask.

'You and Scott,' she says, gesturing back and forth between us with her eyes. 'I've been doing my best to get you two together.'

'*Have* you?' I blurt.

She seems offended I haven't noticed.

'Well, you were doing a terrible job on your own,' she points out. 'Pretending to date Billy.'

'Hang on, you *pretended* to date Billy?' Scott chimes in.

'No, Billy pretended to date me,' I point out. 'I didn't ask him to say that, he just came out with it.'

'So, say he's lying,' Scott says. 'When he said it. Why did you not say that he was lying?'

'I didn't want to embarrass him,' I reply.

'No, you just wanted to use him, just like you always have,' Kay chimes in.

I feel my jaw drop.

'I don't use Billy,' I say. I turn to him. 'Do I?'

'Yes, you do,' Kay replies, before he has a chance to speak. 'You always have. You must know that he fancies you, that he'd do anything for you. If not, then you really are just so oblivious. I can't take it any more. I care about him so, so much, and does he even notice? No, he's obsessed with *you*. We'd actually grown much closer recently, I thought something was going to happen between us, finally, but then he got all caught up in your drama again.'

I look at Billy. His cheeks are bright red and his eyes wide. He looks frozen on the spot.

'It's the same with Scott,' Pippa chimes in. 'I know, he'll go mad at me for saying this—'

'Pippa, leave it,' Scott insists, a real look of panic in his eyes.

'No, she needs to hear this,' Pippa insists. 'Because Kay is right, she is oblivious. She rocks up, thinks she can have any part she wants, any man she wants. But Scott and I were... well, we were, you know, getting close, well, getting *together* most nights. Until Emmy turned up and he dropped me.'

'Right, that meant nothing to me,' Scott insists to me, rather cruelly. 'She's exaggerating.'

'You two were sleeping together?' Alison says,

her jaw dropping, although she's probably more shocked that she didn't know about it, rather than because it was happening. 'Oh, this group has some serious issues.'

'You were trying to get Emmy and Scott together,' Kay reminds her. 'You even warned Tel off.'

'What?' I squeak in disbelief.

'Some of us were worried he was distracting you from Scott,' Alison says. 'The one you were meant to be with.'

'Alison, I appreciate you trying to help, but that's just way over the line,' I tell her.

'You're probably the reason Billy is in plaster,' Kay says. 'Honestly, Emmy, I think we've all had enough of your selfishness.'

I'm not a selfish person, I can't be, or I wouldn't be standing here, in this house, doing this pantomime, throwing my sister a wedding, but they might be right about one thing, I am oblivious. I had no idea Billy had a crush on me – and I never would have put Scott and Pippa together. The revelation has definitely cemented my feelings that

Scott is not the person for me, so at least there's that.

'Erm, the reason Billy is in that chair, I'm pretty sure, is because of *her*,' I say, pointing at Pippa. 'She was out to get me that day. From staining my dress and trying to pin it on the kids to thinking she shoved *me* through the curtain. I saw how guilty she looked when she realised it was Billy.'

Pippa rolls her eyes.

'OK, look, fine, I did try to shove you through the curtain,' she says. 'I wasn't trying to push anyone into the hole in the floor, not even you, I just lost my temper. You've waltzed in and replaced me.'

It is satisfying, to hear Pippa own up, but Kay is on a roll with her now. It turns out, harbouring such strong feelings for Billy all these years, while he apparently was feeling that way about me, has built up so much resentment in her.

'So, it *was* your fault he fell,' Kay says.

'You can't just steal people's parts,' Pippa says with a manic intensity.

I just stand there for a second. I don't know what to say.

'Wow, you could cut the party atmosphere down here with a knife,' Tel says as he joins us.

'I was looking for you,' I tell him.

'I gave Gracie a lift home, she'd had a couple of drinks, so she didn't want to drive,' he replies. 'I've had to promise her I'll go over next week and remove my bit of finger from her wall. I'll just have to pretend, make her feel better. She invited you too. She said she'd make dinner to say thank you.'

He laughs at how absurd all that sounds, but then he realises there really is something going on.

'What's wrong?' he asks.

A look takes over Scott's face. An angry realisation of something. He cocks his head curiously.

'I've been so stupid,' Scott says. 'I can't believe I've been missing something so obvious all along. I thought maybe I was being paranoid, but I'm not paranoid at all. You're out to get me.'

He's looking at Tel.

'Kind of sounds like something a paranoid

person would say,' I joke, trying to dispel the tension, but Scott is enraged.

'You're trying to steal my part,' he says to Tel, prodding him in the chest. 'And you're trying to steal my girl.'

Scott prods Tel again.

I think back to what Scott told me, about the theatre being haunted, how the place made actors crazy, paranoid, jealous, prone to sabotage. It freaked me out at the time, but I understand it now. The theatre isn't haunted, it's the actors who are possessed. Not by evil spirits but by their ego, their insecurities, their jealousy.

'She's not your girl though, is she?' Tel points out.

Scott gives Tel a little push.

'Let's settle this like men,' Scott suggests, with an aggression I didn't know he had in him.

'Wow, OK,' I interrupt. 'Men don't settle things by pushing each other any more.'

'She's not even worth it,' Pippa points out. 'We all know she's just after old men. It said so in the papers – Scott, you told me yourself, that you thought she was sleeping with your dad.'

My eyebrows shoot up.

'None of that is true,' Tel says in my defence.

'And how would you know?' Scott asks him.

'Because I know her,' he replies. 'I know, you were friends when you were kids, but I probably got to know her better over the past six weeks than you have over your entire life.'

This is the final straw for Scott.

It's clear Tel has no interest in fighting him but that doesn't stop Scott giving him one big shove. Tel stumbles backwards into one of the new, fancy metal floor lamps I bought for the lounge. He hits it with such a force that it goes flying and, before anyone has a chance to halt the domino effect, the lamp hits my large, old window right smack bang in the middle.

We all just stare at it, as the crack forms. I don't know how long it takes but eventually it shatters.

The whole party falls silent. Someone even turns off the music.

'Oh my God,' I blurt.

'It was his fault,' Scott says. 'I...'

Scott doesn't finish his sentence. He just scarpers.

'Maybe we should all go,' Kay says softly, suddenly seeming like her old self again, even if it is too little too late.

I think the loud sound of the window smashing has knocked some sense into her, snapped her out of her crazed jealousy. She looks like perhaps she might feel a bit silly now.

'Katie's wedding reception,' I say quietly. 'She's having it here tomorrow.'

'If you maybe clean up the glass,' Alison suggests, ever so helpfully.

'It's December and it's freezing,' I point out.

'We should probably go,' she says, grabbing her handbag, pulling herself to her feet.

'Everyone, party's over, get out,' I call out as calmly as I can, but I can hear a little wobble in my voice. 'Everyone, please leave.'

No one needs telling twice.

The room clears out and not one person offers

to stay and help me. Not that I have any idea what I'm supposed to do.

With everyone gone and a huge hole in my lounge two things occur to me. One is: just how cold it's going to get in here in no time at all, because the icy breeze is already surging around my body. The other is: that worse than that, when I told everyone to leave, they did. Everyone. Even Tel. I'm all alone.

42

Sitting on the floor, alone in my lounge, staring at the large hole in the side of my house, I don't know what to do other than grab a throw from the sofa and wrap it around myself. When the window broke, every bit of heat escaped outside. My short-sleeved dress suddenly left me feeling exposed to the weather. By morning, it's going to be totally frozen in here and, with the weather not set to be any warmer tomorrow, there is just no way in hell a wedding reception can take place in here.

I jump out of my skin when I hear the front door open and close.

'Tel,' I say as he walks into the lounge. I quickly wipe my tears from my cheeks, embarrassed he's found me crying again. 'I thought you left with everyone else.'

'I suppose I did,' he says. 'But I only popped next door to get my tools.'

He drops his bag down on the floor. I notice he's changed into his work clothes too.

'I'm not sure you've got anything in that bag that can replace a window,' I reply with a sigh. 'Even if we board it up, it's going to look awful, not like a venue for a wedding. God, I've really fucked things up this time.'

'OK, here's what's going to happen,' Tel says, extending a hand to pull me up from the floor. He rubs my cold shoulders as he tells me what to do. 'You're going to go upstairs, you're going to have a nice warm shower, and then you're going to get in your bed, where it's warm, and you're going to stay there. I'm going to replace your window.'

I raise a sceptical eyebrow.

'I had to replace my window when I moved in,' he says. 'A friend of mine did it, so he knows exactly what we need, and he can arrange it. Plus, he owes me a favour, so he's going to come over and help me fit it. I'm going to get to work removing the old frame and clear up all the glass. I promise you, your window will be good as new by morning, no one is even going to be able to tell this happened.'

I exhale for what feels like a minute.

'Why are you so amazing?' I ask him.

Tel just smiles and shrugs.

'Go on,' he insists. 'I'll be up to check on you in a bit.'

I do as Tel says and, as I head upstairs, I think about how fantastic he's been. He's such an amazing man, so selfless, so talented and generous. Just like that, my worries have evaporated. I would worry that you can't possibly get the exact window we need in a matter of hours, at 10 p.m., but if Tel says we can, I believe him. I haven't had a problem yet that he hasn't been able to solve. Except, of course, the problem I have of what I'm going to do without him when I go back to London. That's really starting to play on my mind.

43

I wake up with a big yawn and a huge stretch. That's when I realise something is different. Instead of lying on my pillow, I'm resting my head on Tel's chest and I've never felt more comfortable.

I look up at him. He's still fully clothed, sitting propped up on the bed. He's sleeping so peacefully. It's rare to see his face so relaxed because usually he's always flashing a cheeky smile, laughing, or even showing when he's feeling frustrated. Tel wears his emotions on his face – that's probably why acting is one of the things he can't do. He can't channel them, he's just too genuine.

Tel came up to check on me a few times during the night. He kept me posted on the progress of the window, never bringing me any news that wasn't positive. Eventually he came up, sat down next to me and whispered: 'it's done'. That's when I hugged him, to say thank you, and I don't know if it was because I was relieved or relaxed but I just stayed there, exactly where I was, and drifted right off to sleep. It seems like he wasn't far behind me.

'Good morning,' I say softly.

Tel stirs before waking up. He seems as comfortable as I am.

'Morning,' he replies.

'I can't thank you enough for last night,' I tell him. 'You are phenomenal.'

'I always hoped a girl would say that to me in bed one morning,' he jokes. 'I just never thought it would be for fitting a window.'

I laugh.

'Sorry if I pinned you down,' I say. 'I'll bet you're dying to get home.'

Tel shrugs.

'I'm pretty happy here, actually,' he says with a smile.

I glance at the clock.

'My alarm is going to go off in twenty minutes,' I say with a sigh. 'Then people will start turning up with things for the wedding. The hired tables and chairs, the caterers and so on. I need to get a few cups of tea down me.'

'At this wedding are you technically staff or a guest?' he asks curiously.

'On paper, I'm a guest who just happens to be hosting, but I don't have to do any work, or so I'm told. Dad has called a few times to say he's taking care of everything.'

'You're not close with your dad, are you?' Tel says.

I shake my head.

'With his new family he acts like he's this doting family man,' I say. 'I don't buy it. I'm dreading spending a day in the same room as him.'

'Well, if you're technically a guest, and this is *your* house, does that mean you're allowed a plus-one?' he asks.

'I suppose it technically means I'm allowed a plus whatever I want,' I say with a chuckle. 'But I'd settle for a one.'

'I do love a wedding,' he says. 'I'd love to be your plus-one, if you'll have me?'

I don't have time to even think about what I'm doing before I scoot up the bed, place my hands on Tel's face, and kiss him – and I mean really kiss him. He kisses me back, scooping me up and sitting me down on his lap, holding my waist in his hands. I wrap my arms around his neck as we kiss for a few minutes but then he stops me.

'Wait, wait, wait,' Tel says. 'Don't you have a wedding to get ready for? I don't want to distract you. I don't think we can take another disaster.'

Now I have no choice but to think about what I'm doing. God, what am I doing? I don't know what came over me, I suppose I was just so over-whelmed by how incredible he's being, and so re-lieved he wants to be at this wedding with me, keeping me sane, and... just so sure that I want him more than anything.

'I've got fifteen minutes before I need to get up,' I tell him. 'So, stop wasting time and kiss me.'

'Fifteen minutes? That gives us ten to spare,' he jokes.

We start kissing again.

I appreciate Tel's dedication to the cause, and wanting to avoid another disaster, but if there's one thing I am sure of, it's that this, what we're doing now, is anything but disastrous. Nothing has ever felt so right.

44

'It really is amazing,' I tell Tel. 'This window...
you'd never believe what happened last night.'

'Did you doubt my skills for a minute?' he asks
through a smile.

'Of course not,' I say.

I plonk myself down on the sofa.

'So, how are you feeling?' he asks me. 'The ceremony should be finished now.'

'Yeah,' I say with a sigh. 'It's so strange, thinking
about my dad in church, walking Katie down the
aisle, giving her away. With her, he's like a real dad.'

Tel squeezes my hand.

'You're doing an amazing thing, letting Katie have her wedding here,' Tel says. 'Without you, this wedding wouldn't be happening.'

'Well, it wouldn't be happening without you either,' I tell him.

'*Well*, that just means we make an excellent team,' he replies.

I rest my head on his shoulder.

'They'll all be arriving soon,' I tell him. 'I just want this whole thing to be over.'

'Are we talking about the wedding?' he asks. 'Or the pantomime too?'

'Both,' I reply. 'I don't know, maybe I should let Pippa take my place. I don't think Felix wants me to be a part of it any more.'

I don't want to repeat exactly what he said.

'That doesn't sound right to me but, regardless, I think a lot of people have paid to see *you*,' he says. 'You have to do what's right for you. I'll have a word with Felix later, try and work out where he's at with all of this.'

'I think he wants it all to be over too,' I reply.

'Emmy, there you are,' Dad says as he walks in.

He's wearing what I assume is a new navy-blue suit and a smile the size of the causeway.

'Here I am,' I reply.

'It was such a bloody gorgeous ceremony,' he says. 'It's a shame you had to stay here and get things ready. I'm so proud I could burst.'

'I'm glad it went well,' I say politely.

'I've got Katie and Lewis outside, they wondered if they could have the house for a moment? Their photographer thinks it would a great location for the family photos,' he says.

I assume Lewis is Katie's new husband. I've never met him.

'Erm, OK,' I reply. 'I'll nip upstairs for a bit.'

'I've got something I need to sort at home,' Tel says. He stands up, kisses me briefly on the lips, and heads for the door. 'I'll be right back.'

'OK,' I call after him.

Dad sits down on the sofa for a moment.

'That your fella?' he asks me seriously.

'Oh, don't do that,' I say with a snort.

'Do what?'

'Pretend you care,' I reply. 'Pretend to be my

dad. You're Katie's dad. Her perfect dad – or so she thinks. You don't give a shit about me so let's just skip all this.'

Dad hangs his head for a second.

'I know you think I'm a bastard, but I'm not,' he says.

I open my mouth to speak but he stops me.

'I *was* a bastard. I'm not any more,' he says. 'At least I try not to be. I appreciate how hard it must be for you. I was a crap dad to you – I still am, because I don't think I can ever make it up to you. I ruined all of our lives, I know I did. But your mum is happy now and Gracie has her family. I know how lucky I am to have a second chance with Patsie and Katie. I really am doing my best because I won't fuck up again.'

I don't know what to say.

'I will never be able to apologise enough for what I did to our family,' he continues, swiping a tear from his cheek that he thinks I haven't noticed. 'Never. But you have to be happy. You have to trust, you have to love. This Tel sounds like a good lad, your mum has told me a lot about him. She tells me a lot about you – all the things I'm too scared to ask you myself.'

Dad takes my hand in his and, for the first time in a long time, I don't snatch it back.

'Emmy, I am so unbelievably proud of you,' he tells me. 'Of what a fantastic young woman you've grown into, of how talented you are, of how generous you are. What you're doing for Katie today is a bloody incredible thing. I can't make up for the past, but I can make it up to you for what you've done for Katie, if you'll give me a chance?'

'It's nice to be able to help my sister,' I tell him with a smile. 'I'm going upstairs, to check my phone, if you want to take your family photos.'

'OK,' he replies. 'But don't be too long, OK? You're family too, we want you in them.'

I head upstairs, somehow feeling exactly the same way about my dad, but with a difference. I'm still mad at him for what happened in the past, and I still don't know how to forgive him, but perhaps there is a way to have him in my future.

When I get to my bedroom, I'm surprised to see six missed calls from my agent. Uh-oh! I wonder if

Alex has reported back to her about the party last night. I noticed he was very quick to leave, when it seemed like things were kicking off. I'll bet Jane is calling me to (as she usually calls it when it's bad news) *have a word*. Normally, my heart would be in my mouth. I'd be feeling sick at the idea of calling her, seeing what kind of trouble I'd caused, but what's actually going to happen, is she going to find me less jobs than no jobs?

With no time like the present, I tap to call her.

I admire my floor-length black dress in the new full-length mirror in my bedroom but I only get a second or two before she answers.

'Emmy Palmer, where have you been?' Jane asks angrily.

So, it is bad.

'Sorry, it's my sister's wedding day,' I reply.

'I thought Gracie was already married?'

'The other one,' I say.

'The child?'

I laugh.

'The *other* other one,' I tell her. 'My dad's other daughter.'

'Anyway, I'm not calling for your family tree, I'm calling with news,' she says. 'Emmy, we got him.'

'We've got who?'

'Danny Terrence,' she replies. 'And we don't *have* him, we *got* him, like we've nailed him – oh, you know what I mean.'

Jane gets frustrated.

'Your sexual harassment showrunner is officially no longer running the show,' she eventually says.

'Oh my God!' I exclaim. 'How?'

'Sexual harassment, would you believe?' she says. 'Other women came forward. It's very hush-hush, as you can imagine, but when they called me up to tell me, I told them, Danny is the reason you got killed off, because you rejected him, and they could see us in court or they could give you your job back.'

This is all so much to take in and not a call I was expecting to receive today at all.

'Sorry, did you just say I could have my job back?' I say, because I'm pretty sure she did, but it sounds too good to be true.

'Absolutely,' she says. 'So, what are you doing on the twenty-fourth?'

'On Christmas Eve?'

'Yes,' Jane replies blankly.

'I'm doing Christmas Eve,' I tell her.

'Not any more you're not,' she says. 'You've got a 5 a.m. start and a day of reshoots. It does mean you can't do your little pantomime tomorrow, if that's still a thing, because I'm booking you a train ticket for tomorrow. Sound good?'

'Jane, you're making my head spin,' I say before puffing air from my cheeks. 'Can I think about it, let you know in the morning?'

She laughs wildly for a few seconds then stops in an instant.

'You're not kidding?' she says. 'Emmy, you're killing me. OK, fine, take the night. But they want you back, Emmy. They. Want. You. Back.'

I exhale deeply again. I don't know what to say.

'Right, go to your sister's wedding, and call me in the morning,' she says. 'And say yes.'

'Talk to you tomorrow,' I reply.

I hang up the phone and flop backwards onto my bed.

I never, ever, ever thought this was going to happen. I thought Danny was going to get away with it. Well, the affair rumours died down, and they were only ever based on a photo of the two of us looking close on set, and anecdotal evidence from a source – now I'm wondering if it might have been someone else he was involved with, someone who maybe knew he'd tried it on with me and was either jealous or trying to expose him. I suppose it might seem like he is getting away with it, in a way, but he's off the show which, really, is the only thing he cares about after himself, and people talk in this industry. Hopefully, no one will ever call him again.

'Emmy, your dad asked me to get you,' Tel says, peeping his head around the door. 'He says they want you for a photo.'

'Right, yes,' I say as I sit up.

'Are you OK?' he asks me. 'You look like you've seen a ghost.'

'Something like that,' I reply. 'Don't worry, I'm fine.'

It's funny, I have seen a ghost in a way, and it isn't just down to the resurrection of Princess Adelina, it's the ghost of my life in London. I'm being given the chance to retcon the past six weeks. I can go back to London, back to my showbiz life, to my swanky flat and my famous friends. I can take back my old job, hopefully clear my name when word gets out about Danny. I can put this entire nightmare behind me, but it comes at the cost of giving up starring in the panto.

'You really do look smoking hot in that dress,' Tel says as we walk down the stairs.

That's when it hits me. It comes at the cost of the panto (which I'm not sure anyone wants me to be a part of any more anyway), but I'd also lose Tel.

I've got a lot to think about.

One of the best things about hosting someone else's wedding is that they feel entirely responsible for cleaning up the aftermath. Well, not them personally, but by the time all the staff from the wedding had packed up and gone they'd taken away any sign they were ever here.

Katie and Lewis' wedding was great in the end. Despite cancelled venues, house renovations and last-minute broken windows, we all really pulled it out of the bag.

The main reason I enjoyed it (and, let's be honest, the only reason it was able to go ahead) was Tel.

I sat with him to eat. I introduced him to people and he charmed the backside off them. We drank and we danced and it just felt so natural and so easy. The night really would have been perfect, if I hadn't had my old job offer dangling in front of me. An offer I'm seriously, seriously thinking I need to take.

I haven't mentioned it to Tel yet. We were having such a lovely time at the wedding, and then we ended up in the bedroom right after everyone else left. Well, when is a good time to tell the man you're falling for that you're packing your bags and moving back home, hundreds of miles away? During the speeches? When we joined in on the first dance to Westlife's 'Flying Without Wings'? When he was kissing me, carrying me upstairs, throwing me around the bedroom all night? And he wasn't there when I woke up so, I guess, now's the time to find him and tell him.

I'm sheepishly walking through the dining room when I'm stopped in my tracks. The first thing I notice is that the table is laid with breakfast foods – one of my main weaknesses – and, my gosh, it smells phenomenal. I can hear Tel singing (his big musical number from the panto, hilariously) in the kitchen. He must have been out because I know I didn't have all this food in. There's fresh fruit, pastries, whipped cream, syrup, Nutella, and I can smell either pancakes or waffles – please, God, let it be waffles.

As I scan the table, I notice something else – the table. This isn't the old kitchen table that I've been using in the dining room, oh no, this is Granddad's old table, safely returned to where it belongs, only lovingly restored with a sleek, colourful river of resin running through the heart of it. Tel walks in with a plate (yep, it's waffles) and the loving barrage of all of the above makes talking to him now feel impossible.

'Wow,' I blurt. 'Wow. Wow at the food but, oh my God, wow at the table.'

'It looks great, doesn't it?' he says. 'I'll tell my mate Ben you like it. We're really proud of this one.'

'You're amazing,' I tell him. 'Too amazing.'

Tel walks over, takes my chin between his thumb and finger and kisses me on the lips.

'You're the amazing one,' he tells me. 'Do you think I'd do all this for just anyone?'

'I kind of do, to a degree,' I tell him. 'You're just this incredible, generous, gorgeous, talented man. I don't deserve you.'

I should have added perceptive to that list because Tel reads the room in a split second.

'You're binning me off,' he says, taking a step back.

'No, no, I'm not, not exactly,' I reply. 'I really can't overstate just how strongly I feel about you but, I have some news, and I just need you to look at the bigger picture.'

'OK,' he replies.

'I've been offered my old job back,' I tell him. 'The showrunner I told you about, he's gone. He's been exposed, other women on the show came forward. So, I can have my job back.'

'That's good news, isn't it?' he replies with a cautious smile.

'It is, except they want me to head back later today, so I won't be here for Christmas – which I'm sure my family will understand.'

Oh, God, my family. I'm sure they will understand but with Granddad missing from the table this Christmas, I'm sure my absence too will be felt more than ever.

'I won't be able to do the pantomime either,' I add.

'Ah,' is all he says. 'So, what are you going to do?'

'I think I'm going to head back to London today,' I reply cautiously, because I think he already knows I'm going to say that, and I can see from his face how disappointed in me he is.

'You're just going to let everyone down?' he asks me plainly.

'Listen, I was all for this pantomime, and I thought the dress rehearsal performance went amazingly, but then Felix took me to one side and basically told me I was crap and he didn't want me playing the part, he wanted Pippa, which was an absolute slap in the face.'

'Oh, really?' he replies, kind of dismissively.

'Yes, really,' I continue. I'm starting to get a bit ranty now. 'I don't know who he thinks he is, giving me advice like that, and then there's Alison, meddling in my life, Scott who is starting to seem like a bit of a player who pretty much just wants to live in my flat and get cast in my TV show. Kay hates me, everything Billy has ever done has been with a view to sleeping with me. Pippa literally tried to kill me – and I mean literally. Billy has a broken leg! This theatre group has just been nothing but a pain in my arse. These people are nothing to me. I don't owe them anything.'

'Is that really what you think?' he replies.

'Well, yeah,' I say. 'We can't all be noble and selfless like you.'

Tel frowns – something I'm not used to seeing him do. Maybe that was too far.

'You think no one cares about you? Fine,' he replies. 'I'm out of here. I'll be at the theatre later, no matter what. If you're there, you're there. If you're not, well, good luck, safe trip back to London. It worked out really well for Felix when he did the same.'

I follow Tel to the front door, unwilling to let him have the last word.

'Felix is the one who told me he doesn't want me in the panto,' I remind him. 'He told me himself. If you don't believe me, that's on you. I know I'm telling the truth.'

'I believe you,' Tel replies, still walking towards the door, still intent on leaving. 'But I couldn't understand why you thought Felix wanted you out, so I called him this morning. You're really not piecing this together, are you?'

'What?' I call after him.

'You told me yourself, Felix knows the network people on your show,' he replies. 'Turns out he overheard you telling me about the showrunner a couple of days ago. He was horrified and then, after you did so much for him, getting him and Anita back together, he really wanted to help you, so he called them up and told them what was going on. It sounds like, when they asked around, he'd done the same thing to other women. They thanked him and let him know they would be making sure you got your job back. I guess it worked. He told you what he told you to encourage you to take it. He knows his theatre could go down, in spite of everything we've done, and he doesn't want to take you down with him. That's what Felix does. I told you, he's like the tide, pushing people away when what he's really trying to do is hold them close. You think no one cares about you, Emmy? Look around.'

As Tel vaults over the dividing fence between our gardens, like he always does, and heads for his own front door, that's when I notice the wooden boards where his lounge window should be, and the protective plastic sheeting blowing in the wind.

'Shit, Tel, wait,' I call after him, but he doesn't listen. He heads inside and closes the door behind him.

So, that's where you get a custom-sized window at short notice. He gave me his window, oh my God, he *gave me his window*. He was right, that night he made me spaghetti, when he said the beauty of him living next door was that he could just pop over and get whatever I needed. He didn't even tell me, he didn't want any credit, he just gave me his own actual window from his house, leaving him waiting for a new one to be made, however long that takes – how wild is that?

He is too good for me. Really, he is. So is Felix.

I've really, really got this so wrong this time. My life has gone so far off-track, I need to do something, I need to work out what I'm going to do. I'm just not sure how yet.

46

The two parts I have available to me at the moment don't really compare, do they?

On the one hand, there's the panto. Sure, as Cinderella, I'd be playing the lead, and a crowd of nearly two thousand is decent, especially given the fact that every last ticket has been sold. But it's a panto. A one-night-only show in a crumbling, old theatre, alongside a cast of amateur actors, in a seaside town no one has really heard of. Plus, I wouldn't even be getting paid to do it.

Then there's my old job. Princess Adelina. She's a feminist icon adored by fans all over the world. I don't just get praise and recognition for the part; the financial compensation is all I need to set me up for life. I get to travel the world and star alongside acting legends as well as talented up-and-comers.

There really, really is no comparison. That's why I can't stop laughing to myself as I make my way through the theatre, heading for the dressing rooms, ready to step into my rags and make this shit legit. Screw *Bragadon Forrest*, I'm a theatre actor now.

Before I get to the dressing room I bump into Felix in the corridor.

'Oh, Emmy,' he says, realising the choice I've clearly made.

'Oh, *Felix*,' I reply with a smile. 'I don't know, thinking you can manipulate me like that. I'll give you this, you're one hell of an actor. I totally fell for it.'

'You're one hell of an actor too,' he replies. 'Which is why I'm so incensed that you're here, for this, this abomination. Yes, it may well be the best pantomime out there, but it's still panto, my love. Panto is not theatre.'

'I don't know, I think it is,' I reply. 'And I think you're on to a good thing here. Marram Bay needs this theatre. Sure, it's a pantomime today but, who knows, in the spring it could be *Waiting for Godot*.'

'I admire your optimism, my dear,' he replies. 'I hope to bring you that news someday, although I fear you'll be the one who is waiting.'

'Well, I hope I'll be waiting here, helping you,' I tell him. 'I've decided to stick around for a bit so, if there's anything I can do, just ask, I'll be at a loose end. Now, if you'll excuse me, I've got a series of ugly dresses to get into while I deliver a performance of *Cinderella* so good it's going to make your head spin.'

'On the subject of dresses, the big white one, the one you said was your favourite,' Felix starts. 'The skirt is pink now. We couldn't get the red paint out so blending it in was our only option.'

'You're still not getting rid of me,' I tell him with a laugh.

I grab him for a hug and I squeeze him so

tightly. Felix has given me more than he'll ever know. The only person who has given me more (the window clinched it for him) has just stepped out of the room behind him.

'I'll give you two a moment,' Felix says. 'Apparently, I'm the only one young Billy fears enough to keep his eyes open while Steve applies his eyeliner.'

God, that sounds like fun to watch.

'You came then,' Tel says.

He's dressed in the black outfit he wears for hiding behind the curtain, supposedly making him even harder for anyone to spot, while he's singing for Scott.

'You gave me your window,' I reply.

'It was a loan at best,' he tells me with a smile. 'You'll be getting my bill for the new one.'

'Stick it on my tab,' I reply. 'Tel, listen, I'm sorry. Obviously, I wasn't talking about you earlier, I know how much you've done for me, and you've got to let me off the hook with Felix, the man has three Olivier awards, for God's sake. I believed every word he said.'

'I don't know what that is, but I'll let you off the

hook,' he replies with a smile. 'I'm sorry too. I acted out. I'm not the noble, selfless person you think I am. I *am* selfish. I didn't want you to leave.'

'Lucky I'm not leaving then,' I say. 'I'm sticking around for a bit.'

Tel plays it super-cool.

'Oh, nice,' he replies. 'Maybe I'll see you over the garden fence for a cuppa one morning then.'

'Maybe,' I reply. 'But for now, I need to get in that room, and I need to get everyone back onside.'

'I don't think that's going to be a problem,' he replies. 'With the exception of Pippa, everyone is just so scared it's going to be a disaster without you, and I think they're all feeling guilty about the night of the party.'

'Well, let's get in there and try and pretend that's true,' I reply.

I peer round the doorway before stepping inside. Everyone is in their first costumes and each person looks more nervous than the next.

'Oh my gosh, Emmy,' Alison says. She springs to her feet and runs over to me. 'Everyone, it's Emmy, she's here, it's Emmy.'

'Hello,' I say in kind of a dorky way.

'Emmy, I'm sorry,' she says, practically sweating pure relief. 'I was meddling and I'm sorry.'

'I'm sorry too,' Kay says. 'I was kind of a jealous psycho, if we're being honest. We're all so freaked out and I let it all get to me.'

'Me too,' Billy says. 'I'm thinking this leg might be karma for trying to lie my way into a date with you.'

'Yeah, and I probably fucked up the worst,' Scott adds sheepishly. 'With the window and everything that came before it, and after it. I'm sorry for the way I reacted. This theatre really does make people crazy.'

We all look at Pippa.

'I'm not apologising to her,' Pippa says. 'Until she turned up just now, I was going to get to play the part that should have been mine in the first place. No way am I apologising.'

'Can we at least call a truce?' I ask her. 'I understand how you're feeling, I do. Let me do this tonight and I'll find a way to make it up to you.'

She remains unconvinced.

'And we'll put the whole trying-to-assault-me thing behind us, if Billy is happy with that too?'

Pippa looks embarrassed now.

'Already forgotten about it,' Billy says. 'Literally, actually, turns out I hit my head on the way down.'

'OK, fine, Emmy can play Cinderella,' she says.

By the time we're all in our costumes and ready to begin, I suddenly start to feel a little nervous.

'Shit, I just had a peep through the curtain,' Steve tells us, yanking up his corset as he runs back towards us, in the most unladylike fashion. 'There's more people out there than there's padding in my bra.'

'A full house,' Felix tells us. 'For those not privy to the contents of Steve's dress.'

We all stand in a circle, psyching ourselves up.

'OK, we're going to do this, and we're going to be amazing,' I tell them.

Everyone echoes my sentiment with a 'yeah' or a 'woo'.

'Everyone, break a leg,' Tel says. 'No offence, Billy.'

We all just laugh.

It's nice, to have the theatre family back together, and to know that I'm not abandoning my actual family for Christmas too. When they eventually find out I've finished on my show I won't tell them why I was killed off in the first place, or that I was offered my job back. I'll just tell them that I decided to stay.

Jane was upset, obviously, but only from a professional point of view. She was horrified when she found out what had happened to me on set, back when we found out I was getting axed, so she totally understands why I'd want to take a break for a while.

I feel so sure about my decision to stay. I don't want to leave my family. I don't want to leave my lovely, new house. It's time to try something different, even if it's not what I'm used to. This decision has to be the life equivalent of Billy trying to pull off a dress and Marc trying to pull Cinderella. It might not be what you were hoping for or expecting, but it works out just fine. As we say in the industry, the show *must* go on.

47

I am happy to be upholding the Christmas tradition of the entire family gathering at Granddad's house for Christmas dinner.

We're all sitting around the large, fancy resin dining table, polishing off the last of our dinner. And by we, I mean everyone. Me, Gracie, Darcy and Oscar, Carl, Mum, Roy, the twins, Bev, Uncle Richard, Vee – and she brought Ken with her which was a surprise to us all. Dad even dropped by earlier and it wasn't the usual uncomfortable ordeal, it was actually kind of nice, which I never thought I'd say. And then there's Tel, sitting next to me, fitting in seamlessly with my weird extended family, pulling crackers, laughing at jokes – he was even brave/polite enough to try some of Vee's infamous Christmas cauliflower cheese (she makes it with gorgonzola, and not only does it stink, but after you eat it, it acquaints you with the bathroom in ways you never imagined). Of course, when I pointed this out to him, something as simple as me using the word cheese in a sentence was enough to trigger an echo of 'Cheeeeeseaiiiir' around the room. You can always trust your family to keep you grounded.

Yep, I think I've found myself a good one. I think I've found myself a good everything. It's funny how something that seems like a bad thing, like losing my job, could put me on the path to something fantastic. I was lonely in London, with fake friends, living in an apartment that was unreasonably small for the price. Up here I have my family, I have a big house, and then there's Tel.

The only thing missing is Granddad. It's so strange, having Christmas without him, but even though I feel his absence, it doesn't quite feel like he's gone. I'll always have my amazing memories. Oh, and four bedrooms bursting with his stuff upstairs. I can't wait to start sorting through it all, reminding myself of how wonderful he was.

'Right, who wants Christmas pudding and who wants chocolate pudding?' Mum asks.

Everyone shouts their orders at her and, amazingly, she seems to absorb them all. I don't think I caught any one person's reply, apart from my own. Chocolate all the way.

'I'll give you a hand,' I tell her.

We leave the rabble in the dining room and head to the kitchen.

'Emmy, I never would have said this to you before, but you moving home is the best Christmas present I could have asked for,' she says through a big smile. 'I know it's selfish of me, but I'm just so much happier when you're around.'

'I'm happier too,' I tell her. 'Staying near you, living in this house, Tel...'

'He's something else, that man,' she replies. 'You've certainly landed on your feet there.'

I laugh.

'Thanks, Mum,' I reply. 'You know, you were right, when you said that if I moved back into this house I might fall in love. I do really love it here.'

'I wasn't talking about the house,' she says through a smug smile. 'Now, help me plate up these puddings.'

Mums are always right, aren't they?

48

SIX MONTHS LATER

I never thought I'd see the day this house – *my* house – was finished, but it finally came.

After the initial pre-Christmas rush to get the downstairs done, work slowed down a little. Well, I've been pretty busy, and so has my number one workman.

I was nervous, after I turned down my old *Bragadon Forrest* role, terrified about what I was going to do for money, or just to keep me sane, but after the pantomime was such a huge success, and as even more work on the theatre was completed, it became more and more like a real place – a real place with real plays. In a bit of a departure from what I'm used to, rather than starring in the shows, I'm actually directing them, leaving Felix free to manage the theatre and spend lots of time with Anita. They must still feel like they have so much making up to do.

It may not be *Waiting For Godot*, but we're putting on *Little Shop of Horrors* this summer, and even though Felix offered me the part of Audrey, I decided to give it to Pippa. Well, I did promise I'd make things up to her. The whole squad is on board – even Tel, who will be donning his black outfit to hide behind the curtain, this time to play Audrey II, because it turns out his voice acting is as fantastic as his singing.

I have to say, things are going a lot smoother than they did with the pantomime, mostly because we've all sorted our personal stuff out. That night of the party, the night the window smashed, I think everything just came to a head. We all flew off the handle. And while everyone was just so relieved when I turned up for the panto anyway, we did have to spend a little time rebuilding old bridges and figuring out where we all stood, but we're all friends again now – most of us just friends, although we do have three new couples. First of all, there's Felix and Anita, who have been like a pair of loved-up teenagers since they got back together. They didn't waste any time dating, seeing what happened, nope, it's as though they've never been apart. Then we have Kay and Billy who have finally got it together – I may have derailed things slightly when I turned up but once things settled down, and Billy was off his super-strong painkillers, he realised what a mistake he was making ignoring Kay for me. And then there's me and Tel...

After what happened at the last house party here, needless to say, I haven't been in a rush to have another one. It's been six months, but tonight finally feels like the night to give it a go, safe in the knowledge we're all friends. Not just because the house is finished, but because my final episode is airing, so we're having a watching party in the garden. So, we spent the day celebrating the house, hanging out in the sunshine, eating barbecue food and enjoying drinks together, and now that it's dark, there's a projector beaming the *Bragadon Forrest* season finale for all my friends and family to see. It's funny, because no one apart from Tel actually knows that this is my final episode, so no one has any idea I'm about to be brutally murdered. It's also completely embarrassing because I never stopped to consider how awkward it would be to watch this final scene with my entire family and everyone from the theatre group, because the fact it happens during a sex scene somehow completely slipped my mind.

'Wahey, get stuck in girl,' Auntie Vee calls out as my sex scene with Alex picks up. 'If I were ten years younger.'

If she were ten years younger, she'd still be old enough to be Alex's mum, but you're only as old as you feel, and she's still feeling Ken. I'm also happy to report that, now that she's found love, she's stopped talking about getting surgery.

I'm doing my best to keep my eyes on the screen. I usually hate watching myself but it's better than watching other people watching me.

'This is great,' Tel whispers to me as he runs his

hand up and down my back. 'I wish I'd watched it now.'

'This is so awkward,' I say through a laugh that proves as much.

'Everyone knows it's just a TV show,' he reassures me. 'Plus, I've got a present for you when it's over.'

'Well, that's exciting,' I say with a smile.

'And it's not as embarrassing as your Cheeseair advert,' Gracie leans over to reassure me.

'Thanks, sis,' I reply sarcastically.

She's probably right.

The last six months with Tel have been amazing. We took things slowly at first, going on a few dates, having a cup of tea over the garden fence most mornings, like we said we would, although that rarely happens any more, now that we're official, it's rare we don't spend the night together here or next door. I want to say that being with Tel feels so wonderfully normal but that makes it sound average, and there is nothing average about being with Tel.

'This is for Varitan,' Edrym's voice booms through the speakers.

The garden is otherwise completely silent, until the sound of me being decapitated echoes around us, shortly followed by a combination of screams and gasps.

Roy, who is probably my biggest fan, jumps to his feet.

'Emmy, no,' he says, clearly upset. 'No, no, no. They can't do that. They can't kill Adelina.'

'I thought Adelina and Edrym were always going to be endgame,' Dad chimes in, which takes me aback, just a little, because I didn't know he watched it, never mind the fact he's invested in it, and clearly shipping 'Edalina' (hardcore fans merge our names together to talk about us as a couple) like the rest of the fandom.

Everyone looks at me for an explanation.

'Hey, I don't write the show,' I insist. 'And, well, if I hadn't been killed off, we wouldn't all be sitting here, so...'

'So that's wonderful,' Mum insists. 'I'll drink to

that. Even if I did just see my daughter being beheaded.'

'And here's your present,' Tel says, popping a box on the table in front of me.

I pop off the lid and look inside. I see myself staring back up at me.

'Ahh, just what every woman wants,' I say. 'Her own severed head.'

'I knew you'd want it eventually,' he tells me. 'And I do want to use it to freak people out on Halloween.'

'Fair enough,' I say with a chuckle.

I lean forward and kiss him. He's right (he's always right), now that I see things differently, I do actually want to keep this weird souvenir, because it represents so much more than my time on the show. I remember reading once that there are certain animals capable of regrowing their own heads if they lose them, and while I may not exactly be doing that, I do feel like a whole new person, and this head symbolises the old me. Plus, Tel is right, it's going to terrify people on Halloween, especially if they see the real me walking around first!

I am happier here. So much happier. And if I've learned anything it's that the fancy job isn't always the best one to take. The person you have the most history with might not be the right person for you. Home really could be where your heart is. Take chances. Go with your gut. Don't hold grudges because the only person they will make feel bad is yourself. Grab your grandparents and hug them because you never know which hug will be your last. Most of all just do whatever it is that makes you happy. Oh, and if you're ever offered a job advertising aerosol cheese, say no, because no one will ever let you forget it.

ACKNOWLEDGMENTS

Massive thanks to my brilliant editor, Nia, to Amanda, and to the rest of the wonderful Boldwood Books team.

A huge thank you to my lovely readers and all the reviewers who take the time to read my books and share their thoughts.

As always, thank you to my family and friends for all their support. Massive thanks to Kim and Audrey for being my biggest fans, thanks to Pino for his support, to James for all his tech support and to Joey for always listening to me bang on about weird book stuff. Bonus thanks to Rachel,

Rebecca, Belinda and my sistah Lynsey, and a special shout-out to Darcy for being the best.

Finally, the biggest thank you of all goes to my husband, Joe, for always being incredible. I couldn't do any of this without you.

MORE FROM PORTIA MACINTOSH

We hope you enjoyed reading *Will They, Won't They*? If you did, please leave a review.

If you'd like to gift a copy, this book is also available as an ebook, digital audio download and audiobook CD.

Sign up to Portia MacIntosh's mailing list for news, competitions and updates on future books.

http://bit.ly/PortiaMacIntoshNewsletter

Discover more laugh-out-loud romantic comedies from Portia Macintosh:

ALSO BY PORTIA MACINTOSH

One Way or Another

If We Ever Meet Again

Bad Bridesmaid

Drive Me Crazy

Truth or Date

It's Not You, It's Them

The Accidental Honeymoon

You Can't Hurry Love

Summer Secrets at the Apple Blossom Deli

Love & Lies at the Village Christmas Shop

The Time of Our Lives

Honeymoon For One

My Great Ex-Scape

Make or Break at the Lighthouse B&B

The Plus One Pact

Stuck On You

Faking It
Life's a Beach

Will They, Won't They?

ABOUT THE AUTHOR

Portia MacIntosh is a bestselling romantic comedy author of 15 novels, including *My Great Ex-Scape* and *Honeymoon For One*. Previously a music journalist, Portia writes hilarious stories, drawing on her real life experiences.

Visit Portia's website: https://portiamacintosh.com/

Follow Portia MacIntosh on social media here:

facebook.com/portia.macintosh.3

twitter.com/PortiaMacIntosh

instagram.com/portiamacintoshauthor

bookbub.com/authors/portia-macintosh

ABOUT BOLDWOOD BOOKS

Boldwood Books is a fiction publishing company seeking out the best stories from around the world.

Find out more at www.boldwoodbooks.com

Sign up to the Book and Tonic newsletter for news, offers and competitions from Boldwood Books!

http://www.bit.ly/bookandtonic

We'd love to hear from you, follow us on social media:

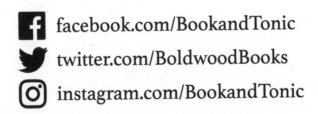

facebook.com/BookandTonic

twitter.com/BoldwoodBooks

instagram.com/BookandTonic

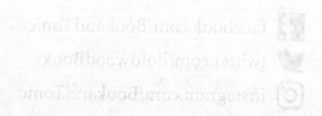

Lightning Source UK Ltd.
Milton Keynes UK
UKHW040802271021
392898UK00003B/179